THE FOUR'

Secon

Lauren(

Book One of "The ~~

Copyright 2009 Laurence Moroney

This book is dedicated to my family: Rebecca Moroney, my wife and confidant; Claudia Moroney, the first person ever to read this book, and a seriously wonderful daughter, and my Son, Christopher, who is just an awesome dude.

Cover Art by: Bradley Wind
Special Thanks to: Liz Tipping who backed this book right from the beginning

Chapter 1: Fintan

Are you sure it's the right time to take him? He's immature.

He's more insecure than immature, and you know that is one of the side effects of-

You think they are involved?

I'm sure of it. And if we put him in the school, we'll be able to watch him closely.

But so will they.

They're doing that already.

Poor kid.

"Cough it up space boy, or I'll put my fist down your throat," growled Brian Delaney. It probably wasn't possible to do, but Fintan figured Delaney would still try, so he didn't argue. Besides, with his arm twisted painfully behind his back, and remembering prior times with the bully, he decided it was best not to fight back.

"Right coat pocket," he croaked.

Delaney threw him to the ground and pushed his knee into Fintan's back while rummaging through his pockets. He pulled his hand out and inspected his prize.

"Only 3 Euro? Mommy's getting cheap with lunch money for her precious boy, isn't she?"

"It's all I have."

The response was Delaney's knee driven harder into his back. Lights blinked in Fintan's eyes and a hot flash of pain burned through his back.

"Speak when you are spoken to, you little maggot," said Delaney. "It'll have to do." Roughly, he stood up, causing another bolt of pain to shoot down Fintan's back. He sneered, and as Fintan tried to get up, Delaney kicked him in the arm, dropping him to the ground again.

"You can stay here until I'm gone. Little maggot. Little *worm* can crawl on the ground."

When he was safely gone, Fintan got up and dusted himself off. He inspected his school uniform. Nothing ripped or pulled. He sighed with relief. There was no visible evidence of the incident he would have to explain to teachers or parents. They *said* he should always report bullying and they *said* he would be protected, but they had *no idea* what the repercussions of snitching would be. It was easier to lose the money and leave things as they were.

Afternoon classes were miserable for Fintan. He wasn't sure which was worst between the pain in his back, the hunger in his stomach or the smug grin from Delaney who licked his lips and patted his belly thanking Fintan for the free lunch. After what seemed like an eternity, the bell rang, and Fintan grabbed his backpack and ran for the door. If he wasn't quick the bullies might find him again.

He ran all the way home.

*

Fintan always loved late summer and early autumn in Ireland. The nights were cool with clear skies, and if he stayed up late enough, he could see the stars in all their glory. He had just finished dinner and came out to sit in the fields behind his house. He watched the sky darken and change through its brilliant colors, from dark blue, through rusty reds and finally to black. His favorite part was when he got to watch the stars twinkle into view one by one.

His back still hurt, but he decided not to let it bother him.

His chest tightened as looked at the sky. Only the brightest stars were visible now. Polaris to the North was bright as always. He imagined generations of sailors looking up to it, comforted by its presence and its stability, always showing them the way home. A feeling welled up in his chest. It was like he was inflating and the sky was lifting him up. He couldn't name the feeling but he loved it. It was like the stars were calling to him. Like he *belonged* there, but was stuck *here* on Earth.

Stuck in a miserable life, in a miserable town, with a miserable family.

He shook his head. No point in worrying too much about it. It would only depress him.

Someday. Someday I won't feel so helpless. Someday I'll be my own man, setting my own path in my own life. Someday I won't have to put up with bullies, and school, and a brother who hates me and parents who don't care for me despite what they say.

*

On Sundays, Fintan usually helped his mother with shopping for groceries at the local market. Fintan Senior, his father, would usually sleep off his hangover from the night before. For the afternoon, Fintan would stay out of the house, wanting to avoid Father's temper, and would take a walk down to the cliff tops nearby.

It was a land of bleak beauty, with the roar of waves crashing below, and the bare limestone rocks peeking out of a deep green covering. He always liked to come here to sit and think. To the west he could see the sun setting, and the growl in his stomach told him it was getting late.

He returned home to find dinner in the microwave.

An empty package stood on the dinner table. It was addressed to him, but his parents had opened it. He sighed, not surprised. Of course they would disrespect his privacy. *Of course.*

Mother came into the kitchen. She ran to hug him. "Oh here you are," she said.

Fintan held up the empty package. "What's this?"

"Great news!" she said. "It's a school for gifted children. They want to talk to you in Dublin, tomorrow, *all expenses paid!*"

"Can I see it?"

"Oh they sent a check with it. Your Father took it out to cash it."

"And the letter?"

"He took it too."

"It was addressed to *me*," said Fintan.

"Sorry, we thought it was for your father, so we opened it."

Right thought Fintan. *Like I am stupid enough to believe everything you tell me.*

Mother took his silence as an accusation. "Oh don't be like that! He'll be home in half an hour."

Half an hour passed, then an hour, and then two hours. Mother was high and excited, but Fintan was too angry to even think, much less hang out with the family. His older brother Dermot was smirking at Fintan's unease. By midnight Father still wasn't home, and Fintan went to bed.

*

Father finally turned up in the small hours, and his drunken singing and clumsy banging of doors woke Fintan. Finally, when all was quiet, Fintan crept downstairs.

Father was asleep, snoring loudly on the sofa. The stale, sour smell of alcohol filled the room. His jacket lay sprawled on the floor where he had dropped it. Some crumpled papers were sticking out of the inside pocket. Fintan grabbed them and retreated upstairs before Mother or Dermot came down.

He straightened the papers out carefully. There was a letter, addressed to Fintan.

```
Dear Mr Reilly,
```

I am pleased to inform you that have passed the
selection process for entry into the 'Young Boys
Elite School of Ireland'.

Our entry requirements are strict, you are one of
only a handful of students from around the country
who is eligible to test for entry.
In order to enter the school you will be required
to pass an interview and admissions test.

Please present yourself at our administrative
offices on September 19 at 10:00AM. Directions and
address may be found on the other side of this
page.

Enclosed are expenses for travel and accommodation
for you and your family. An overnight stay may be
necessary.

Punctuality is expected.
   Yours,

   Mr Smith, BOE.

September 19 was *tomorrow*. To get there by 10AM, he'd have to
leave his house by 7AM, which would mean getting up in just a few
hours. How was he going to sleep? Worse, how was he going to wake
Father?

Chapter 2: Mister Smith

The poor kid has a wretched life, doesn't he?

And yet he tests off the scales. So much for nurture being greater than nature.

But how? I mean the rest of the family isn't too sharp, and the father is downright nasty.

That's evolution, isn't it? Sometimes a random mutation can change the direction of a species. Or a family.

But what happens when the mutation isn't random?

Groggy and hung over, Father somehow dragged himself out of bed and got them on their way. They made it to the station just in time to catch the train to Dublin. The cheap tickets were sold out, and Father had argued noisily with the ticket officer, but there was nothing he could do.

Had they gotten there earlier, there may have been a chance, but for now it was either pay the higher fare, or wait for the next train.

Again, Fintan could feel the frustration ready to boil over within him. They had been sent more than enough money for the whole family to travel *first* class, with hotel accommodations and meals. Despite this, Father was considering missing this train and being late for the interview just so they could save some money, which would be spent at the nearest bar later.

Reluctantly, he agreed, but only after yelling at Fintan for '*dragging your feet*' and being late, lazy and every other cliché he could think of. He was still telling Fintan off loudly as the train departed. He finally stopped as the drinks cart arrived and he helped himself to some beer.

Finally, with some peace and quiet, Fintan was able to catch up on some sleep.

They arrived in Dublin without further incident, and made their way to the given address.

They were greeted at the entrance by a prim-looking secretary. They showed her the invitation letter and she discreetly ignored how crumpled it was. "Please take a seat," she said. "Someone will see you shortly."

It was a plain office, but Father looked around it, impressed. As a factory worker, any place where people sat to work impressed him.

The secretary's phone rang. "Yes," she said. "Yes, I'll send them in."

She brought them to a back-office where a man was waiting. He was tall and slim with thinning gray hair and sharp blue eyes.

Introducing himself as "Mister Smith", he shook Father's hand vigorously before turning to Fintan. He held Fintan's gaze a moment.

"I'll get right down to business," he said, addressing Father. "Fintan junior is here to be tested for a *very* special and very *exclusive* school. Needless to say it's *only* for the best and brightest."

He glanced briefly at Fintan before continuing, while Father beamed with pride. "We've been following his progress through primary school, and feel he has the right stuff, not just to enter, but also to succeed."

Before Father could say anything, Smith spoke again, in a firm tone. "Do note there are tests, and Fintan will have to pass these tests before he is admitted."

He passed a permission slip across the table to Father.

"Please be clear Mister Reilly, this school is expensive. If he enters, we want him to complete his education. He'll be away from home, out in the country. Should Fintan junior pass the tests, and accept entry, you will have sign a document legally passing parental rights for him over to the state. We will care for him until he becomes of adult age."

Father looked to Fintan. His eyes glazed over, calculating.

"Of course," said Mister Smith "that is why the whole family was invited, so it could be a family decision. But, as the only parent present, and head of the household, you have the authority to decide."

"Where is the school?"

"I'm not at liberty to disclose the location," said Mister Smith flatly.

"You want me to sign my kid over to you, but you won't tell me where the school is?" Father asked. His voice was getting louder. "What if I say no?"

"Then you will never find out where the school is, and Fintan junior will no longer be invited to attend."

"So he'll just go to school back at home then," said Father, dropping the pen.

"And be doomed to a life of mediocrity," said Mister Smith. "He'll likely go through secondary school, and do well, but, will there be money for University?"

"He'll get a scholarship," said Father.

"Will he?" Do you know how good you have to be to get a scholarship these days?"

"He's good enough," said Father.

"Maybe," said Mister Smith, "but I noticed Fintan's brother has had to take a part-time job to help out at home, and bring some money in. I assume Fintan junior will have to do the same when he's 14?"

Father said nothing.

"And do you know how badly his grades will suffer? Studies have shown once a child starts working, they drop at least 2 grade points.

So an 'A' student like Fintan will drop to be a 'C' student. Do you really want that for your Son?"

"It's none of your business," said Father.

"Correct, Mister Reilly, but it is *Fintan's* business, and I want you to understand what you are passing up just because we will not tell you the *location* of the school. It suggests to me your pride is being dented, and you would sacrifice your son's future for its sake. Am I wrong?"

"No." said Father, emphatically. Then, with a little less strength, he repeated, "No. This has nothing to do with my pride."

He picked up the pen.

Fintan held his breath.

Father put the pen to paper, and paused.

"What are the chances of him going to University after this school of yours?"

"We haven't had anybody drop out yet," said Mister Smith.

Father signed the paper and threw it back at Mister Smith. Fintan finally breathed.

Mister Smith said "Thank you," sweetly, with just a little hint of sarcasm.

He then put his professional face on and told Father the testing would likely take several hours. He took Father's cell phone number and told him they would call when they were done.

"And what should I do while I wait?"

"There are several pubs within walking distance," said Mister Smith, "I am sure you will enjoy them."

Father left, and Fintan was alone with the mysterious Mister Smith.

Chapter 3: The Tests

You're good. You're playing with his head already.
I just did what I had to do to get him into the test.
You think he's worth it? He's damaged goods.
Nothing that I cannot repair.

The first words that Fintan said to Mister Smith surprised even him.

"I don't like the way you spoke to my father."

"Really?" Mister Smith answered, a smile creeping onto his lean face. "I thought that you would enjoy seeing him put in his place."

Fintan's silence was an answer in itself.

"For the next few hours you will be tested," said Smith, changing the subject. "And I will not entertain any questions until the end of the testing. Do I make myself clear?"

"Yes," said Fintan, and Smith led him through a door at the back of his office.

Behind the door was a room with a simple computer terminal. Fintan sat at the terminal and Smith left the room.

The screen was blank.

Is this the test? Fintan wondered. Smith had not given him any instructions other than not to ask any questions. Was that also a part of the test?

Fintan figured that if he touched a key on the keyboard, he would be showing initiative, but he would also be showing curiosity, and perhaps a lack of respect. This was after all, their terminal, and they hadn't given him permission to use it.

But if he did nothing, it would show a lack of initiative, and the need to be led and instructed on everything.

He reached to touch the space bar on the keyboard, hesitated a moment, and then pressed it.

The screen came to life. It said: `Welcome, Fintan Reilly,` and then turned off.

Mister Smith entered, holding a stopwatch.

"Two minutes, thirty six seconds," he said, and then harrumphed as he led Fintan to the next room.

This one looked the same as the first, and again he showed Fintan where to sit before leaving. This time, without hesitation, Fintan reached out and touched the space bar. The screen came to life and said:

```
What is the password
Enter password here:
```

They wanted Fintan to enter a password. But they had given him no sign of what it was.

Fintan thought frantically. Could it be 'Smith', 'Mister Smith', or 'Fintan'? He had no idea.

Fintan looked around the room, guessing there must be a clue, but the walls were featureless and bare.

He looked again at the screen. There *had* to be a clue.

And then he noticed that something was missing -- there was no question mark at the end of the first statement. That made it a statement, instead of a question: *What* is the password.

Fintan carefully typed it in, making sure that he capitalized it correctly. He pressed the 'Enter' key.

A light came on, the door opened, and Mister Smith stood there applauding slowly and quietly, a mocking look on his face.

"So, you've passed the first two tests. That gives you the right to go towards the real testing," he said with vigor. He led Fintan out of the room and into a windowed corridor. Through the windows Fintan could see what looked like a video games arcade with each game station having at least one technician in a white coat standing nearby.

"These are the real tests," said Smith, "tests of dexterity, imagination, strength, stamina, and even intelligence. Don't worry, and just relax. You may even enjoy them."

He was right. The first few tests looked like simple computer games, but once he started playing them, they weren't as simple as they first appeared. They didn't have any logical rules. One involved flipping tiles to reveal colors, a little bit like a child's pair-matching game, but, the colors weren't always consistent, so the first time Fintan flipped a tile it might be orange, and the next time it might be green. Every time he flipped, the score went down.

But soon Fintan began to see the pattern, and deduce the algorithm the programmer used to decide the color rules. It was complex and multidimensional, sometimes depending on which previous tile had been flipped, sometimes based on its color, sometimes based on how long Fintan took (in moves as well as seconds) in flipping it.

He could see where it would be easy to get frustrated by its randomness, but once he began to figure it out, Fintan was able to start clearing the board quickly. The more he cleared, the easier it got.

Finally, he finished the board, exhausted. He looked at the game clock. It had taken nearly two hours.

Smith was eyeing him closely.

"That was fun," said Fintan.

More, similar tests followed, all being bizarre games, but, Fintan discovered that if he didn't get frustrated, and focused on the task at hand, he could quickly find the solution. Some involved him needing to interact physically with the games console, lifting and twisting bizarre controls to navigate a ball through a maze. Others involved a sensory overload as they forced him to wear a headset that projected virtual screens.

After several exhausting (but exhilarating) hours Fintan finished all the games. Mister Smith was waiting for him in front of a large black door.

Fintan was feeling a little cocky, "Is that all you've got?"

"That was a question Mister Reilly," was the only response.

One of the techs handed Smith a sheet. Fintan saw many tick marks on it, and his name at the top. Fintan figured this was a good sign.

Smith spoke again "For the final test, you will go through this door, and you will continue down the corridor on the other side. At the end, there is a hatch. Enter it, and you will find a small room. You will see a headset. Put it on, and I will use it to direct you what to do next."

Fintan nodded, and opened the door.

Chapter 4: Flight Simulator

They're getting closer aren't they?
Are they?
That's why you're taking these risks.
Maybe.

A long black corridor lay in front of Fintan. He followed it as directed, turning several times. It was a long walk, taking him perhaps fifteen minutes. At several points along the way, the corridor led through hatches, which Fintan struggled to open.

At the end, as promised was a small room. It had painted foot impressions on the floor, and a thin metal rail behind them, which was about four feet tall. It made Fintan think of a bar stool, but without a seat. It was clear that he was to stand where marked, and the metal rail was something that he could lean back against, but not sit on.

Hanging on the rail was a headset. It looked like an oversized pair of skiing sunglasses, with angular rims around the lenses. Tiny speakers locked down over his ears and a small boom microphone extended from one side.

On either side of where he would stand were two raised columns, with polished black surfaces that angled towards him.

Fintan stood on the footprints and leaned back slightly against the rail. It was strangely comfortable, and although tired, he felt relaxed. In this position he could rest his hands on the tops of the columns comfortably.

Investigating his headset, he felt a small button on the left side. He pressed it and the headset came to life.

A virtual display overlaid his field of vision. Now, instead of plain walls, he could see a star field, and as he moved his head around, the gray curve of the moon came into view. He could also see the two black columns, but, through the headset they were lit up with many and varied controls.

To Fintan it felt like he was floating in space. His heart fluttered. This was awe-inspiring technology.

Mister Smith's voice spoke through the headpiece. He coached Fintan in how to activate the console under his left hand. This console gave different views from inside or outside his ship. The console on his right hand controlled the ship, but the method of piloting was unfamiliar.

"You are the pilot," said Mister Smith, "but you don't fly the ship like you see them do it in the movies. It is all about programming the right course, and telling the ship to go there. It will do the rest."

On the right hand console he found a trackball and experimented with it. He quickly learned that he could use it to 'draw' where he wanted the ship to go on his display.

"Moving in space isn't like moving on the ground," said Mister Smith. "When you're in deep space, if you push the ship in a certain direction, it will keep going in that direction until either you, or something else pushes in the opposite direction."

"So, to stop the ship moving, I push the ship in a direction opposite to its current movement, right?"

"You got it." Smith paused. "Just remember that gravity can also take effect if you are near something big, like the Earth or the Moon. Think about what happens when you throw something. It starts moving in the direction you threw it in, but soon falls away towards the ground. The same will happen here, so you must take gravity into account. Think about throwing – the harder you throw, the more time it takes before gravity pulls the ball down."

"Ok" said Fintan. "I have to *understand* the best trajectory with limited fuel. Anything else?"

"Well, there's the effect of other forces, inertia and the like, but wait until you learn about them in school. Not to mention the funny math when you have to consider the changing mass of your ship when you use fuel to move it."

Fintan figured that if a smile had sound, then he could hear Smith smiling. He was a different man now. It seemed that Fintan had passed Smith's personal test, and he hoped he could do as well with this simulation.

After playing with the controls and moving the spaceship around a little, and after crashing several times into the surface of the moon, he started to get the knack, and picked arbitrary targets and locations. With practice it did get easier, but Fintan was beginning to realize that while it might be easy to do the basics, it would be a lot harder to *master* flying the ship.

The screen went blank and Mister Smith spoke up again.

"Are you ready for the test now?"

"Yes" he replied.

The screen came on again, and it was a much more detailed and realistic star field than that Fintan had seen earlier. The ship was still in a parking orbit above the moon.

"You will run through several scenarios. The first involves a rescue mission; your monitor contains the details. Please get to this location in less than three minutes."

Some coordinates popped up on the screen. Fintan instantly recognized them as being on exactly the opposite side of the moon from his current location. He could reach it easily, but slowly, by following the parking orbit. For speed, he would have to spend fuel to climb away from the moon, and then dive back towards it as he moved around the moon towards his target. Using the trackball he drew a curve that took the ship into a high orbit, and then dived back down. He activated it, and the ship began to move.

The clock was ticking down faster than he would have liked, but he felt confident that he'd make it.

But when his ship approached the top of the curve it was beginning to slow down, pulled back by the gravity of the moon. If Fintan added thrust, it would change his course, and he may not have time to readjust.

With only thirty seconds left he reached the summit of the curve, and like a rollercoaster the ship turned around and tore downhill towards its destination.

Just in time, he arrived at his goal. Fintan breathed a sigh of relief. *One down.*

Scenario after scenario followed each one progressively more difficult than the last. Sometimes he had to reach multiple destinations against the clock, sometimes with little fuel or a damaged spacecraft. Sometimes he had multiple points of reference to deal with as he was between Earth and the Moon, and had to figure out which one gave the coordinates of the location to reach.

For the final test, Fintan had to catch two drifting objects and put them into a parking orbit around the Earth. He had to do it with little fuel, so he would need to be perfect. There wasn't enough fuel to do each separately, so he needed to come up with a way to tow the two of them together.

In the end the solution was deceptively simple. He played snooker with them. Using about half his fuel in one shot, Fintan put the ship on a trajectory that would strike the first one towards the second, hitting it, placing them both in a parking orbit around the Earth. The simulator made it easy for him to project this and tweak it until it was perfect. The ship would recoil from the first impact and drop into a wild orbit, but, it wouldn't take much to adjust. He hoped.

The course laid in, Fintan changed from projection to real mode. He watched as the ship shot around the moon and approached the first object.

And then it seemed all hell broke loose. He could see from the monitor that his ship had collided with the first object and sent it earthward, but, the impact had damaged his ship. Parts of the simulator were shutting down, and some of the controls were not responding. He could see that his ship was falling towards the moon in a rapidly tightening spiral.

The projector was broken, so he would have to set a course manually. Fintan calmed himself by breathing deeply, fighting the urge to scream. This was just a simulation.

"Be calm and you'll be fine," he whispered.

And then he saw it: The way out.

In a moment of perfect clarity he guessed a direction and thrust that would get him out of this spin, and send him Earthward. It would be the ideal time to perform this thrust in a little over a minute. Only a few seconds later the ship would crash into the moon, so the timing would have to be perfect.

He started a countdown from ten in his head. At five most of his screen panels were gone. At three, the whole room began to vibrate.

At zero, he punched the actual mode, and the vibration worsened for a few moments before subsiding and finally stopping. Most of the viewport was out now – huge parts of the sky showed instead as white hexagonal cells – the underlying computer monitors.

After a few moments Mister Smith's voice came through the headset again.

"Thank you Mister Reilly," he said. "You'll find a small ante-room at the back of this chamber. You can take your headset off and go there to rest while we calculate your scores. I'll be in to get you in less than an hour."

The ante-room contained a small bed. Fintan lay down on it, exhausted from the day. Within seconds he was sound asleep.

*

He was woken by Mister Smith, placing his hand gently on Fintan's shoulder. He was smiling.

"Congratulations," he said, "you passed"

Fintan was speechless. A smile crept across his face.

"You are welcome to attend our school. However, you must understand something. You cannot tell anyone, ever, what the school is, or what you are studying there. You must agree to secrecy. You must not even tell your family."

Fintan nodded.

"There's one more thing," he said, pulling out the paper that Fintan's father had signed earlier. "The choice is yours now. Nobody else can legally tell you what you can and cannot do with respect to this school. If you say 'no', you can go home and nobody will know the better. If you say 'yes' and sign this paper, then you are agreeing to attend, agreeing to secrecy, and agreeing to extreme punishment should you break this secrecy. You will be given a believable cover story of a normal school that you can tell your parents and friends, but they must never know the truth. Is that clear?"

Fintan nodded affirmation.

"So, Mister Reilly, will you join us?"

Without hesitation, Fintan signed the paper.

"Good," he said, "you will of course need to go home and pack. Term starts in two weeks. This is the greatest decision you have ever made, as you will see in time."

He clapped Fintan on the back and led him to the exit.

"The simulator," said Fintan, "that's the most amazing technology I've ever seen. Will we be using equipment like that again?"

"Oh yes" answered Smith. "That's one of the core parts of the curriculum."

"It's amazing," repeated Fintan, "it felt like I was really in space, piloting a space ship."

"Ah" said Mister Smith. "That's because you were."

Chapter 5: Ayako

So he passed the unpassable test. I bet you didn't expect that?
He has a high ceiling, that's for sure.
He almost died.
But he didn't did he?
That's not the point.
Oh, but it is.

Father went home earlier, so Mister Smith had organized transport for Fintan. A nondescript car picked him up at the office and took him home. His body was tired, so he was happy not to worry about trying to catch a train and call his parents for a pickup.

As he arrived at his doorstep, butterflies were dancing in his stomach. There's no way that his family were going to swallow the cover story. But it didn't matter – Father had signed him over to the state, and regardless of *what* they accepted, his parents had no choice but to let him go.

Father and Mother were waiting in the living room. Dermot was still out with friends.

"I passed," said Fintan.

Father smiled and clapped Fintan on the shoulder. It felt unusually good. Mother cried.

"You don't have to go if you don't want to," she said. "You can stay here with us."

Father shot her a dirty look.

Fintan raised his hand before they could start bickering.

"It's for the best," he said. "I'm going."

They both fell silent. Mother nodded. "I know, but I'll miss you."

"I'll miss you too," said Fintan, surprising himself in realizing that he meant it, "but I'll be back for Christmas and for the summer."

Mother nodded. Father looked thoughtful.

*

There wasn't much to prepare, as Fintan's instructions had been for him to bring as little as possible. However, Mother had to trot him around her extended family showing off the brochures and exclaiming how proud Fintan had made her, Father had to introduce Fintan to all his drinking buddies, an endless cycle of pointless socializing.

However, the time went quickly and for that, Fintan was grateful.

On his last night, his family hosted a dinner in his honor, and for once Fintan felt like he was part of a family. Father was sober, talkative and funny. Mother was genuine and warm in her admiration for Fintan, and Dermot had gotten over his early jealousy, even mumbling a heartfelt congratulations.

What stopped Fintan from crying and tearing up his school papers was the memory of being *in space*, and the likelihood of going back. Excitement welled up in his chest, tempering his sadness at leaving home.

*

The day came. After melodramatic goodbyes at the train station, Fintan made his way to the ministry building, alone, as told. A black car was waiting for him there. It whisked him to the airport where, before he knew exactly what was happening, he boarded a flight for New York.

New York thought Fintan, stunned. But it wasn't to be his final destination. He got off the plane and changed to another, headed towards Las Vegas, walking through a disappointingly scruffy terminal. Once on this plane, dead tired, Fintan fell asleep and didn't wake until it landed.

At the gate, a normal looking man wearing a normal looking suit met and greeted him. The man didn't say much, just small talk as he led Fintan through the terminal. While most passengers went to baggage claim, the man took Fintan in the opposite direction.

 "We'll take care of your bags, don't worry," he said, in response to Fintan's unspoken comment.

Confused, Fintan followed the man, who led him through the maze of passengers and tourists, through the business lounge areas to a nondescript office with a woman sitting behind a desk.

The man flashed his security card at her. She inspected it closely, and a door opened in the wall behind her. Fintan didn't know how she did it – there was no visible button or other control.

The door led to a large open area, which was clearly another terminal, much smaller than the main one, but looking unlike a typical airport terminal. There were no shops, no bars or other amenities. The people didn't have the look of tourists, and looked more like commuters. Many were in military uniform.

Scattered around, were a bewildered-looking children, guided by escorts like his own. Fintan guessed that he looked just like they did.

The man guided Fintan to a gate, and bade his good-bye. And just like that, Fintan was on another plane. This time with no idea where he was going. There were no announcements or signage that might give him a clue.

He took a window seat in an empty row about halfway back. He had no ticket, so he figured that it was fine to take any seat.

The plane began to fill up, but there was little conversation. Sometimes people would pass Fintan's row, see him sitting there, and getting a knowing look on their face would walk on by, leaving him alone. Fintan assumed they didn't want a newcomer questioning them.

A girl about his age got onto the plane, which was now almost full. She walked down the aisle, looking left and right for an empty seat. She was short, so she couldn't see over the seat tops too well. She reached Fintan's row and looked at the two empty seats beside him. After a moments calculation she took the aisle seat without a word, sitting primly with her hands on her lap.

She had the classic Asian look with thick, silky black hair that flowed to her shoulders. As she turned her head, the way her hair moved was enticing. How it could be so thick, so black, and so shiny but just fall in place was mesmerizing to Fintan. People in Fintan's town commonly joked about Asian's having 'yellow' skin, which sounded unattractive to Fintan, but hers was bright and clear and had a healthy glow.

She turned to look at Fintan, and her eyes were large and brown.

He realized that he was staring and that she had caught him. Fintan quickly looked away, embarrassed and blushing. She didn't say a word.

Since the flight simulator test, Fintan had gotten the habit of mimicking the gestures of flying a ship, using an imaginary thumbstick with his left hand, and trackball and buttons on his right. In an unguarded moment he started to do it again on the arms of the airplane seat.

The girl gasped, and pointed at Fintan's hands.

"You've done that too," she said, curiosity tinting her voice.

Fintan figured that he owed her an answer, but he didn't know what to say.

"We're not allowed to talk about it," was the best he could do.

She nodded, but she was smiling, as was Fintan.

"I'm Fintan Reilly," said Fintan, offering his hand, and feeling like a fool when she stared at it.

She then took his hand gently in hers, which was small and cool to the touch.

"Ayako," she said with a mild Japanese accent. "Ayako Katsuragi."

"You are from Japan?"

"Yes," she said, "Tokyo. This is my first time in your country."

"It isn't my country," Fintan said defensively, "I am from Ireland."

She looked a little blank for a moment. Fintan heard her say 'Ireland' and then start translating it phonetically into her language. Understanding finally dawned on her.

"Ireland," she said, "In Europe, right beside England. I have seen it in books. It is beautiful."

"You think so?" Fintan asked sarcastically.

The sarcasm clearly went over her head, so instead he said "It has some beautiful places, and some ugly places. I come from one of the ugly places."

She laughed. "It sounds a lot like Japan!"

"This is my first time in this country too," said Fintan, pointing out the window at Las Vegas. "It's an interesting place, isn't it?"

From their window they had an excellent view of the Las Vegas strip. At one end stood the huge 'Mandalay Bay' and 'MGM Grand' resorts. Between them they could see what looked like a fairytale castle and a huge black pyramid.

Ayako leaned over slightly to see out the window.

"Beautiful" she said.

"The Pyramid is called the 'Luxor'," said Fintan. "Because it is a pyramid it doesn't have elevators, but 'inclinators' that go up the angle of the wall. They might be fun to try."

"Yes," she said, "perhaps one day we will try them together."

Fintan gulped. His heart felt like it skipped a beat.

"And the Castle. That's called the 'Excalibur'. It's from an English legend."

"You know a lot about Las Vegas," she said, "you must be very smart."

"Nah," he said casually, "I just read it in this brochure I picked up in the airport." He held up a glossy paper.

They laughed. It was a nice moment. She took the brochure and started flicking through it.

Another boy had gotten on the plane. From his brand-name clothes and confident stride, he was clearly American. Ayako noticed him too, and as he got closer, it was obvious that he was eyeing the seat between her and Fintan. Deftly she stood, and took the center seat, letting the new boy take the outside aisle seat.

"Thank you," he said in a thick and loud American accent, while looking her in the eye.

She nodded and returned to her brochure. Fintan went back to looking out the window.

"Zack Adams," the boy said, offering his hand. He shook Fintan's vigorously.

"Fintan Reilly," answered Fintan, without the same enthusiasm.

He then offered his hand to Ayako who politely took it and gently shook it.

Trying to be friendly, Fintan opened a new conversation.

"So, any idea where this plane is going?"

"Well, it's all supposed to be a big secret," said Zack, "but I think it's pretty obvious."

Ayako raised an eyebrow.

"C'mon guys," Zack said incredulously, "look at this plane. It's small, with limited range, probably only an hour or two flight time."

Fintan and Ayako said nothing, waiting for more.

"We're in Las Vegas, right? So where do you think we'd be going in such a small plane?"

He paused, searching their confused expression.

He smiled, and whispered "Area 51 of course!"

Chapter 6: Area 51

And so the die is cast.
Time is getting close, we have to take risks.

Zack smiled smugly as the plane took off. As it turned, Fintan watched the long dark shadows the sun cast on the tawny desert ground.

"We're heading north," he finally said.

Zack was nodding and grinning widely. "Area 51," he said, "I knew it! This is just so cool!"

Ayako's eyebrows furrowed. She cocked her head to the side, facing away from Fintan, and towards Zack. Fintan felt a pang of jealousy like a sharp knife sticking beneath his ribs. In her soft but lilting voice she asked "What is this Area 51?"

"Sorry," said Zack smiling a broad, confident grin, "I'm just geeking out on all this."

He paused and took a breath.

"Area 51 is the most secret military base in the country. Many people believe that our Government has made contact with aliens, and that they are in this base."

"Oh," said Ayako, disappointed. She returned to the brochure of Las Vegas.

"Oh?" said Zack. "Is that all you can say? We are going to *Area 51* and all you can say is 'Oh'?"

He shrugged, and looked at Fintan, his eyes speaking inaudibly "What's with this girl?"

Ayako looked at Fintan. "Do you believe in aliens?"

Suddenly he felt like he was choking. A hot flush emanated from his lower back and quickly went up to his neck and his face. He was sure he was blushing as he saw Zack hide a snicker.

"Er," said Fintan.

She was looking him right in the eye. Her eyes were a deep black, like a midnight lake, and he was swimming in them, trying not to drown.

"Um," said Fintan.

"Well I don't," said Ayako, "I mean think about the diseases that aliens would carry. If they landed on the Earth, we'd all die."

"Unless," interrupted Zack, "we kept them in a top secret base out in the middle of the desert where they wouldn't mix with the general population."

Ayako turned back towards him. Her hair flicked near Fintan's face. He suddenly remembered how to breathe.

She said nothing, and conceded the point.

*

Fintan mulled over the previous conversation. "It makes sense that we'd be going to a secret base though, right? You saw the papers that we had to sign to get here."

Zack nodded. "Not to mention *where* we did our final test, assuming you guys did the same test as me?" He pointed upwards, towards the sky, towards space.

Ayako nodded slowly. Those magnificent eyes of hers were lost in thought.

*

The plane turned to climb over a mountain range, hitting some rough turbulence. Through the window Fintan could see a sparse rocky desert. So different from where he had grown up, but so beautiful in it's way. Having crossed the mountains, gradually the landscape began to change.

The ground beneath gave way from pebbled slopes to a flat, white plain that stretched towards the horizon in every direction.

"Millions of years ago, this was ocean," said Zack, "all that is left after the waters receded or evaporated is the salt. Area 51 is actually built on the bed of an ancient salt sea called Groom Lake."

"For something so secret, you know a lot about it" said Fintan.

"The Internet is a wonderful place you know," winked Zack.

The plane was beginning to descend.

"We're landing," said Ayako.

Peering out the window they could see as the plane descended towards the white ground. It touched down smoothly, and then taxied for a long time to approach a cluster of buildings. In the distance Fintan saw some fighter jets, but on the whole the base was nondescript.

The plane finally halted, and without ceremony an attendant opened the doors and the people filed out. Fintan saw other children on board, and as they left, the attendant handed them a pair of sunglasses with a warm smile.

When it came to be their turn, they also received sunglasses. Once he passed through the door, Fintan could see why – the glare of the sun, reflected off the white sands was overwhelming. He slipped his glasses on gratefully.

Fintan looked around, openmouthed, in awe at the natural surroundings. The white flat landscape was surreal and except for the distant brown craggy mountains that surrounded the base, and the rich blue sky, he could have believed he was on the moon.

With a whoosh he heard the plane move away behind him. It turned surprisingly quickly on the runway and raced away, taking off with a dull boom. One thing struck him about the plane – it was nondescript and unmarked, being a simple white jet with a red stripe down the side.

A uniformed attendant led the children – besides Fintan, Zack and Ayako there were perhaps half a dozen others on this flight, towards a nondescript and unmarked hanger. The other passengers just went their separate ways into the different buildings that dotted the area around the landing strip.

"Secret military base with Aliens," whispered Fintan to Zack. "I expected something a bit more, you know – modern!"

Zack was quiet. Fintan figured that this wasn't a typical state for him.

*

The building was set up to be a simple staging area or waiting room. It was full of curious children, just like them. Fintan did a quick count, and estimated there were around a hundred of them, all around the same age.

Zack grunted and pointed towards some empty seats near the back. Excited, they sat, listening to the speculation and buzz going around the room. Zack spotted a buffet area, and went to get them some drinks. Another stab of jealousy hit Fintan as Ayako rewarded Zack with a beaming smile.

*

"Not what I expected of Area 51," said Zack, louder than necessary, "I mean, other than my Irish friend here, there ain't no little green men!"

A few kids nearby snickered, but the adults paid no attention.

A door on the far side of the room opened, and there was a bright light behind it. It was hard for Fintan to see, but some shapes resolved out of the glare. Four soldiers marched into the room in full combat gear. He had never seen men as big as these. It wasn't just their size, but their very presence was intimidating and was the epitome of strength.

Another man walked into the room behind them. He walked past them to a low dais in the center of the room. The soldiers fell into place around him and knelt, facing outwards towards the group.

"What, are they afraid we'll hit him with a spitball," whispered Zack to his new best friend, a tall gangly kid with the same goofy grin.

"Good morning," said the man. "And welcome to Groom Lake. My name is Mister Jones, and I'm what you might call a member of the school board. It is nice to meet you, and I'm looking forward to knowing you better. We will enter the main part of the school shortly, but before we do, I just have a few safety notices."

The crowd paused, waiting for more, expecting a long boring lecture.

Jones took his time, slowly gazing around the room, meeting them all with a look in the eye until he owned the room, and the anticipation for what he was about to say was building.

"No running," he grinned. "Now, let's go."

The inner side of the room, that being furthest from the door, and close to where Fintan was sitting, opened with an enormous groan, peeling away to reveal some ordinary-looking escalators leading downwards.

*

Zack elbowed Fintan gently in the ribs. "Mister Jones, " he snorted. "Now how much are you willing to bet that that is not his real name?"

They stepped onto the escalator and rode it down to a large elevator lobby. All the elevators were open, and the kids were directed to enter them.

"I don't think I've ever been in a lift before," said Fintan.

"A what?"

"A lift," said Fintan. "You know this thing."

"A *lift*," said Zack, shaking his head. "That's what you call an *elevator*?"

The elevator interrupted their conversation as it jarred to life, and started to move downwards, slowly at first, but quickly picking up speed.

"We're going pretty deep," said Zack.

"If it's just black walls outside," said Fintan, "why are the walls of the elevator made of glass?"

Beyond the elevator walls they could see the darkened rock of the elevator shaft moving past. And it was moving *fast*.

There was a gasp, and the elevator suddenly became glaringly bright. Fintan fumbled for his sunglasses and put them on. He turned around to see the back of the elevator and his stomach jumped into his mouth.

"That's impossible," said one kid, a short dark skinned boy with an Indian accent.

Through the glass wall, Fintan could see that they were high up in the air, descending rapidly towards a huge city far beneath them. It was disconcerting – they were underground, but it felt like they were flying.

He looked around to see the city was surrounded by green fields. He followed the fields towards the horizon where he saw a dark wall that surrounded the city, forming a perfect circle.

The wall must have been hundreds of feet high, and on top of it, covering the entire city and surroundings was a dome that curved upwards and over Fintan's head.

He guessed that it could be as much as ten miles across and maybe two miles high.

Above their heads, in the center of the dome was a bright light, illuminating the city and the lands below. It was like a small sun, providing light and life to the world below.

Between them and the city, far below, was a circular platform, empty in the middle like the rim of a wheel, and standing on the ground with four legs like a giant dinner table.

The elevator approached this platform, slowly grinding to a halt. Shocked and awed, Fintan joined the others in leaving the elevator, and, with the other kids, they entered a large reception hall, with a view in every direction of the city below, and the roof above.

Mister Jones spoke up. "It's called a *geofront*," he said, "and it will be your home for the next few years." He paused before continuing. "We're buried beneath the Nevada desert, but here is where the future of humankind is waiting to be born."

Zack's face spoke volumes to Fintan. It didn't take much to deduce that the American boy was as stunned and as shaken as Fintan was. He looked at Ayako who was pale, and staring around openmouthed.

"Are we still alive," said Zack. "Is this real?"

They left the lobby and walked out towards the main platform that they had seen from the elevator. The sides of the rim spread out before them, meeting at the close of the circle, perhaps half a mile away. They could look down through the center of the rim at the city below, or over the outer edge of the rim to see the outskirts of the city and the countryside leading up to the rim wall.

Fintan looked down at the city. Several skyscrapers occupied in the city center, and he could see trains snaking their way between them. Hundreds of smaller buildings surrounded them; tapering out in density as well as height the further you got from the city center. He did notice four large dome-shaped buildings spaced evenly around the circle of the city center. Each one had train lines leading to and from them, and each one was a hive of activity.

Far below, he could see the dots of people walking around on their daily business.

I belong here he thought. *They want* me *here.* A great rush of pride welled inside him, bursting over him like an ocean wave. He shuddered, and couldn't help but smile. A tear crept to his eye.

*

"The show's about to begin," said Mister Jones.

As if on cue, the bright light far above them began to dim, and lights started to twinkle in each of the buildings. The domes that Fintan had noticed earlier lit up brightest of all, with searchlights that penetrated the rapidly darkening sky and diffusing in the roof above in a splash of colors. Each dome had its own distinctive color. One was Red, another Blue, another Green and the last one Yellow.

Out of the searchlights, Fintan could see small objects beginning to move. They made small trails of light and darted around like angry insects.

"Some type of ship," muttered Zack.

He was right. As they got closer, Fintan could see that they were small aircraft, but they moved like nothing he had ever seen. They turned and banked easily and effortlessly as they zipped their way around the sky, trailing light behind them.

In an instant the ships fell into a formation and flew directly at the observation platform. The crowd gasped as one as the ships whizzed over, under and around the platform, bathing it in light.

The ships were moving so fast it was hard to see their shape. But then a group of them broke formation and hovered just above their heads, spinning silently, with only a faint whoosh of air giving a cooling breeze to the onlookers.

They were disk shaped, metallic, and maybe ten feet across. A bubble at the top center contained the pilot.

"Flying saucers," said Zack. "Flying saucers!"

Fintan felt like his chin was going to hit the floor.

The saucers broke formation and continued with the light show. For the next few minutes they banked and turned, performing stunts, spinning, flying in tight formations before breaking in an array of glittering lights that made the crowd laugh and cheer.

Not for the first time, Fintan forgot to breathe, and gasped as a trio of red saucers buzzed the platform only feet away from him.

A tear was running down Ayako's cheek. He stood closer to her, and their hands touched. She held his hand for a moment, squeezing him tightly before letting go.

Fintan's chest tingled.

The show's climax came with the ships clustering beneath the platform, in a huge bright dancing group. They went still, and the kids peered over the edge. Then, in a choreographed maneuver, the ships exploded upwards and outwards, skywriting the word 'Welcome' in many different languages.

The group cheered and applauded loudly. Fireworks started exploding in the sky below them, and from the city they could hear the faint cheers of a large crowd, lost in the distance.

Around the platform, lights came on slowly, and as the sky-written words faded away, the center of the ring turned opaque, and a boy walked out onto it. He looked to be about fourteen, and wore a dark gray uniform with three red stripes on his right arm.

"A force field?" Zack wondered out loud. Ayako shushed him.

"Welcome to Area 51," the uniformed boy said, smiling enthusiastically.

The silence broken, some students began to applaud. And then some cheered. Quickly the area became a cacophony of noise as the students cheered for the display that they'd just seen, and the secret world that they knew they would be a part of.

"On behalf of the Area 51 flight school, we want to welcome all our new students," he said in a rehearsed manner. "You've come from many different countries and cultures, but together, here, we are all the brotherhood and sisterhood of humankind."

Another cheer went up, this one much louder than the first. Fintan felt Zack grab his hand and hold it high cheering with all his lungs.

When it subsided, he continued. "Before we begin our welcome meal, the principal of the school would like to meet you. Do you want to meet her?"

They answered as one "Yes!"

A small figure in a silver, hooded robe walked out of the crowd. Fintan couldn't make out if it was a man or a woman. It reached the microphone, faced them and lowered its hood.

Its skin was gray in color and hairless. Its head was much larger than Fintan would have expected on an equivalent sized human body.

It had a small mouth, filled with tiny white teeth, and large, almond-shaped black eyes.

The principal was an alien.

Chapter 7: Nizhoni

We've been looking, but haven't found any hard evidence that they're here yet.

Well that's good news.

Yes, but let's stay vigilant. Things will deteriorate quickly if they find us.

I understand.

On another note, the new crop of kids is promising.

Evolution at work again, providing the best genes at the time we need them most.

The principal raised its hand in greeting, and all fell silent. It wasn't far from Fintan, but there were some taller kids in front of him so he had to strain to look. It moved its head smoothly, looking around the room, and as it breathed he could hear a soft rasp. What looked like an air bladder on the side of its head inflated and deflated as it breathed. This made sense to Fintan – its body was so slender that it wouldn't be able to hold large lungs. It would probably be more efficient for the lungs to be close to the brain too.

It spoke out, with a voice that Fintan didn't know how to describe. It had a beautiful quality to it, like a rushing wind, or flowing waters.

"Welcome," it said, "I understand you have many questions, and I assure you, they will be answered in time. For now I will cover the basics. My name is Trichallik, and I am what you would call, an alien. And, before you ask, I am female."

Her little mouth smiled, and then she paused, surveying the room once more. She gazed directly at Fintan and he felt funny in his stomach.

"But in time you will drop that title and learn that despite our differences, we are just like you and you will call my people your brothers and sisters from the stars. We have been working with your people for some time, with a single goal in mind. To protect your species from extinction by helping them go to the stars."

"You see," she said, "a few decades ago, your people, in this nation, discovered and used the deadliest weapons your world has ever seen. Nuclear weapons. You already used these weapons once in a war. We could not allow that to happen again. Using them on a wide scale would destroy all life on this planet. You were spiraling downwards towards self-destruction. So we acted."

She paused. The room was silent, rapt.

"We unveiled ourselves to your leaders and told them of the dangerous path that they were on. Your leaders were wise, and chose to hide our existence. They chose to work with us, in secret, to build a new future. On one planet, your species was vulnerable to extinction, but should you go to the stars and colonize them, this could never happen."

"And thus our project was born. Since then, every year we take the best and brightest from your children and teach them the skills that they will need to reach the stars, and handle what you find there."

"This is why you are here. This is what you will learn. This is who we are."

She ended, and left the stage.

"You got your aliens," said Fintan on seeing Zack's stunned face.

"I never guessed,"said Zack, trailing off, "I never guessed."

Mister Jones then took the podium. He gestured towards large doors on the right hand side.

"I'm sure everyone must be hungry for food as well as answers," he smiled. "Refreshments are available through here. At each seat you'll see a small device that looks like a bracelet. Please put it on and follow the instructions it gives you."

"Food," said Zack. "Perfect, I'm starving!"

"We've just seen aliens," said Fintan, "and all you can think about is food?"

"Yep," said Zack. "Squeet!"

Ayako cocked her head in confusion. "Squeet?"

"Squeet," said Zack. "Let's go eat. Say it quickly. Squeet."

"Ah" said Fintan. "Squeet."

Ayako looked confused but complied. "Squeet," she said.

They followed the crowd into a large hall, laid out with a welcome banquet. Zack was grinning ear to ear.

They grabbed three chairs and inspected the bracelets. While the two boys started wolfing into the waiting food, Ayako tried her bracelet on.

She winced. "It scratched me," she said.

The bracelet came to life and a clear voice came from a tiny speaker on its side. "Ayako Katsuragi," it said, "Red Squadron."

A jewel placed in the center turned from white to red and the bracelet went silent.

Fintan took his bracelet and slipped it on. It scratched him too, and he was ashamed to react with a bigger jump than Ayako had. "Ouch," he yelled while the bracelet said, "Fintan Reilly, Red Squadron."

Ayako smiled. At least they'd each have a friend in their new squadron.

They saw other kids trying theirs on, and the jewels turning different colors. Some were red, but others were blue, yellow or green.

"The same colors as the ships we saw," said Zack through a mouthful of sausages. His bracelet still lay on the table.

"It's taking a DNA sample," said Ayako. "That's how it identifies us."

"Here goes nothing," said Zack. He picked up his bracelet and looked at it gingerly. He slipped it on and winced as it scratched him.

"Zack Adams," it said, "Red Squadron."

He had been holding his breath and let it out. "Thank goodness," he said. "I didn't want to go looking for new friends!"

Now they were able to relax and discuss the events of the day over food. The conversation went from the light show to Trichallik and the aliens.

"I wonder how many of them there are," said Ayako. "We've only seen one"

"So far," said Zack. "But we only just got here."

"So much information in such a short time," added Fintan. "Makes me feel I've been here a lot longer."

Ayako smiled. Zack laughed. "You nailed it there buddy."

As the meal wound down, Mister Jones directed them to another elevator lobby that led them down to a train station, where they boarded color-coded trains to take them to their squadron barracks.

The barracks were designed with a large central dorm containing a common area for eating and general gatherings. Two smaller domes, one for the boys and one for the girls were connected to this, and the sleeping areas were small two-person rooms connected to these. They'd be mixing in with the older kids in the rest of the squadron, but enough rooms had been reserved so the newcomers could find a place to stay. Ayako went off towards the girls dorms while Zack and Fintan claimed their sleeping quarters.

The first order of business for the newcomers was getting their uniforms made up. This was a simple process – they stood in a glass chamber that took pictures of their bodies from several angles. When Zack and Fintan had claimed their sleeping room and signed into their provided terminals, the uniforms were delivered. There were two different uniforms for them to wear – 'day' uniforms that were to be worn at school and on duty, and 'casual' wear which was suitable for other times.

They tried on the uniforms and admired how smart they looked. The uniforms looked familiar – the boy that had welcomed them earlier had been wearing one. They were shale gray, with a red stripe that ran up each arm and across the shoulders. Around their right arm was a single red band, beneath which was the flag of their country of citizenship. Zack had the stars and stripes of the USA, Fintan the Irish tricolor.

On their breast was a patch with their name on it. Fintan liked the look of it. "Fintan Reilly," he said, reading it out.

Zack looked at the band around his arm. "I guess it's because we are first years," he said. "Next year we'll have two, the following year three."

Both terminals beeped. Fintan signed into his to see an e-mail waiting from Ayako.

"She figured it out pretty quick," said Zack, "didn't she?"

"She's not here because she's dumb," said Fintan, smiling.

Zack nodded. He smiled. "So what do you think?"

"About what?"

"You know. A girl like her and a guy like me?"

"I think you're crazy," said Fintan, smiling.

Zack returned the smile and nodded towards the terminal, "What does she want?"

"Go down to the common area and meet her new roommate before rack time."

"Oh," said Zack. "What's rack time"

"Sleep," said Fintan. "I guess she's picking up the military terminology"

They went down to the common area, which was already a bustle of activity. Many older students were remaking acquaintances and new students like Fintan and Zack were staring around, wide-eyed.

Zack was grinning.

Fintan looked at him, an eyebrow raised. "What?"

"Look at the girls!"

The girls were also in uniform, which was similar to the boys', except they wore skirts instead of the trousers that they guys had. And they looked good. They looked *good*.

Fintan elbowed Zack who was staring. "You're drooling," he said.

"I know, but I don't care," said Zack. "This just isn't fair, there's no way I'll be able to concentrate with all this," he stopped as an older blonde girl walked past and flashed him a smile.

Fintan smiled too. He elbowed Zack again. At a table on the far side of the room sat Ayako and another girl, who were sipping tea and quietly taking in the surroundings.

As they approached, Ayako's face lit up as she waved towards the boys to join her.

Fintan and Zack sat opposite the two girls.

"Nice uniforms," said Zack.

Ayako's face flushed a little. She smiled and said 'thank you' quietly.

The other girl scowled.

Zack, ignoring her expression turned to face the other girl. "And who is this lovely lady?"

Ayako answered. "It's my roommate, Nizhoni".

Fintan read 'Nizhoni Benally' on her name tag.

"Wow," said Zack, "you Japs all have such beautiful names. Ayako, Nizhoni. It is very nice to meet you." He stretched out his hand.

Nizhoni looked at him emotionlessly. She didn't take his hand.

Finally she spoke, with a quiet, but powerful voice.

"I'm not Japanese," she said. "And it's pronounced Nee-shaw-Nee."

The silence lingered. Zack looked at her, and looked at his outstretched hand, embarrassment spreading across his face.

"And I'm not a 'Jap'" said Ayako coldly.

Silence spread around the table like an icy blanket.

Fintan spoke up, hoping to break the mood.

"Navajo," he said, and Nizhoni broke eye contact with Zack and stared at him in surprise. "Nizhoni is Navajo, right" said Fintan. "You're –"

Zack interrupted "You're native American! An Indian! Oh wow! I'm so sorry, you just look so much like you are–"

Nizhoni interrupted, but she didn't take her gaze off Fintan. "We prefer to be called Diné, or *First Nation*. We're not *Indian*, despite what the early European explorers thought." She showed the flag on her sleeve. It was yellow and had some map-like shapes on it, with a red and green rainbow covering them.

Zack stopped talking again. Embarrassed, he looked around and gulped. "Where'd you guys find the tea?"

Ayako pointed, so Zack got up to go and get some, escaping the awkwardness.

Ayako looked at Fintan. Fintan looked at Nizhoni. Nizhoni looked at Ayako. They all looked at Zack fumbling a teapot at the tea counter. They looked at one another again. And laughed.

Nizhoni reached her hand out to Fintan. "You must be Fintan," she said. "It's nice to meet you."

"And you, too," said Fintan. "It's really nice to meet you."

"He's coming back," said Ayako. "Look serious".

Somehow they straightened their faces, looking upset and hurt. Fintan could feel tears in his eyes from trying not to laugh.

Zack placed a teacup on the table for Fintan, and started sipping his own.

He sat, started to speak, stopped and started again. "Ayako, Nizhoni. I'm sorry, I think I just got too excited, and when that happens, I run my mouth off. I'm really sorry."

Fintan snorted and nearly choked on his tea.

Confused, Zack blurted out "What now?"

Fintan started to giggle.

"Hey," said Zack. "C'mon Fintan, help a brother out here"

Ayako and Nizhoni cracked up too. Zack looked at each of them.

"Oh," he said. "I get it."

Ayako and Nizhoni looked at each other. Ayako winked, and both girls turned to him. "Typical American!"

Ayako stuck her tongue out at him.

Chapter 8: Hazing

He's making healthy friendships.
He needs them. They'll help bond him into our family.
Yes, but families always have a cost.
A price we'll have to pay.

"Classes begin *tomorrow?*" said Zack, reading from his terminal. "They don't give us time to settle in do they?"

"It's been a long day," said Fintan. "I'll worry about classes in the morning."

*

All his life he'd had dreams, and this night he had a nightmare. He dreamed that he was swimming upwards to the surface of the ocean. When he reached the surface he tried to breathe, but something felt different. He couldn't figure out what it was. He looked at his body, but it wasn't human. He was an insect, a grasshopper or a locust with a grayish body and dry hard skin. He could feel the exoskeleton clicking as he moved his legs in the water. He looked all around, but there was water in all directions. Then he saw a disturbance in the water, waves began to fan out from the disturbance and bubbles began to rise. At first they were tiny, but they got bigger and bigger as something was approaching from underneath. The water broke with a roar and a great, ugly creature surfaced. It had a large maw with sharp teeth, but its eyes were intelligent. It made him think of a Chinese dragon as it turned towards him. Its eyes met his as it closed on him. Its maw opened, revealing row after row of sharp teeth, ready to consume him, closing fast. He could smell sulfur, like there was fire within it.

And then he woke up, cold sweat clinging to his skin. The clock read 6:00. Time to wake up.

"You alright?" said Zack from the other side of the room.

"Nightmare," said Fintan. "Sorry."

"Scary huh?" he asked as he sloped off towards the shower.

"You have no idea."

*

The first class of the day was *Cosmic History*. Fintan was excited at first, thinking he'd be looking into aliens and other civilizations around the galaxy, but it turned out to be a lot more boring. It was the 'real' history of the world over the last few decades, starting with the crash of an alien ship in Roswell, New Mexico, and going up to the present day.

The teacher, Mister Sinclair, was the classic, clichéd English man. He was formerly of the Royal Air Force, tall, thin and gangly, with a superior air that had him looking down his long nose at the students.

Those that he liked he would speak to with some likeness of respect, and to the others his voice dripped with sarcasm.

His style was to read from the textbook in his boring, monotone voice. He'd stop at random, and ask someone in the class a question. If they got it right, the reward was a gruff acknowledgment; otherwise it was a withering look.

"Who was the President of the United States at the time of the Roswell crash?" he asked out loud, scanning the classroom. His eyes rested on Fintan's and he pointed.

"Reilly, isn't it? I can spot an Irishman anywhere," he said dryly.

Fintan gulped. He had no idea about American presidents.

"We're waiting, Mister Reilly. You can answer that *simple* question, can you not?"

Time for a wild guess thought Fintan. "Truman?"

"Hmm," said Sinclair. "Lucky guess, I'm sure"

Zack whispered from behind his hand "Was that a snarl?"

As the class ended and they left, Fintan strode ahead of the others.

Zack ran to catch up with him. "What's up buddy?"

"Darn it, he hates me already," said Fintan.

"I think," said Nizhoni, catching up, "he hates everyone."

"He's English, I'm Irish," said Fintan, "it's special in my case."

Zack smiled. "Don't worry about it. Back in California my pranks are...what's the word?"

"Terrible?" asked Ayako.

"Legendary," said Zack, ignoring her. "Mister Limey Englishman Toffee Sinclair will be my first target."

*

The first day of school behind them, Zack, Fintan, Ayako, Nizhoni and the rest of the first-years made it back to the dorm, expecting dinner, but instead the rest of the squadron was waiting for them.

A tall, thin boy, wearing the stripes of a fifth-year hushed everyone and approached the confused first-years.

He spoke with a similar drawl to Mister Sinclair.

"Welcome freshers," he said, with a tone that was anything but welcoming. "I'm Simon Saint-john, your squadron captain. You've had your first day of school, but now you're going to have your first night of being a real member of Red Squadron."

"We're a squadron of what?" he asked.

"Bravery!" answered the crowd.

"And what makes us Brave?" he asked.

"Combat!" came the answer.

"And where do we find combat?"

"Anywhere, everywhere, Anywhere, Everywhere!"

He turned back to the new kids. "Tonight we'll see just how brave you are."

They only had time to drop their bags, and then it was back outside. Simon led them back to the train station and they boarded a train that was outbound towards the rim wall. When they had reached the final stop, he led them off the train and across some fields and some uncultivated earth and wasteland towards the wall. It was a long walk, and the younger kids huddled in near silence.

"Don't worry," whispered Zack to Ayako, noticing her concern. "It's just a hazing"

"Hazing?" she asked. "I am not familiar with that word."

"It's a prank that they play on newcomers to scare us, but they're not going to harm or hurt us."

Nizhoni shrugged. She didn't believe him. "Because we're kids? You forget that this is a military school. Be on your guard." She pressed on in grim silence.

Simon flashed his eyes in their direction. He didn't need to say it, but it was clear that he was telling them to be quiet.

They approached a part of the wall that looked a little different from the rest. The wall itself was a couple of hundred feet high and in sections was both broader and thicker. Fintan guessed that these were support points to help hold the weight of the dome.

As they got closer, he could see some hatches and doors on either side of the wall section. Simon led them to one hatch, made of thick steel and opened it by spinning a wheel at its front. He gestured for the kids to go through.

"Where are we going?" asked one kid, Raj, the small dark-skinned boy Fintan had seen in the elevator a few days before.

Simon just smiled and gestured again. It was time to go in, not time for questions.

Zack strode to the front of the group and walked through the door. There was some hesitation, but eventually the others followed, with Fintan, Ayako and Nizhoni taking the lead.

The door banged shut and Fintan could hear it squeak as Simon locked it from the other side.

They were alone, in near darkness, a dim light showing them that they were in a cave of some sort. The walls were dark and damp, and the floor sandy and strewn with rocks of different sizes. Fintan could hear Zack's voice ahead. "It's a tunnel, not a cave," he called out. "There's a light up here. It's probably the way out."

"I don't like this," said one girl.

"Don't worry," said Fintan. "I'm sure Zack is right and this is just a silly hazing."

They stepped carefully over rocks as they made their way through the dim tunnel. Despite the darkness, Fintan noticed how light Nizhoni was on her feet and how she deftly navigated her way through. She quickly went ahead of the group, catching up with Zack. The darkness didn't bother her. She trotted back towards the main group.

"There's a large cavern up ahead," she said. "The light is coming from there. We should go."

She went ahead again, stopping at the entrance to the cavern to wait for the others to catch up.

Fintan was one of the first there. She looked him up and down, measuring him with some degree of admiration. "I walk the beaches near where I live," said Fintan. "They're quite rocky, so I've learned to balance."

She smiled and nodded. Fintan felt his heart flutter.

Zack had walked into the cavern which was a good forty feet across and twenty feet high. Dim lamps, recessed deep into the rock ceiling cast a pallid light. He was striding around, in a challenging pose, arms held out.

"Come on guys, is this all you've got?"

His answer was a low, menacing grumbling noise. Something else was in there with them. Something *big*.

"Oh ha-ha," said Zack, defiant. "You make some monster noises and you think I'm scared?"

The grumbling grew louder. Fintan heard someone gasp. Behind Zack, the shadows jumped.

It was behind him, and he didn't see it.

Then it shuffled into the light, roaring as it did so. Monstrous and over ten feet tall, all teeth and fangs it lumbered on two back legs towards Zack. Its forelegs stretched out like the claws of a crab, and were equipped with long, sharp, talons.

Zack screamed and ran for cover. The monster, or whatever it was, continued lumbering towards the group. There was no cover in the tunnel that they had come from, so the only hope for escape was to go forward into the cavern and hope to go *around* the monster, or climb higher than it could reach. There was chaos as they scattered, screaming.

Fintan fought the urge to scream. He was quivering with fear, and it felt like the world slowed down as the beast moved towards him. Then something kicked into action within him and he saw a trail that led upwards and away from the cavern floor. He darted towards it, but it was shorter than he expected, and he reached its end quickly. There was no further way to climb, so he could only hope to hide. There was a large rock near its end, and he found Raj there, cowering in the dark. He leaped behind the rock and huddled up with the smaller boy.

Neither of them said anything, afraid the monster might hear and might find them. They could hear it shuffling across the cavern floor, and they could hear the screams of the other children.

Fintan closed his eyes as tightly as he could. He reached for his bracelet, wondering if he could use it to call for help, but it was dead. Raj's was too.

He couldn't help but wonder what had happened to the others, so, peeping out from his cover, he saw Ayako and Zack on the other side of the cavern. They were climbing upwards towards what looked like an artificial path around the rim.

And then he saw Nizhoni.

She had no escape route, and she ran out of space behind. The monster had cornered her and lumbered slowly towards her, roaring as it went. From his vantage point, behind the monster and a little to its right, he could see her face, emotionless and still as always. She was slowly crouching down to try to grab a rock. She wasn't going down without a fight.

A rush of bravery hit Fintan and he screamed, climbed over his rock and charged straight at the monsters hindquarters. Seeing a stick on the ground he grabbed it, and swung with all his might at the creature's right leg.

He must have missed, because with the strength of his swing he found himself corkscrewing into the ground and falling in a cloud of dust. Disoriented, he tried to pull himself up, to see Nizhoni pulling back with the stone and throwing it hard and straight at a point behind Fintan.

He heard breaking glass.

The monster vanished.

There was laughter, followed by a voice. "I don't believe it, she broke it!"

The lights came on in the cavern, and Simon stood in the center, smirking. Other, older kids wandered in from their hiding places around him.

"You spoiled my little joke, didn't you, little girl?" he said, facing Nizhoni. If he was trying to intimidate her, it didn't work. She stared back, unblinking.

Not getting any traction, he turned to Fintan. He laughed. "Nice swing there, ace. You should play baseball!"

He laughed and mimicked an umpire yelling "Steerike One!" The others laughed along; one clapped Simon on the back.

He moved in for more abuse. "Trying to save the little woman and he ends up on his butt in the ground. How *embarrassing* for our little hero."

"Shut up," said Nizhoni.

Simon looked back at her, and raised an eyebrow. He advanced on her, his hands closing into a fist.

"Did you say something?" he snarled.

"I said 'Shut up'" she responded.

Fintan could see Simon's body tense up as he approached her. Fintan climbed to his feet and ran to stand between them. Simon was much taller than he was, so he was looking up towards the older boy's chin.

"Leave her alone," said Fintan.

Simon stopped in his tracks and looked down at the smaller boy. He smiled. Laughed.

"Oh you kids are just too funny!" He bent over, double, laughing hard, slapping his knee. The other older kids laughed too. Nizhoni put her hand on Fintan's shoulder, gently pushing him aside so she could stand *beside* him instead of *behind* him.

Simon continued laughing at them, pouring on the humiliation. Fintan was getting angrier by the second. Bu Nizhoni took his hand and led him away without a word. She wasn't going to confront Simon on this.

Fintan realized that she was being smart, walking away. The image had changed from Simon laughing in their faces, to him standing alone in the cavern, laughing and looking insane. Simon also realized this, and stopped. He wasn't going to talk to their backs, so instead gestured for everyone to come closer. He had to take control of the situation again.

"Ok, first years," he said. "Party's over. Let's get back to the barracks."

Chapter 9: Draft

The girl is impressive. Is she one of yours?
Surprisingly, no.
But her kind are always strong and noble, right?
Her kind?

"You," said Zack, mouth full of breakfast, stabbing a fork in Fintan's direction, "made an enemy last night."

"Actually," said Ayako. "I think he made a friend."

Nizhoni said nothing.

Zack raised his eyebrows, smiling.

"And," said Ayako, "I didn't see you doing anything to help her. She was trapped."

"I was busy helping *you* escape," said Zack. "Only one damsel in distress at a time!"

"I don't remember asking for your help," she said. "And, if I remember right, I was climbing out faster than you were."

"Oh, I was just going slowly so I could be beneath you, to defend you."

"No," she said. "It was so you could look up my skirt!"

"No!" said Zack, but Ayako was laughing.

"It was because I was staying between you and the monster-"

But she continued laughing. Even Nizhoni was smiling.

Zack buried his head in his hands. They had gotten him again.

Fintan yawned.

"Late night?" asked Ayako.

"No, I just didn't sleep well."

"Didn't sleep well?" said Zack "You were groaning all night. That was some dream you had."

"Dream?" said Nizhoni. "What did you dream?"

"I don't remember," said Fintan. "I've been having strange dreams since I got here."

"Strange dreams, blah, blah, blah," said Zack. "Look, we can psychoanalyze them to death, but the answer is obvious. Look around us. We're living in a giant underground city, and aliens are teaching us to fly UFOs. I think your mind has to deal with it somehow. For you it's dreams. I wouldn't worry too much about it; they're just silly dreams after all."

"Dreams are not silly," said Nizhoni. "Sometimes they try to tell us what we need to know."

She turned back to Fintan. "Try to remember. I believe it could be important."

Zack rolled his eyes. "Native mumbo jumbo," he grunted beneath his breath.

"I'll try," said Fintan, ignoring him.

She nodded and smiled. It was time to leave so they got up and went to clear their plates.

On the way, Zack whispered in his ear. "You made a friend all right, nice one buddy. Now if only I could get Ayako to talk to me like that!"

He was smiling.

"I'm sure it will happen," said Fintan.

*

It was exciting. Today they'd start flying for the first time. Instead of the usual classrooms, they made their way to a given address in the city.

They arrived at a large dome, nestled beneath and contrasting with the tall skyscrapers.

"Oh look, another dome," said Zack. "These architects have no imagination, do they?"

Inside, a large room containing several car-sized machines awaited them.

"Flight simulators," said Ayako.

"Flight *simulators*," said Zack. "Aw darn it. I was hoping for the real thing."

"You're not ready for the real thing," came a voice from behind him. A tall, dark skinned, but fair-haired woman walked past and through the crowd of students. "I'm Iara" she said. "While it is spelled I-A-R-A, it is pronounced EE-Ara. Understood?"

Zack nodded, eyes fixed on her.

Tall, and statuesque with a perfect figure, long wavy blonde hair contrasted her dark brown skin. On her right arm, her uniform had the Brazilian flag on it.

Zack's eyes said more than Fintan needed to know. The boy was in love.

Iara had them each take a flight simulator and run through various drills. Fintan recognized it as similar to what he had flown during his testing.

He set himself up, placing his headset on and activating the display. Small windows popped into his view, containing the faces of the other pilots. One larger window opened, containing Iara's face.

"Listen up," she said. "You might think you can fly a saucer because you passed the test, but don't forget that it was just a test, and you didn't pass every part of it. Also, that ship was tuned for someone who had never flown before. Going from that to one of these is like going from a bicycle to a sports car so *pay attention*"

"Yes ma'am, paying attention." Said Zack. "Definitely paying attention. I mean, like, you have all my attention. Not you, but what you're saying, right? I mean I'm paying attention to your lesson. Ok, so you haven't started the lesson yet, but I'm paying attention while I wait for you to start the lesson, and, well, I'm ready, so when you're ready to start the lesson, I'll be paying attention. Ok?"

"Zack," said Iara.

"Yes ma'am?" said Zack.

"Clear the channel."

"Uh, what does that mean ma'am?"

"It means shut up," said Nizhoni.

"Oh. Yes ma'am. Shutting up now. I mean clearing the channel now."

The windows of the other students cleared from Fintan's display, and a star field showed in their place. Iara's window remained open so she could direct them.

"Now let's take it slowly," she said. "Assemble at this point."

An icon blinked on the screen, showing the needed assembly point.

"Oh come on!" said Zack, a window with his face popping into view on Fintan's screen. "That's too easy!"

The simulator was smart. Fintan turned his head around and could see Zack's saucer in formation behind him. It started to move forward slowly, and then suddenly accelerated.

It collided with another saucer and bounced off in a wild direction. Fintan heard him say "Oops" as he tried to adjust. He then tried to move forward again, but again collided with another saucer. On his display, Fintan could see Zack's head as it bounced around, recoiling from the impact shock. He was grunting. His ship was bouncing like a pinball in a machine before shooting off in a random direction. Zack screamed.

And then his ship stopped, and vanished off the screen, before returning to its initial position.

"I forgot to say," said Iara, smiling slightly, "that as these simulators are used for in-atmosphere training, there are no inertial dampeners, so you will feel *every* collision as if it was real."

"Right" said Zack, quietly. "Ouch."

Iara smiled again.

Class was only a couple of hours, but even in that time Fintan began to get a feel for the ship and how it could fly. Despite this, he was no match for Nizhoni, who flew like an expert, right out of the gate.

"Impressive" said Iara. "Have you been in one of these before?"

"Never," said Nizhoni. "I just listened to my teacher."

Iara nodded. Zack made a slurping sound.

Nizhoni bumped her ship against his, hard. "Ow!" said Zack. "You did that on purpose!"

"No," said Nizhoni. "We're just trainees, it was an accident."

"Grr" said Zack.

*

It had been another long day, and at the end, they were glad to make their way back to the barracks. "I wonder what surprises your friend Simon has in store for us tonight?" said Zack.

They returned in time for dinner. The buffet line was snaking around already.

"Great, we're late," said Zack. "All that will be left is yucky vegetables."

They got in line behind a fifth year boy.

"Some show last night," the boy said to Nizhoni and Fintan.

Nizhoni glared at him.

"No offense, but you have to realize that Simon is our group captain, and under his leadership Red Squadron has won the Starball tournament four years in a row. Tonight is the Starball draft, so he needs to show that he's in charge with you freshers."

"Starball?" said Zack.

"It's everything here" said the boy. "You might think we're here for school and lessons and *Cosmic History* but it's all about flying, and Starball is for the best of the best flyers."

Ayako looked intrigued and interested. "Tell us more" she said.

"Starball is everything," he repeated. "It's a game, played using the saucers, flying inside the dome. It's hard to explain – it's best just to watch it, there'll be a game at the end of this week. Every year the first and second place teams from the year before play an 'exhibition' match in the first week, to kick off the school year as it were."

Zack nodded thoughtfully.

"The draft is tonight, after dinner. It's a big deal. Students graduate, and need to be replaced. We lost two of our best players this year, so the draft will replace them. The new draftees will have to play in the exhibition game, which makes it more challenging for the leader – he only has a few days to get the new team together and working as a unit. Tryouts and the games proper will begin next semester, in late January. Then we play every squadron against every other until a winner is determined."

"Is there a prize?" asked Zack.

"Oh yes," said the boy. "A field trip."

"A field trip?" said Zack. "Oh whoopee, that sounds amazing. Not."

The boy shrugged. He then pointed at the door that led out of the dome, towards the train station. "You see those rocks?" he said, gesturing at a couple of display cases with basketball-sized gray rocks in them. "We picked them up on the last field trip"

"Great," said Zack. "Rocks. Where'd you get them? Nevada?"

"We got them on our field trip," repeated the boy. "On the *Moon*."

*

Dinner was full of thoughtful silence from Zack. He had Starball on his mind, not to mention a field trip to the moon. He hadn't said as much, but Fintan could read it all over his face.

"I guess I was always on the sports teams at school," he said finally. "I wonder how I can get to be on the Starball team."

"They might draft you," said Fintan.

Ayako smiled. "You probably don't want to be *drafted*," she said. "I can't imagine leader Simon will be happy with untrained freshers on the team. We'll have a chance when they have tryouts in January."

After dinner, Mister Sinclair, who was their squadron owner as well as *Cosmic History* teacher, took to the podium at one end of the dining hall.

"Everybody, can I have your attention please" he said loudly.

All eyes turned on Sinclair, as a large screen unfurled behind him. On it was a video feed of the leaders of other squadrons. Fintan elbowed Zack pointing out Iara who was on-screen as the leader of Yellow squadron. In the center was Trichallik.

"Let the draft begin," she said in her hissing alien voice.

She held up a simple looking bag. "As yellow finished fourth, they shall go first" said Trichallik. She pulled a name out of the bag and read it "Morgan Wilson". There were cheers on-screen in yellow squadron's room, while there were groans all around them in red's.

"He was their best reserve. They just got much stronger!" said one boy. The draft went on through green squadron, and then blue, which had to replace three players.

As each name was called out, Fintan could see Simon putting his head further down in his hands. The draft had been kind to their rivals, with experienced players being pulled from the hat.

"Blue is looking strong now. I think they'll take it this year!" Fintan heard somebody say.

And then it became Red squadron's turn.

On-screen, Trichallik reached into the bag. She pulled out a name and read it.

"Nizhoni Benally," she said. "First year student."

"What?" shouted Simon, incredulous. "A first year! A *fresher*? You've got to be kidding me! She doesn't even know how to fly!"

"Actually," said Iara, from the screen. "She's in my class, and she's pretty good."

Simon stared at the screen. "She's a first year" he repeated, softer this time.

Mister Sinclair put his hand on Simon's shoulder. "It's a random draw," he said. "Luck is against us, but we don't need luck. We are red squadron."

"And," he continued. "There's another name to come out of the hat."

Trichallik nodded and reached into the bag once more. She pulled out a name and read it.

"Fintan Reilly," she said, without emotion. "First year student."

Chapter 10: Nizhoni's Plan

I never thought you'd rig the draw like that.
You probably won't believe this, but I didn't
Really?
Really. Fate can play a strange hand, can't it?

"So you guys are the little freshers who think they can fly with us, huh?" said Simon to Fintan and Nizhoni at breakfast the next morning. "I haven't forgotten your pathetic defiance in the cavern. You will not defy me like that again, understood?"

"Hang on," said Fintan. "We didn't choose this. You saw Trichallik pick our names out of the hat."

"Don't answer me back like that!" said Simon, anger bubbling up in his voice. "You will now call me *sir* and ask me for permission to speak. Do you understand?"

Fintan didn't answer.

"I said, do you understand?" he yelled, slapping the table for emphasis.

"Yes, sir," said Nizhoni flatly.

Simon looked to her. She met his gaze. If he was looking for sarcasm or irony, it wasn't there.

"Practice is at the launch dome at 1700," he said to her. "You know how to get there? You can read, right? And make sure the other greenie kiddo is with you, ok?" he said, jutting his thumb in Fintan's direction.

*

Cosmic History was even more boring than usual and it was hard to concentrate when Fintan was worried sick about what would happen with Simon later in the day. I didn't *ask* for this, he thought. I didn't *want* to join your little team.

It seemed that Mister Sinclair had a sixth sense for when Fintan wasn't paying attention and asked him question after question. Each one Fintan got right, but that wasn't enough for the teacher, who kept asking.

Finally, Fintan got one wrong. With glee Sinclair doled out detention for Fintan's "lack of attention".

As he had practice that evening, he would have to serve late detention, after dinner.

Fintan sighed. This was not a good day.

He walked out of class in a dark mood, wanting just to go back to his bed and hide his head under the covers. Zack smiled and joked and mimicked Sinclair, but nothing was going to work. The more he tried, the more Fintan felt a knot in his stomach, tightening, making him want to scream.

He felt a touch on his arm. It was Nizhoni. "Can we talk?" she said.

Fintan nodded, and Zack said "Sure! What's up Nizhoni?"

Ayako elbowed him. "She wants to talk to *Fintan*"

Zack's mouth made an 'Oh' and he winked as he walked off with Ayako.

When they were gone, Nizhoni looked him in the eye.

"I told you he hates me" said Fintan.

Her answer was a slap to his face. Not a hard one, but enough to shock him more than he ever thought he could be.

"Wake up," she said. "You're better than this."

Fintan put his hand to his face. It felt hot where she had struck him. "Why-"

She didn't let him finish. "Because sometimes that is the only language you understand. Listen with your heart Fintan, not your brain, and sometimes things previously hidden will be unveiled."

"Are you telling me he doesn't hate me?"

She sighed. "I'm telling you it doesn't matter what he thinks. You are in control of what matters in your life, not him. He cannot *touch* you, he cannot *hurt* you, he cannot *harm* one who has dreamed a dream like yours."

She smiled a rare smile. Tears were in her eyes. And suddenly tears were in Fintan's eyes too.

She touched his face again, this time more gently.

*

Last class of the day was Astronomy with Miss Parmour.

Fintan had always loved the stars, but this class terrified him. Miss Parmour was *huge* and she was *warty*. Her dirty blonde hair fell to her shoulders and her pig-like eyes seemed to have no whites in them. She liked to scream in class as she recited data about star after star.

Red giants in particular got her excited.

"I'm sure she's an alien" said Zack. "You know like it's a disguise that she's hiding in."

Fintan snickered, but stopped quickly as she cast her piggy gaze towards him. She squinted before going back to her lecture on the life span of red giants.

"Deep inside there's a big slimy lizard just waiting to get out" whispered Zack.

Fintan snorted. Again she looked his way and he tried not to cry from keeping the laughter inside. He bit his lip so hard he thought it was bleeding.

"The blob from the planet Mungo" whispered Zack.

Finally Fintan burst out laughing, but by some stroke of luck his laugher was drowned out by the bell.

He sobered quickly. It was 1700.

As they left class, Zack and Ayako bade their goodbyes and Fintan and Nizhoni made their way to the flight center.

They were a few minutes early, but Simon showed up on the stroke of the hour. He was friendly and cordial with the rest of the team, shaking hands, exchanging hugs and discussing the summer gone past and the upcoming game.

But then the moment passed and it was time to get down to business.

"By now, you know who we got to replace Jack and Paulinha" he said to the team. "Two greenie freshers. Two pinpricks who are useless to help us."

He paused and stood before Fintan, towering over him. "Two *pilots* who will be nothing but a weight around our necks."

"Well," he continued. "Let me ask if these babies understand that when we are practicing and playing Starball, that they are under my command and my word is law?"

"Yes sir" said Nizhoni. Simon smirked and looked at Fintan.

"Yes, sir" croaked Fintan.

"Good" said Simon. "I have my first orders for you. So simple, even you can understand."

He pointed to the door, and yelled.

"*Get out!*"

*

Fintan was ready to protest, but a subtle elbow in the ribs from Nizhoni stopped him. Wordless, she turned and walked out the door. Fintan followed, reddening as he thought of Simon's smirk.

She was waiting for him outside.

"That nasty son of a-"

She cut him off with a stern look. "We follow orders without question," she said.

"Without question?" said Fintan, incredulous. "Does the squadron owner know that he'd kick us out?"

"You forget who the squadron owner is," said Nizhoni, raising an eyebrow. "I'm sure Mister Sinclair would *love* to hear your concerns."

"Besides," she continued. "Without question means without question. End of discussion."

She strode off towards the train station.

Fintan followed "But-"

She stopped, looking up at the signboards showing the different platforms for the different train lines. Her eyes furrowed as she searched. Then, with a little grunt, she found what she was looking for and began to walk towards a staircase that was ahead of her and to her right. She walked a few steps and then stopped, turned around and gestured for Fintan to follow.

"But, that's not the right way," he said.

"I know," she answered. "Come."

She boarded a train that was heading closer to the city center, away from the barracks.

"Where are we going?" asked Fintan, confused and dazed.

"To practice," she responded.

At the next stop she got off, looked around, and then headed towards a large, low, nondescript building not far from the station.

At the gates, she swiped her wrist bracelet over the security scanner. It beeped green and the gates yawned open, granting her access. Fintan did likewise and followed her in.

Inside the building was a vast, noisy and cavernous hall. Lights were flashing and noises were pounding everywhere. Fintan looked around and all he could see were games. Some reminded him of those from the testing, but there were many others that looked far more complex. Some were solo games, others involved teams of players huddled over large consoles, directing the action within. One thing stood out, all the kids were older. There were no first years here.

"Wow," said Fintan.

Nizhoni gestured towards another area. Large black doors separated it from the game room. A swipe of their bracelets granted access. And inside were flight simulators like the ones Simon had kicked them out of.

"You're a genius!" said Fintan. "How did you know about this?"

"I have some friends in the school," said Nizhoni, not elaborating further. "They told me."

They grabbed a couple of the simulators, and Nizhoni started programming the settings. "I'm setting it for Battle mode," she said. "You and I will be dog fighting. This is practice time, and this is how we will practice."

Fintan entered the simulator and put his headpiece on. Immediately the screen filled with a beautiful desert scene. He was flying above canyons and mesas. The view was amazingly realistic, and it was easy to believe that he really was flying over the desert.

He'd never flown in-atmosphere before so needed to experiment with the controls a little. As he would be fighting, he also needed to get used to the gun controls.

"The ship is a saucer," said Nizhoni in his headset. "You can shoot a narrow beam in any direction along the axis of the ship, forwards, backwards or whatever. Or, you can shoot a blast downwards from the center of the ship. Understood?"

Fintan experimented a little. He could get behind another ship and try to take it out with his beam, but because the saucers were thin, they were hard to hit. Alternatively, he could try to get above and then shoot a barrage directly downwards with devastating effect.

He did a little target practice on the ground and got the hang of it quickly.

"Ready?" she said.

"Ready," he answered.

The landscape reset, and now she was nowhere to be seen. Taking his ship low to the ground, hugging the contours, he searched for her. However, the simulation was so accurate; he blew dust off the ground, giving away his position. Nizhoni came screaming out of the sky, obscured by the sun, and blew him to pieces.

The fight had lasted maybe five seconds.

"One – Zero" she said, and the simulator reset.

Fintan wasn't going to be fooled again. He also knew that she was smart enough not to try the same trick twice. Flying close to the ground would throw up dust and give away her position, so he guessed there was only one choice – the canyons.

Again she was too smart for him. She *had* hidden in the canyons, but as soon as he entered, she shot straight up and waited for him to pass beneath before blowing him to pieces.

"Two – Zero."

At least he had lasted a little longer this time. That was encouraging.

"You've done this before, haven't you?" asked Fintan.

"No" she responded. "This is my first time. But it's like any combat, and *that* I have done before."

Fintan made a guess this time that he might have more experience in the tight confines of a canyon than she did. Both her kills came from open air. He saw a rock arch, and tried an experiment. He flew his saucer into the arch, stopping under the bridge at its top, and then gently flew upwards until his saucer was hovering, partially obscured by the bridge.

He waited.

After a few minutes, he spotted Nizhoni. She was smart, knowing he was trying something different and thus plotting random courses, trying to be unpredictable. Finally she seemed to decide that he was in the canyon and started 'buzzing' it, flying close to the edge, trying to lure him out.

He waited.

He was going to try an edge shot, with his beam weapon. He held his breath as he waited to line up the ideal shot.

She edged closer to his position, still not seeing him. When she was in range, he fired, and realization dawned on him that this was his first time using the weapons.

But it worked -- her ship was blown apart.

"Nice shot," she said "Two – One"

After that, their fights were a lot more even. The next time was a good old fashioned chase, and the ships were too fast and too thin to take each other out with beam weapons. However, Nizhoni made a mistake, flying under an arch, allowing Fintan to blow the top off it, burying her ship and scoring a kill.

"Two-Two" she said, reluctantly.

It was exhausting, but fun. Their time ran out at 18:30, and they had to stop. By then they had killed each other half a dozen times.

"Good practice!" said Fintan, and she answered with a smile. He'd never seen her smile like this before, and it made him feel special. Somehow, after that, detention didn't hurt so badly. Even Sinclair's scowl didn't bother him.

Chapter 11: Starball

Are you sure it's him and not her that we should be interested in?

Yes.

But she is the best we've seen in years.

I know, but I don't understand it but when I look forward, I see him being the One.

The One. Sounds so religious.

Not religion, fact. But again, most real religions are based on fact, are they not?

Nizhoni had asked Fintan not to tell anyone about their practice session. So, when the following morning Zack had asked them how practice went, Fintan answered "Great", but didn't elaborate.

For the rest of the week, they followed the routine. They'd turn up at practice, only for Simon to throw them out, and then go on to practice in the games arena.

On Friday, the day before Starball, Nizhoni programmed the machine differently. She dropped in a data crystal that set the machine up to simulate a Starball arena.

So this is what all the fuss is about thought Fintan as they looked at the arena. It was simple, being a perfect cube made up of force fields. Hitting a field would be like hitting a wall. Your ship could be damaged or even destroyed. Being a cube, it had eight corners. The 'goals' were in opposite corners, with the playing field stretching across the diagonal width of the cube.

"If it helps" said Nizhoni, "think of the cube as resting on one of its pointed corners instead of one of its flat sides. Then, one goal is at the bottom, and the other is at the top."

Fintan nodded. That *was* a good way of looking at it. The aim of the game was simple. Get the ball into the goal by any means necessary. While the saucer could carry the ball, a collision would cause the ball to drop. Additionally a saucer could fly fast and drop the ball, in which case it would continue along the trajectory the saucer had been heading in, carried by its inertia, like dropping a ball out of a moving car. Thus, to score one could either carry or drop the ball into the goal.

They practiced carrying and avoiding collisions with each other. Then they practiced collisions to see how the ball would break free, and if there was anything they could do to protect it or get an advantage in recovering it. They practiced flying around the bounds of the arena as quickly as possible, without crashing into walls or corners.

It was exhilirating! They were getting it, and knew that they would be able to compete in the game.

And with that, Saturday came, and it was time for Starball.

*

Saturday morning's breakfast was quiet at their table.

"Nervous?" asked Zack.

Nizhoni nodded. Fintan croaked a weak "yes".

Simon stood by their table.

"So, nuggets," he said. "Report to the arena at 1000, suited up and ready to play. Do you understand?"

"Yes, sir" they both replied.

Simon smiled, amused, and turned to Fintan.

"I see your little squaw has been teaching you about respect. Good that you've been learning *something* after I kicked you out of our practices. Be there, and don't be late."

He walked off.

Zack had his eyebrows raised. "Kicked you out of practice?" he mimicked.

Fintan stayed quiet and looked down at his breakfast.

"When did he do that?" asked Zack, more insistent this time.

Again, Fintan didn't answer.

"Every day," said Nizhoni.

"What?" said Zack. "What did you do? Why didn't you tell us?"

"Because," said Nizhoni "it was necessary to keep it a secret."

"A secret even from us?" said Zack, sounding hurt, and looking towards Fintan. "I thought we were friends".

"We are," said Fintan, but by then Zack had gotten up and walked away from the table, shaking his head.

Ayako had said nothing, but was also looking at Nizhoni, hurt in her eyes.

Nizhoni said nothing.

"I'd better go see if Zack is okay," said Ayako, getting up and following him.

And then they were alone. As always, Nizhoni was calm and unbothered. But then she melted a little. "We can tell them after the game, but, there will be many questions, and I cannot answer them all yet."

*

They assembled in the team ready rooms a quarter of an hour before the game.

"So," Simon said to the team, fully assembled for the first time. Rules didn't allow him to throw Fintan and Nizhoni out, and the rules of the exhibition game meant that he had eleven players only, and all must suit up and play. "It's the Nine of us against a full strength Blue Squadron."

The other players shuffled a little, casting the occasional glance at Nizhoni and Fintan.

"Yes, sir" they said, but not in unison.

Simon fell silent and forced them all to look him in the eye.

"We're a squadron of what?" he asked them quietly.

"Bravery!"

"And what makes us brave?" he asked.

"Combat!" came the answer.

"And where do we find combat?"

"Anywhere, everywhere, anywhere, everywhere!" they chanted.

"Anywhere and everywhere!" said Simon. "And today we will go into combat. Nine against eleven."

He called up a virtual display of the Starball cube. It was arranged in the same way as Nizhoni had explained it, balanced on one corner, with the Red squadron goal at the top, and the Blue squadron goal at the bottom.

"You two" he said, gesturing to Nizhoni and Fintan, "will cover these corners." He pointed at the four corners of the cube that were not goals and that were furthest from the action. "You are not to touch the ball at any time. Is that clear?"

Fintan looked at the corners. They had no strategic value in the game, and were as far away from the action as was possible. He was putting them on the field, but he didn't have to play them.

"Stupid freshers will just get in our way" he said. "So stay in those corners well away from the action. Do you understand?"

"Yes, sir" said Nizhoni.

Fintan shrugged, unhappy, but followed her lead. "Yes, sir"

*

The game began with Red and Blue squadrons feeling each other out in the center of the park. Each squadron would hold the ball for a little while, trying to penetrate the other team's side of the cube, getting a little closer to the goal each time, but not committing.

Nizhoni popped up in a window in Fintan's field of view. A red dot in the top right hand corner of the window showed that she was in 'private' mode, and that nobody else could hear their conversation.

"They're feeling each other out, right?"

Fintan nodded. "When Blue figure out why we're here, they'll realize they have a two-ship advantage. Red's only chance is to score before then, and try to hold out defensively."

Almost on cue, Red got more aggressive, pushing deeper and deeper into Blue territory, but leaving their goal untended.

"I wish I could hear what they're saying," said Fintan. "But they even cut us off from communications."

Nizhoni was watching the game play out. "One thing I have to say about Simon" she said. "He's a heck of a flyer."

Fintan watched as the captains ship darted in and out of the Blue formation. He was clearly acting as a diversion, hoping for the other team to double or triple team him and regain the advantage.

"It might suck that he's treating us like this, but he sure can play the game."

On his screen, Nizhoni nodded.

And then Simon stopped being a decoy and made a run for the other team's goal. He had gotten in front of the others and Red 2 sent the ball in his direction. His saucer caught it, spun on its axis, and without stopping the balls momentum, propelled it off a wall and into the corner of the goal.

It was 1-0 to Red, despite being outnumbered.

Fintan turned on the external feed. The crowd was going crazy. Two fifth years, one from Green and one from Yellow acted as commentators. They were in awe at Simon's flying, but curious about the tactic of keeping Fintan and Nizhoni in neutral corners.

"Sure they might be useless due to their inexperience," said one, a blonde American girl from yellow squadron. "But he could at least have them guarding the goals."

The game started again, but instead of sitting back and defending their lead, Red pressed its advantage. Their attack was devastating, and Blue was reeling backwards before Red 3 caught the ball and shot a *curving* shot around the last Blue ship and into the goal.

"Wow," said Nizhoni. "Did you see that? He spun his ship as he released the ball, causing the ball to spin, and then curve past the keeper. Amazing."

Fintan looked at the clock. Over Eleven minutes of the twenty allotted for the game remained.

"Long way to go," he said. "And Blue are not dumb. They'll catch on soon enough."

Blue squadron had started triple teaming Simon, keeping him out of the game. Everywhere he went, even when he slipped back into his own half they shadowed him, and slowly they started putting on pressure. Whenever Simon would drop back into his half, Blue 7 would break off from marking him and make for the Red goal. Blue Leader had an accurate shot and would shoot the ball down the field trying to catch him open. Red had to keep dropping ships back to stop being stretched.

And then Simon made a mistake. He pushed his ship forward, trying to catch Blue leader off guard, but Blue leader was ready, and lobbed the ball downfield, off the force shields. Blue 7 caught it and shot into the undefended goal.

"There's plenty of time left, and now the deficit is just one goal. It's looking more and more like Red are playing 9 on 11, keeping the two newbies out of the game," said the commentator. "It was a bold move, but will it last?"

As the seconds ticked down, Blue were now pressing more and more. Simon and the rest of Red squadron were fighting a brave game, defending their goal like crazy, and content not to attack, but to punt the ball towards the other goal whenever they got it.

With only two minutes left, Blue broke through again and scored. Red 6 made a sloppy mistake as she tried to shoot the ball downfield.

Blue were ready for the move, intercepted and used their two ship advantage to pass the ball into the gap behind Red 6 and score.

Fintan was glad he couldn't hear the rest of Red's communication. He was sure that Simon was angry and using some interesting words at this point.

"If the game remains tied, it will go into sudden death overtime," said Nizhoni. "First team to score wins."

"We've as good as lost."

"I have an idea," said Nizhoni.

"I don't like the sound of that," smiled Fintan. She smiled back.

"No time to explain, but cover my back."

"Always."

There were just a few seconds left on the clock. Red had blocked another Blue attack and punted the ball again downfield towards the Blue goal. As the goalkeeper came out to pick it up, Nizhoni's ship darted out of her corner.

She flew in an arc, heading for another corner, but while on the way she shot the ball with her beam weapons. It bounced away from the goalkeeper, off a wall and spun back heading roughly across the field, but slightly towards the *Red* goal.

Fintan saw what she was doing. She had hit the ball with a precise shot, forcing it to backspin off the wall in her direction. She was following Simon's orders by not touching the ball, and was staying out of the area of action by flying towards another corner. The trajectory of the ball was taking it closer to her, allowing her next shot to be more powerful.

Blue Leader seemed to catch on to what she was doing. He had laid in an intercept course to block her from shooting it.

And then Fintan acted. He laid in an intercept course of his own.

His ship darted across the arena and hit Blue Leader cleanly. Fintan's ship jarred violently and he fell from his pedestal. He bumped his head hard on the side of the console. Dizzied, he quickly scrambled to his feet to regain control.

Just in time to see Nizhoni shoot the ball with a full blast from the underside of her ship. She shot the ball on its side, causing it to spin, and it curved around the goalkeeper and into the net.

There were only 3 seconds left, and no time for Blue to come back. The score was 3-2. Red Squadron had won.

*

They landed in the Red Squadron landing zone amid cheers from the full squadron. Dismounting their ships they could see that everyone had come out to cheer them on. Fintan searched the crowd for Zack and Ayako, and of course they were right at the front, cheering on their friends.

He rushed to them, and Zack enveloped him in a big bear hug. "Sorry about earlier," he said. "I know that you'll tell me when the time is right. And, uh, nice *waiting around* out there. Never saw anybody do so little but still decide a game!" He winked.

Ayako and Nizhoni were hugging and sharing some quiet words too.

Simon didn't look too happy. "Squadron," he said. "Debrief in my ready room, now!"

They entered the ready room, smiling and jovial until they saw Simon staring at them. The rest of the squadron looked stunned by his attitude. Fintan guessed that they were thinking that holding Nizhoni and Fintan in reserve until the end of the game had been part of a brilliant plan.

"You disobeyed orders," he said to them. Mostly to Nizhoni.

"With respect sir, I didn't," she responded.

"I told you to stay out of the way and out of the game."

"No sir," she responded. "You told us not to touch the ball, and to stay in the corners well away from the action. Neither Fintan nor I touched the ball. We stayed exactly where you told us to."

"Don't get funny with me little girl," he said.

He was raising his hand to slap her, when something snapped in Fintan and he stood between them. "Take your hands off her," he yelled, pushing Simon in the chest.

Simon countered with his right fist, catching Fintan in the jaw.

The blow knocked Fintan off his feet, and his head cracked against a table on the way down. He hit the ground, out cold.

Chapter 12: Secrets

Interesting game.
Yes, Red Leader was impressive wasn't he?
That's not what I'm referring to.
Are you sure?

He was standing on the side of a hill with woods stretching upslope from him. The sky was a crisp blue, and the air was cold and fresh. He looked around to see purple mountains on the horizon in all directions.

He heard a voice calling him. It was faint and distant, carried by the wind. He looked around, trying to catch the direction. The voice called out again, unearthly, but still warm and with genuine love in its sound.

He decided that downhill would be the way to go. As he started walking he looked down at his feet. They weren't his feet – instead he looked down at brown-haired claws. He caught his reflection in a small pool of water.

A bear.

The voice called him again.

I'm dreaming he thought. But he didn't wake up and the voice kept calling him. He continued down the hill, into a large and wide canyon.

It was *beautiful.* The earth itself was painted in many colors, from deep reds through yellows and browns. The trees accented it with deep greens. He never wanted to leave here.

The voice called him again. It was louder now, and female, cadenced with such warmth. He wanted to meet its owner.

He walked around the curving canyon.

A tower came into view. It was like a skyscraper, but natural. He'd seen rock stacks before, but this one was impossibly high and impossibly straight. Its strata showed horizontal stripes leading up into the sky.

He reached out to touch it. White light filled his vision.

*

The light began to dim, and to resolve itself. There was somebody's face there and it was calling him. He could make out dark hair, but no features yet. It was too blurred.

He felt his hands. *His* hands. Someone was holding his left hand in both of hers.

Hers. He looked to the face again and could hear her speaking his name.

Fintan it said. *Wake up.*

His vision cleared and the face resolved itself to a girl. She was pleasant-looking with dark reddish skin and a mane of thick black hair.

I know her.

She said his name again.

Fintan, wake up. Come back to us, please.

"Nizhoni," he croaked, surprising himself. "Nizhoni." *So that was her name.*

The face turned to the side. "Doctor," it said. "He's waking up"

His vision cleared some more. He was in a bed in what clearly looked like a hospital. Nizhoni was sitting by the bed, holding his hand talking to him. A man rushed in, wearing a white coat. He looked at some instruments, and then reached over Fintan's head to adjust something. It hurt when the doctor touched him. His head pounded.

"Ow," said Fintan.

"Sorry," said the Doctor. "But you took a knock to the head. You're lucky to be awake so quickly."

"What happened?"

"When you crashed your ship into that guy," said Nizhoni, "you cracked your head badly. And then, afterwards you collapsed and hit it again."

"There's also a bruise on his jaw," said the doctor, quizzically.

"On his way down, he bumped it," said Nizhoni. "I told you already."

The doctor harrumphed, clearly not believing her.

"Well he needs more rest," said the Doctor.

"Which is why you won't disturb him with interrogations," said Nizhoni.

"He's in good shape now, best to let him sleep," said the Doctor. "Please, leave him. I'll call you when he's ready to talk some more."

Nizhoni looked disappointed.

"No," croaked Fintan. "I want her to stay a little longer."

The doctor sighed. "All right, but just a few minutes," he said, before leaving.

When he left, Nizhoni turned back to Fintan and smiled her rare smile.

"Better than any medicine," he said.

She raised an eyebrow.

"Your smile," he said.

She rewarded him with a larger smile. But then it stopped, and she grew serious.

"Fintan," she said. "Thank you. Thank you for having my back both in the game and in what happened afterwards. But, you have to know, you don't need to protect me from a bully like Simon. I can do that myself. I'm sorry he hurt you."

"You didn't want the doctor to know that, did you?"

"No." she said.

"Why not? That jerk should be punished for what he did!"

"Please try to relax," she said, "or the white-coated tyrant will be back."

Fintan smiled.

She continued. "If we push the point, the truth will come out. And the truth is that you hit him first. He was defending himself."

"That's not true," said Fintan. "He was going to hit you."

"Look at it how teachers would," she said. "You *think* he was going to hit me, but he didn't. Had he done so it would be different, but you are the one who lost his temper and hit first. And think of the story that they could tell. Simon humiliated you by not letting you play so you attacked him. That could get you thrown out of the school," she paused, "and I wouldn't like that."

Fintan thought it through. She was right. "And so he's going to get away with it" he said.

"Not exactly," she said, smiling again. She winked.

"You've been hanging out with Zack too much," said Fintan.

She laughed. He'd never heard her laugh before.

And then it was time for the doctor to come in and boot her out so he could sleep. It wasn't long before Fintan slipped into a deep, dreamless sleep.

*

"I'm sorry," said the voice in his ear.

He must have still been dreaming. It was dark around him. He cracked his eyes open to see a shadow looming over.

"I'm sorry," it repeated. "I don't know how I let it get out of control. You don't know how hard it is to control them. I have to make them fear me. But you were so defiant, and I went too far. I'm sorry, I never meant to hurt you."

The voice was familiar.

"Thank you for pulling that game out of the bag for us. I should have used you better than I did. I'm sorry. I hope you'll find it in your heart to forgive me."

And then Fintan was slipping away into sleep again.

*

He woke, still in his hospital bed. Everything seemed clearer now. He looked around the room. As hospitals went, it was nice. It was clean, and the equipment looked modern.

The doctor peeped in.

"Ah!" he said. "You're awake!"

Fintan smiled and nodded.

"I bet you're hungry too."

"Yes" said Fintan. "I could eat a horse"

"Sorry, horse is off the menu until tomorrow. Can I get you steak and eggs instead?"

"Sounds good."

Breakfast came, with visitors: Zack, Ayako and Nizhoni.

"Nice hat," said Zack.

"Huh?" said Fintan.

Ayako, smiling, pulled a small mirror from her purse. She handed it to Fintan who looked at his face in it. His head was covered in bandages, with only his face exposed.

"Is it Egyptian?" asked Zack. "If so, why didn't you pick one up for us when you were there?"

It was good to hear Zack being back to his usual jovial self.

"I'm glad we're all here" said Nizhoni. "I feel we owe you an explanation"

"It's ok," said Zack. "I'm sorry my ego got in the way, of course you don't have to tell me everything."

"But you are our friends," she said. "And even Fintan didn't know everything, but what he knew I asked him to keep private."

She continued. "There are other Navajo in the school. And these Navajo broke the condition of confidentiality about the school, to help our people. We know that our people can keep a secret, so the Navajo in the school let our friends outside the school know about it, so they have a better chance of getting in and succeeding when they get here."

Zack was stunned. "That's a dangerous game you're playing."

She sighed. "I know. But, you have to understand my people. First, we can keep a secret. There is no way that we would leak something of this importance. And second, you must remember that our people were almost made extinct by outsiders."

"By us," said Fintan.

"Not you, but your forebears," she smiled at him. "There's no hard feelings, but we believe in our culture, we love our culture, and we realized that once the human race made it to the stars, there can be a planet just for us Navajo, where we can be who we want to be and not worry about outside cultures destroying us ever again. We can evolve into what we are supposed to be."

"But isn't that the point of a reservation?" said Zack.

"Have you ever been to a reservation?" she answered.

He shook his head.

"It's a poor compromise," she said. "It's a place where Navajo can be Navajo, but we're surrounded by a culture that could easily destroy us. It feels like we are under siege. It is nice that we can be ourselves in there, but can we expand? Can we grow? All we are right now is a museum or a tourist destination. We've stagnated, and we want to grow."

"So," said Fintan "by having more Navajo in the school, you will grow your power, so when the time comes that we go to the stars-"

"We'll go our own way" she said. "And we'll have what we dreamed of. We'll enter the fifth world."

"That's how I knew about the flight center. That's how I knew a lot about the school. Other Navajo have been here, and went back and told us about it. I couldn't tell, because the secret has never been outside my people before. Can you keep it?"

"Of course" said Fintan. Zack and Ayako also nodded.

Chapter 13: Hospital

I never thought that she'd be so indiscrete
Nor I, but there's a great bond there
Do you think we should do something about it?
Let's wait and see

Fintan's concussion must have been serious, as he stayed in hospital for the whole weekend. He was expecting to get out for Monday classes, but still wasn't released. Still that wasn't a problem as he had double *Cosmic History* on Monday mornings. He was happy not to see Sinclair for the rest of the week.

However, boredom began to set in. He spent the day sleeping, staring at the ceiling, eating the hospital food (his stomach squirmed at the thought) before finally sleeping again. It seemed like an eternity until finally he heard Zack coming down the corridor to visit. He might be only twelve years old, like Fintan, but his voice was deepening and could carry.

He stuck his head in the door.

"Yo!" he said. "Is the sleeping beauty awake?"

Fintan nodded. "Thank God" he said. "I thought I was going to die of boredom."

As always, Ayako and Nizhoni came along. Fintan was so happy he was sure that his grin was loosening his bandages.

"Mister Sinclair missed you this morning," said Zack. "He looked lost and pining for you for the whole lesson."

Fintan laughed. "Yeah, right!"

"He did!" said Zack. "He even gave you a little gift."

Zack dropped some papers on the bed.

"No way," said Fintan.

Zack put on his best English accent, stood as straight as he could and spoke down his nose at Fintan. "Mister Adams," he said, "please make sure that Mister Reilly receives these and ensure that they are completed before next Monday. Just because he's in hospital he's not going to be a slacker."

Fintan couldn't help but laugh, Zack had nailed the accent.

"Slackerrrrr" repeated Zack.

"We've done what we came to do," said Ayako. "Time to go. See you tomorrow Fintan!"

"Woah! Wait a minute!"

Ayako laughed. "Gotcha!"

"Oh you've missed so much good stuff today. I got so much to tell you!" said Zack.

"So go ahead" said Fintan. "Keep me awake"

"First, and this isn't the best part – just wait a bit for that, but you've got to see this" said Zack. "Ayako, go for it!"

Ayako rolled up her sleeve to show the bracelet. "We had a tech class today and they showed us how to do this."

She touched something on the bracelet and the red crystal glowed. Then a small cubic area was projected above Fintan's bed.

"It's like the holographic projector they used when they scared us with that monster," she said.

"So why are *you* showing it to me?" said Fintan. "And not Zack?"

She laughed. "Well, it takes a little while to figure it out, and he's still bumbling around with it."

"Yeah, watch this!" said Zack

He did the same motions as Ayako. A light shot out from it, right into his eyes.

"Ow," said Zack. "It didn't do that last time!"

"Well, what did it do last time?"

"You don't want to know. Trust me," he said.

Ayako smiled. Nizhoni placed her hands over her groin and mimicked an 'Ouch' sound.

Zack went red. "Ok, continue Ayako, let's show him!"

"So is this the coolest part?" asked Fintan.

"No!" said Zack. "It's cool, but it's not the coolest part. Just wait!"

Ayako turned some controls, and the projection lit up with a replay of the Starball game that Fintan and Nizhoni had just played in. She was able to control the game, moving forwards and backwards the play and replay various highlights.

"Now that's cool" said Fintan.

They stepped through one of Simon's more impressive moves. Ayako was able to freeze the frame, show the formation of the other ships and step through just how Simon was able to avoid or deceive them.

"Impressive" said Nizhoni. Praise indeed coming from her.

"Just wait till you see this" said Zack, nodding towards Ayako.

She skipped ahead until the last few seconds. In slow motion they saw Nizhoni's amazing shot to first knock the ball across the field from where she could line up her goalbound shot.

Then they saw Blue Leader's intercept course, and Fintan moving out of his corner. Even in slow motion his ship blurred on the screen. He was moving *fast*. They saw him cut off Blue Leader just in time for Nizhoni to get in the final shot that won the game.

"Now that was cool," said Zack. "You'll have to tell me how you did it!"

"It looks different from here," said Fintan. "In the game, you just do it, you don't think. I told Nizhoni that I had her back, and I didn't want to let her down."

"Aww," said Ayako. Nizhoni blushed slightly.

"First, that's not the coolest thing. I'll get to that in a moment. But, when we were watching the replay, we got to talking about the

Kobayashi Maru, and how we dealt with it, and realized that you weren't part of the conversation, and we'd love to know how you dealt with it."

"The Kobawhatsit?" said Fintan.

"You know the test. The last part. It's impossible to pass, so they want to see how you deal with failure and how spectacularly you burn out. Or something."

"Earth calling Zack, come in?" said Fintan. "What are you talking about."

"You know the Kobayashi Maru. It's Japanese."

"No it isn't," said Ayako.

"Well they said it was Japanese on *Star Trek*."

"Can you start again?" said Fintan. "Maybe it's the bandages, but my head hurts."

"OK" said Zack. "And I will speak s-l-o-w-l-y ok?"

Fintan raised his eyebrow. Get on with it!

"When they tested you for this place, they tested you, like the rest of us with a bunch of games, right?"

"Yeah" said Fintan.

"And then you got to fly a saucer, except you didn't think you were flying a saucer, right?"

"Go on" said Fintan.

"You did a bunch of tests, and blew through them, and then they gave you the impossible test."

"Which one was that?"

"You know the one where there were two balls and you had to put them into a proper orbit, blah blah?" said Zack

"Yeah."

"Well that's the Kobayashi Maru. In Star Trek it was a test of character, to see how you would do in an unwinnable situation. To see what you were really like. I gave up on one ball and just put the other in orbit" he said. "I guess they liked a part success instead of a complete failure."

"I got both in Orbit" said Ayako, "but not the right orbit. After a little while they fell and burned in the atmosphere."

"I shot them" said Nizhoni. "Better than having space junk floating around."

"So what about you?"

"I uh put them into the right orbit," said Fintan. "I guess I passed."

They were quiet.

"Nearly killed myself doing it though. But somehow I got out."

He went on the explain how he had done a billiard shot to put both balls into orbit, but the recoil sent him into a death spin towards the moon. Then he told them how he was able to use his last drops of fuel to pull out and survive.

"Wow," said Ayako.

"Somehow, I'm not surprised," said Nizhoni.

"No wonder they picked you for Starball," said Zack.

"Oh here he goes again with his conspiracy theories" said Ayako. "Zack, you are in the middle of the biggest conspiracy theory on the planet. Why do you have to look for more?"

"They didn't pick me," said Fintan, answering Zack. "It was random."

"Yeah right" said Zack. "You passed the Kobayashi Maru, of course they wanted to see you in action."

Fintan shook his head.

"Anyway" said Zack. "Cool as it is, that's not the coolest part!"

Ayako changed the video to show inside the Red Squadron dome. "Last nights party," she said. "Sorry you missed it."

"Oh thanks," said Fintan. "You guys have a big party to celebrate, and not only am I not there, but you're going to rub my face in it. Thanks a bunch."

"No no no no no no no!" said Zack. "That's not it. Just watch!"

He moved his hands in the air, through the screen. It allowed him to manipulate the image. He picked out the stage, and the members of the team on the stage. He froze the frame and zoomed in on Simon.

The image was very clear. Simon was standing, a little shyly and slightly behind the rest of the team.

"That's odd," said Fintan.

"It's not the oddest thing," said Zack. He zoomed in further. On the screen they could see Simon's face. One eye was blackened and bruised.

"Even that's not the best part" said Zack. He moved forward a few frames to see Simon smile. A tooth was missing too. Zack laughed. "Cool, right?"

Fintan couldn't help but smile, but wasn't sure if it was because of Zack's laughter or because of Simon's discomfort.

"That doesn't make sense" said Fintan, looking at Nizhoni. "We saw him in the ready room, and he didn't have any-"

"He must have" said Nizhoni, interrupting him. "Where else would he have gotten it?" She raised an eyebrow and smiled a little. "And you weren't really yourself, so don't trust your memory."

"But," said Fintan.

Nizhoni smiled a little again, her eyes meeting Fintan's.

He smiled. "You didn't?"

Zack interrupted. "Is this a secret conversation, or can anyone join in?"

Fintan shook his head. "She's right, I must have been disoriented."

Zack looked at him suspiciously. And then at Nizhoni who smiled her best innocent smile.

He shrugged his shoulders in a way that said 'never mind'.

At that moment Trichallik walked into the room. Zack stood back to let her pass. She was much smaller up close, even shorter than Ayako. She nodded to them as she gently eased her way past.

"Hello Fintan," said Trichallik in her unique voice. "I'm sorry about what happened, and wanted to see if you are doing better? I'm sorry to disturb your conversation with your friends, I will leave soon."

She walked closer to his bed. They had never seen her up close like this, and it was unnerving.

As she stepped closer to Fintan he couldn't help but notice her eyes. From a distance they looked to be pure black but as she stepped closer they looked more like mirrors.

It was getting hard for Fintan to breathe. He couldn't take his eyes away from hers. He was looking deeply into them now, and could see that they were compound eyes, like those of an insect.

It was getting too hot for Fintan. He was sweating profusely. Trichallik smiled.

Fintan couldn't be here. He had to get away. He scrambled back in his bed, but was unable to move. It felt like there was a great weight on his chest. He felt a scream rising from low down in his chest, but he fought to surpress it. She reached her hand out and touched his arm. The touch of her skin on his drove him over the edge.

He screamed, and then blacked out again.

Chapter 14: Conspiracy Theory

Not what you expected I assume?
Definitely not. I'm surprised.
This tells us a lot.

"I'm sick of this hospital bed now," said Fintan.

"Well if you'd stop fainting every time you see a perfectly normal alien up close, they might let you out!" said Zack.

"I don't know what came over me."

"That was a fear response if I ever saw one," said Ayako. "No offense, Fintan, but you were clearly terrified."

Nizhoni looked at Fintan, holding his gaze, looking deep into his eyes for a moment. "Are you sure you want to talk about this now? We don't want you to get ill again."

Fintan thought about it. "It's bouncing around my head all the time. If I don't talk about it with you guys, I think I'll go crazy."

They waited, listening.

"Look, this might sound weird," said Fintan. "But when she got up close, I felt like I had seen her before. And I don't mean since I got here. There was something that I couldn't place. And then I couldn't breathe. I just don't get it. I've been trying to figure it out, trying to remember, but I couldn't."

He stopped for a moment, and then continued. "There's something else. Her eyes. When I saw them up close they were different, compound, like those of an insect. She looks almost human so it's easier to accept her as an alien, but when I saw that – I just couldn't deal with it."

"So," said Nizhoni. "You think you've seen aliens like her before?"

"No," said Fintan, "of course not. I've hardly ever been out of my hometown before. Where would I see an alien?"

"There's something else that is odd," said Nizhoni, "How did you know I was Navajo?"

"What?"

"Back when we first met. Zack called me a 'Jap', but you knew I was Navajo," she said. "How?"

"How!" said Zack, holding his hand up. "How. Get it? How! It's how Indians say hello."

Nizhoni rolled her eyes.

"Sorry," said Zack. "Go on"

Fintan thought about it for a moment. "Now that you say it, I have no idea. I guess I had just read about Navajo or something?"

"And that was enough for you to be able to tell which nation I am from, just from my name?"

"Well you do have the flag on your uniform," said Zack. "That helps."

"Zack, you are from California, only 2 states over from New Mexico. Do you recognize this flag?"

He thought about it for a moment. "No," he said, quietly.

"So how did Fintan know about it?" she said, turning back towards him.

Fintan breathed in deeply, and then breathed out again.

"I have no idea," he said. "You have to believe me."

"Are you sure you may not have read something about it? You're a smart guy" said Nizhoni. "And I'm sure you read a lot."

"If I did, I think I'd remember," said Fintan. "I am sure I didn't."

"Why are we interrogating Fintan," said Ayako. "He's our friend."

"Sorry," said Nizhoni. "I don't mean to do that, I just want to be sure there is no rational explanation about how you would know these things"

A tear started crawling down Fintan's cheek. "I don't know," he said. "I don't know."

She took his shoulders in his hands and embraced him to her chest in a motherly way. "I know." she said. "I understand. You see I had the same feeling about you when I first saw you. We have met before. I just don't know where."

She was crying too.

It was a few moments before any of them could talk again.

For once Zack was serious. "There's more here than meets the eye, clearly. I won't claim to understand it, but, I'm your friend. Both of you. Whatever it is, we'll get to the bottom of it. Together."

"Together," said Ayako.

Nizhoni nodded and Fintan agreed too.

"Together," they all repeated.

*

Fintan's condition improved rapidly and within a couple of days he was out of hospital. He got a heroes greeting back at Red Squadron HQ, and a belated ceremony was arranged for his medal reception. He hadn't realized the winners of the friendly game got such an award.

Simon even pinned the medal on Fintan's chest. Up close his black eye was bad. Nizhoni must have hit him hard.

"Good thing you got out in time for Friday," said Zack at breakfast. "Today we're getting our science projects in advanced physics. Mister Singh is going to pair us up. I'm glad you're back, because if we weren't here I might get paired up with, well, you know."

"What?" said Fintan.

"Oh it's nothing, it doesn't matter now," said Zack.

"Spit it out," said Fintan

"Ok. You see. I was just thinking it would be such a nightmare if I got paired up with," he paused, and gulped for effect. "A girl."

Ayako screamed and threw a bread roll at him. He ducked and the bread roll hit the person who had been sitting behind Zack.

Of course it was Simon.

Fintan sighed and shook his head. He couldn't help but smile. Things were getting back to normal.

*

Ayako was the star of Mister Singh's class, so naturally everybody wanted to get her in the science project. They waited in class with baited breath as he doled out the assignments.

Using a projection device much like the one Ayako used in the hospital room he showed a brief vid of each assignment before naming those who would be performing it. Tension was building in the room.

Fintan could hear Zack, who was head down on his desk whispering "Please Ayako, Please Ayako, Please let me get Ayako."

He shook his head and rolled his eyes. Ayako was sitting several desks in front, so thankfully couldn't hear him.

"I can't stand Singh's class," Zack had told him on more than one occasion. "Once we start getting into the math of how everything works, something just goes to sleep inside me. I know I'm going to flunk the project, and then flunk the class, but I need this class if I'm going to continue doing flight."

"And why do you want to continue flight, other than seeing Iara?" Fintan had asked on each occasion.

"Errm. Let me get back to you," was the usual reply.

Singh was blathering on about the next project. It was to mend a crashed saucer. The participants would have to use all of their ingenuity to get it working and flight-ready again. They'd role play being lost in a hostile environment where a repaired ship would be their only means of escape.

"That's perfect!" whispered Zack. "Her brains and my brawn. This has to be set up for me."

"The first project member I pick because she has the academic competence to figure out most of what needs to be done. Ayako Katsuragai, it's your project."

"Yes!" said Zack. "Woo hoo, my prayers are answered."

"She'll be joined by someone who complements her perfectly," said Singh.

Zack pointed at his chest and whispered "Me."

"He's a hard worker, and one who can see beyond just the academics." said Singh

Zack whispered. "Still me."

"And of course, he has great ability in flying, something that will be needed for a ship with ramshackle repairs."

Zack raised his eyebrows. "Cool. He thinks I can fly!" he whispered to Fintan. "Iara must have said nice things about me!"

Singh stopped, and looked at their desk. Zack started to stand up until Singh said "Fintan Reilly, you'll partner Miss Katsuragi."

Zack slumped, his smile frozen on his face.

*

"This sucks," said Zack. "I wanted to work with Ayako. It would be nice to get to know her better."

"You really like her, don't you?" said Fintan.

"Well, you and Nizhoni have something going on. It's nice." said Zack

"It's not like that. There is a bond. I'm not sure what it is, but it's not what you think."

"Are you sure?"

Fintan thought about it a moment. "No," he smiled. "I'm not"

Zack threw a pillow at him.

"I bet you'd like a little bit more alone time with Nizhoni, working on the project together, but she's stuck with me. Ironic isn't it?" said Zack

"Hmm," said Fintan. "I guess."

"She doesn't like me that much either," said Zack. "But I'm thick-skinned. It's ok."

"She likes you just fine," said Fintan. "It's just her way, she doesn't suffer fools gladly."

"Hey" said Zack, "watch who you're calling a fool!"

"You know I don't mean it like that," said Fintan.

"Ha! Gotcha!" said Zack. "You're too easy sometimes."

"You think there's something in all this?" said Zack. "In your reaction to Trichallik, in the way that Nizhoni and you seem to know each other from somewhere else?"

"I don't know," said Fintan, "and I don't believe in reincarnation. I just hope that we'll learn it in time."

"Reincarnation?" said Zack. "Ha. Wouldn't that be funny. Maybe you were husband and wife in a previous life. But of course, she's the tough one, so I guess she was the husband!"

It was Fintan's turn to throw a pillow at Zack.

"You guys will be good together," said Fintan. "I think you'll have a great project."

"If we don't kill each other first."

"Kill each other?" said Fintan. "She's half your size, and she'll still kick your butt."

"No way," said Zack.

"You sure about that?" said Fintan. "Maybe you should have a chat with Simon."

Zack paused. "Really?"

Fintan winked, but said nothing.

Chapter 15: Science Project

So you split them up.

Yes. Healthier that way. They're too young to be so in love.

In Love? I don't think so. Or did you learn something about them that you're not sharing.

It's an adolescent male and a female. Sometimes hormones can be distracting.

So you split them up.

Yes. There isn't a hidden conspiracy in everything I do

Yes there is, and sometimes there are several.

"I'm happy we're working together, Fintan," said Ayako. They were on a shuttle train heading to one of the outlying areas where some land had been reserved to simulate a saucer crashed in the wilderness.

"So am I," said Fintan, "though I think someone else isn't too happy about it."

"Oh Nizhoni is fine," said Ayako "I know she's missing you, but she's practical, and to her it's only a science project."

"I was talking about Zack," smiled Fintan, and Ayako blushed.

"You know she *really* likes you," said Ayako, changing the subject.

"You know *he* really likes *you*," said Fintan, changing it back.

"I know," conceded Ayako "but I don't think I could ever. With an American," she sighed. "It's a long story."

"We will have plenty of time together," said Fintan "but if you are not comfortable, we can always talk about Nizhoni," he said, smiling.

She smiled back, but didn't elaborate.

*

They reached their station and followed the directions out to a field a short way.

"It's always a beautiful day in the dome, isn't it?" said Fintan, looking around to take in the scene. "It looks like it never rains here."

"Yes" said Ayako. "Doesn't need to be so inefficient, the water is in the ground anyway, so they can just pump it up from the ground to feed the crops."

"It's interesting that we use a space like this, which must be expensive, to grow crops. While we don't need to be self-sufficient, it's interesting that we are."

"I guess if things went bad in the world outside," she said, "the project wouldn't stop. This place was built during the cold war after all."

They reached their destination, a force field dome covering a section of the field. Ayako keyed a code into her bracelet, and pointed it at the field. It disappeared, revealing a crashed flying saucer.

"Time to go to work," she said.

*

At that moment, Zack and Nizhoni were on a trail, headed in the opposite direction, towards the city center to meet with their science project coordinator.

"Any idea where we are going?" said Zack.

She shook her head.

"Well, with all your insider knowledge, I thought you might have some idea?"

"None," she said, flatly.

Zack realized that it was time to change the subject.

"I wanted to say 'Thank you'"

She looked at him, curious and surprised.

"For Fintan," he said. "He's my roommate, and I love the guy. His time with you has really helped him. It's only been a few weeks, but he's come out of his shell."

"Yeah?"

"Yeah," said Zack. "I think he had a hard time at home. When he got here he was always having nightmares and he was terrified of everything. That all changed the night he tried to help you against that fake monster."

"That was very kind."

"More than just kind, right? Brave, too. Remember, he was timid, and I believe he had been bullied a lot at home. You really helped break him out of that. "

She smiled. "That's good"

They reached their destination and got out. The conversation had broken the ice between them and they chatted happily as they traced their way through the city looking for the building. They found it and worked their way to the office number that they'd been instructed to seek out.

They entered, and behind a desk sat Trichallik.

*

"What a mess," said Fintan, looking at the wreckage of the ship.

Ayako laughed. "Well we do have a couple of weeks to figure it out."

"You think that's enough time?"

"Well, I can always rig up a time machine that would slow the Universe down so we can spend a couple of years at it if you like?" she said.

"Nah" said Fintan. "Do you want to spend that much time at it?"

"Well, I would be spending it with you, wouldn't I?"

He laughed. "Good point, and pleasant as the offer sounds, maybe we can just get it done in a couple of weeks."

They worked on sorting out the junk for a couple of hours, trying theory after theory about what they can do to fix it. They stopped, exhausted, to break for lunch. It was a short walk back to the train station, where they were able to use a small conference room to sit and eat, as well as break for the bathroom.

"They should put bathrooms on the saucers, shouldn't they?" said Fintan. She laughed.

Ayako had prepared her own lunch instead of taking the packed lunch provided by the dorm.

"*Sushi*," she said. "Would you like to try some?"

"That's raw fish, right?" said Fintan. "Not sure if that's what I want"

"Try it," she said, "you might like it."

He did, and bit down into its soft and sweet texture. It was *good*.

"Wow," he said. "Not what I expected"

He looked back at his sandwich. "Better than this cardboard"

"I'm glad you like it," said Ayako. "That's something that's good about you, you're always willing to adapt to, and try to understand other cultures. That's why Nizhoni likes you so much too."

He laughed. "Likes me as a friend, right?"

She smiled, with fake innocence. "Well of course, what else would I be talking about?"

He smiled too.

She grew serious for a moment. "I guess I should explain more about what I was talking about earlier."

"I was curious about that" said Fintan.

"My family name is Katsuragi," she said. "And in the past, it was a noble clan. Most people with my name don't care about that, but my family does."

She continued. "My family is a military family. Just about everyone has served, and most of them are still loyal to the Emperor. Yes, since World War 2, the country has changed, and we're a democracy now, but we still have an Emperor, and my family, and my father in particular still love him and would die for him, even if he is little more than a figurehead."

Fintan asked "And they don't like Americans as a result?"

"No," she said. "It goes much deeper than that. My grandfather's brother was in Hiroshima when the Americans dropped the bomb. He was burned from head to toe and died a few days later."

"I'm sorry."

"Radiation sickness became a great problem in my family. My grandmother was there too, but wasn't burned. However she did show some signs of sickness, and it became difficult for her to marry. There is just so much bitterness when we think about what happened. We've learned to forgive, but we don't forget." A tinge of sadness entered her voice.

"And you?"

"It's all so long before I was born," she said, "So I just hear what my family say about it. My father is an Admiral in the Japanese navy, so of course he is upset when he thinks about it."

"An admiral," said Fintan "that's impressive."

"He's a good man," she said "and I miss him greatly. If he knew that I was in the USA, working with the American military, I think he'd have a heart attack."

Fintan nodded, and smiled to encourage her.

"But you asked what I think," she said "and I always come back to this. Why did the Americans drop the bombs on us?"

"To end the war," said Fintan. "Japan would never surrender, and an invasion would be costly on both sides, right?"

"That's what everyone says, but that's not my question," she said.

"My grandmother told me that when they dropped the first bomb, on Hiroshima, we were devastated, but defiant, figuring that it was a desperation move by the Americans, and that they only could do it once. When they dropped the *second* bomb on Nagasaki, three days later, we realized that they had more than one, and surrender was our only choice. Hundreds of thousands had died instantly and hundreds of thousands more would die slowly, later."

Tears were running down her face now. "What I don't understand," she said, "is why they had to bomb our *cities*. Surely if surrender was what they wanted, they could have dropped the bombs in the sea where the military and the Emperor could see the force that they were up against. They could *threaten* to use them on our cities, and give us a chance to surrender. But they didn't. They chose, instead, to kill so many people, horrifically, to end the war. How can we trust someone that would do that?"

Fintan was quiet. She had a point. He put his hand on her shoulder to comfort her. She wiped the tears away.

"Sorry" she said. "But I've been bottling it up since I got here. Thanks for listening. I feel better now."

*

Trichallik bade Nizhoni and Zack to sit down.

She handed two pieces of plastic across her desk. One to each.

"These are passes that will allow you to leave the city," she said.

"Report to the main hangar, and take two saucers. You'll fly them out of the city and report to this location."

She pointed out a location on a map that was hovering in the air above her desk.

"That's the Nellis bombing range," said Zack.

"That's right," said Trichallik. "Except we don't use it for bombing. I need you too to become quickly adept at flying small one-person saucers. The terrain here offers enough privacy to allow you to do so."

"Wow" said Zack.

"This is to be kept absolutely confidential," said Trichallik. She glanced at Nizhoni when she said it.

Nizhoni nodded and agreed.

"What's all this for?" said Zack

"All will be revealed in time. For now, you just have to worry about getting some experience flying a real ship, and not a simulator."

She tossed a couple of data crystals across the desk. "These have the exercises that you should master. When you've mastered them, I'll be in touch."

They were clearly dismissed. They gave their goodbyes, stood and left Trichallik's office.

"Now I know why you got me and not Fintan," said Zack.

Nizhoni looked at him, not understanding.

"He'd pass out again once he got close to Trichallik," he said, a smile curling his lips.

"That's not fair," she said, "and it's not a nice thing to say about your friend."

"I was just kidding," said Zack as she sped up her walk a little to leave him behind. He trotted to catch up with her. "You know, trying to lighten the mood."

She didn't reply, and just kept walking.

"I'm sorry," he said. "I always seem to say the wrong thing, don't I?"

"There's a cure for that, you know," she said.

"What is it?" said Zack. "Anything, please tell me!"

"Shut up and don't say anything," she replied.

He stopped. She walked ahead a few paces. She then stopped and turned back to him. Her face was impassive as always. And then she stuck her tongue out, laughed and started running.

*

It was a thrill to go into the hanger and show the credentials that Trichallik had given them. A military officer inspected them, and gruffly nodded. He led Zack and Nizhoni into a hangar where two saucers were parked.

"You're cleared to exit at Gate 1," he said. "Just follow the beacons on your heads-up display and you'll be fine."

They boarded their ships and took off. Zack was a little tentative at first. "It's odd doing this without Iara looking over my shoulder."

Nizhoni didn't answer, and just smiled.

"Actually, it's *nice* doing this without her looking over my shoulder."

Their ships rose above the city, humming quietly as they spun around. They followed the beacon upwards towards the roof where a small gate opened in the dome and they flew through it.

This took them to a smooth sided, dark tunnel. Nizhoni was taking the lead, and had found the controls to start a spotlight that shone upwards into the darkness.

They finally exited the tunnel back into open-air. It was dark outside in the real world.

"Interesting," said Zack. "They have opposite day from night inside the base"

"It makes sense," said Nizhoni. "I assume they fly missions outside the base all the time, and it is easier if it is our daylight, but nighttime in the real world outside."

"And it makes us harder to spot," said Zack, "when we come out of the Earth like this."

Nizhoni punched in the coordinates that Trichallik had supplied.

"Let's go" she said.

Their rally point was in a long valley that ran north to south in the deep Nevada desert.

"The Pintwater range," Zack read out. "Never heard of it."

To the south-west they could see the lights of the highway.

"That's the I-95," said Zack "leading from Las Vegas up to Death Valley. I went there once, when I was a kid". In opening comms with Nizhoni, a window appeared on his heads-up display with her face in it.

"You still are a kid," said Nizhoni, smiling.

He laughed. "And so are you, but, we don't feel like kids here, do we?"

She nodded agreement.

"I'm from Fresno," said Zack. "Just across those mountains. I could fly this sucker home if I wanted."

"And do you want to?"

"No," said Zack, "definitely not."

*

From working with her through the afternoon, it soon became obvious to Fintan that Ayako was *smart*. He enjoyed watching her, and learning that real intelligence didn't just come from book learning, but in how you approach a problem and solve it.

"I'm lost," he admitted. "I thought I was good, but, you're way ahead of me."

She smiled. "Not really. You know how these things go, I'll get only so far, and get stuck, then you'll take over until you get stuck and so on until we have the saucer fixed."

He looked at the array of circuit boards and partially assembled panels in the cockpit.

"I wish I had your confidence."

*

To Nizhoni, Zack had always been a clown. She wondered what Ayako saw in him, and silently agreed with the implicit decision that Ayako had to keep her distance from him. Of course they never spoke about it, but it was easy for her to know what was going on in her roommate's mind.

Zack was bottom in so many classes, but despite this, he was becoming quite popular. In this competitive environment, it was always good to have someone around that was worse than you, when you were worried about so many that were better than you.

But out here, in the real world, she realized that Zack was his own person. He may not be good at the book work, but he outshone her quickly in the field. Even with flying, he struggled in the classroom, but he was already outpacing her in the exercises that Trichallik had given them.

"Now I know why we use flying saucers," said Zack. "Think about it, the typical airplane is arrow-shaped for maximum aerodynamics in the direction it flies."

He paused for a minute, and his ship spun on an axis and zipped in a new direction.

"So to move in a new direction you have to turn so your new direction is forward. If your ship is circular, it's equally aerodynamic no matter which direction it flies in, right?"

She nodded. It made sense. And it helped her understand why Zack was flying much better than her, in fact, much better than anyone. They all flew like they were still in space, thinking in terms of trajectory, gravity wells and fuel. In atmosphere it was a different story, and they flew their saucers like airplanes, with an imaginary nose always at the front. Zack was flying rings around her.

She gained a new admiration for him. Perhaps he wasn't such a clown after all.

*

Dinner at the first year's table in Red Squadron was a lively affair that night. Instead of the students huddling in their own little groups, they were all together and all chatting jovially.

Everyone was talking about their project, complaining about how hard it was, and trashing Mister Singh for giving it to them.

Fintan had barely even heard Raj talking before, but now he was chattering like a monkey, and just as funny. He partnered with Heather, who, if there was an opposite to Raj, it was she. Her tall, fair-skinned, blonde looks contrasted his short, dark-skinned and thick black hair.

But opposites always attracted, and the two got on like a house on fire.

Zack shook his head and muttered under his breath "Even Raj can get a girl."

"I might be blonde," said Heather "but I'm not deaf."

Zack gulped and everybody laughed.

Fintan noticed that Zack and Nizhoni weren't talking much about their project. But whenever he would begin to ask them, the conversation would shift in another direction.

Later that night, he lay in his bed, looking at the ceiling. It had been a good day, and he and Zack were swapping stories about their classmates and laughing themselves to tears.

As they quietened down after lights-out, Fintan had a strange feeling in his chest. He thought about Zack and Ayako and Nizhoni and everything that had been going on. It gave him a light-headed feeling that just felt like it was tugging him upwards, and that he could fly.

I guess this is what they call happiness he thought before falling into a deep and dreamless sleep.

Chapter 16: The Chase

How goes the construction?

Fast, but not fast enough.

It's not like you to be so concerned.

The expression I like to use is 'Hedging my bets' or 'Not having all my eggs in the same basket'

Trichallik contacted Zack and Nizhoni by means of their heads-up displays. Her alien head looked strange on their screens.

"Congratulations," she said. "You learn quickly. Here is your next assignment."

She downloaded some data to their ships and vanished. Zack played it over his intercom. It was a signal, full of electronic noise.

"She has a great taste in music, doesn't she?"

"It's an encrypted signal."

"Then I guess we have to decrypt it."

Nizhoni pulled the signal into her on-board computer and ran some decryption algorithms on it. Nothing.

"It wouldn't be that easy," said Zack. "I think we have to do it by the seat of our pants."

"How?"

"Just watch papa go to work," he answered. She heard him cracking his knuckles.

*

Fintan looked at the ship. They'd been working on it for nearly two days and it still looked like a pile of junk.

"I don't think this is going to work." he said

"Sure it is," said Ayako. "Look, they just asked us to fly it, not take it into space, right?"

She pointed out the makeshift sealant around the engine compartment. "The engine insulation was in pieces, so we could take the sealers off the ship's hull panels and patch the ship up with them."

"The engine wasn't in bad shape, but doing that cut it off from the control room," said Fintan.

"So we drill a hole through the insulation here and that allows us to run the control cables."

"But that breaks the insulation."

"It does, but if we double insulate here, it protects the pilot from any excess radiation."

"So we strip the control cables from the main console, and extend them back towards your little contraption-"

"Exactly."

"So, it might look like garbage, but it's almost done."

"I don't think there are any marks given for tidiness," she said.

"The question is, will you be able to fly it?"

"Me? Why not you?"

She batted her eyelids. "Because I'm a lady, and you're a big strong man."

"Yeah, right."

"Besides," she said "you're a much better pilot."

*

"There's a pattern" said Zack. "Right there."

He had drawn a spectrogram of the signal on their heads-up display. They were still hovering over the Mojave Desert. He drew some circles at some points.

"Look what happens when I split out the signal into different frequencies."

"There's a correlation."

"Right. It's encrypted, but, it's a 1:1 encryption, meaning the letter A will always be encoded to the same value, as will B or C."

"How do you know this?"

"Because when I break it down into discrete values, there are only 26, but they are spread out across different frequency spectrums. So instead of hiding with a complex cipher, they are hiding with a few simple ciphers."

"So we're back to square one," she said.

"Not necessarily," said Zack. "Computers are good at doing simple chores quickly, and doing many of them over time. I just have to program the computer with all these patterns, and get it to go through each to figure out the likelihood about which signal being which letter."

"But you don't have a frame of reference," said Nizhoni. "Any letter could be any value."

"I don't have an absolute frame of reference," said Zack. "But I do have a relative one. There are 26 letters, so it is likely English. It's a long message, so we know the 26 letters probably meet the rough distribution of letters that any text will have."

"What do you mean?"

"For example, the letter 'E' is the most common letter used in the alphabet, so the odds are the most common signal we're seeing matches to the letter 'E' and so on."

"That's brilliant."

"Hey sweetcakes, I'm not just a handsome face you know."

"You're not even a handsome face mister, now get to work."

"Roger Roger Ma'am."

After a few moments Zack was still deep in concentration. Nizhoni wasn't happy with his facial expression.

"Is there a problem?" she said

"It's taking a little longer than I thought. I'm taking some of the other systems off-line to increase computing capacity."

"That's not a good idea," she said.

"It's ok," said Zack. "Main propulsion is still online, so I'm not going to fall from the sky."

"So what did you take off-line."

"Err…" he paused. "Everything else?"

"That's not a good idea."

"What could go wrong?"

Zack's headseat crackled. "Attention unidentified flying craft, you are in a restricted military airspace. Respond." The voice was firm and hostile.

"That wasn't you was it?"

"Not unless I suddenly became a man."

"We are authorized to use deadly force unless you land immediately," said the voice. "This is not an exercise, this is not a drill. Respond."

"Uh oh," said Zack. "I have two bogies on my heads-up. Closing fast. They're the US air force."

"We can easily outrun them," said Nizhoni.

"Not easily," said Zack. "My systems are off-line, remember?"

"But you said propulsion was online," she said.

"It is, but navigation and everything else is off-line. I can hover but not much else."

"ETA to contact is thirty seconds," said Nizhoni. "Can you get it online before then?"

"Negative."

Something beeped on Zack's display. "Oh that's not good."

"Radar lock," said Nizhoni "They have me too"

"Does that mean what I think it means?"

"If you mean radar guided missiles to blow us out of the sky, then yes."

"Oh crap."

"Stay here," said Nizhoni. "I'm going to engage them."

With that Nizhoni's craft left Zack and headed towards the two aircraft.

"As if I could do anything else," he said, under his breath.

From his display he could see Nizhoni darting towards the two craft. They split up to avoid a collision, and one turned to follow her, while the other continued its intercept course at Zack. She immediately reversed course to follow it, overtaking it and 'buzzing' it, forcing it to break off.

"Unidentified craft, this is your last warning. Your actions are considered hostile, and we will use deadly force without further warning."

Deadly force thought Zack. *Deadly force indeed, I could blow you from the sky, but you are my people, you are American, I will serve you, but I will never hurt you.*

The computer beeped at him, his decrypt programming had stopped running, and the rest of his systems were coming online. It was a message but he had no time to read it. There was something else too. His proximity sensors had picked up something, buried in the desert beneath them.

His shop had extra sensors that he didn't expect it to have. They were doing a deep scan on the buried whatever-it-was. He'd only need a few more seconds for them to finish. Nizhoni was doing an admirable job of keeping the air force planes occupied, so he decided to wait.

Those few seconds seemed to last an eternity. Finally, they beeped and the lights went green. Their scan was complete. "Nizhoni," he said. "Go straight up. These planes are likely F-15's which have a ceiling of about 65,000 feet. All we have to do is get above that, and we'll be free of them."

He saw her nodding, and then her ship disengaged from the plane that had been closing down on Zack. Like him, she changed her course and shot straight up. Both planes tried to follow, but then fell back.

"You don't know how many UFO stories I read where the USAF traced unknown craft which escaped by shooting upwards into space," said Zack. "I never thought I'd be in one of them."

*

"It doesn't look pretty, but I think it'll work" said Fintan, looking at their hastily reassembled craft. "We still have a couple of days to go before we have to hand in the project. Are you sure we want to do a test flight today."

"We have to," she said. "If it works, we still need to do refinement, and if it doesn't, well, we'll have to start over."

"Hmm," said Fintan. "Ok, let's give it a shot. You should go back to the station and stay in touch via bracelet comms. Don't want you to be too close in case anything goes wrong."

She nodded, and reluctantly withdrew.

Fintan climbed into the cockpit and took his place at the somewhat familiar controls. Around him the control room looked like a computer workshop with circuit boards and cables everywhere.

Ayako's voice came through his headset "Can you hear me?"

"Yes," said Fintan. "Here goes nothing."

He activated the switch to start the engines. "You see anything?"

"Yes," said Ayako. "The ship has started to levitate; you're about six feet above the ground."

"Good," said Fintan.

"Oh," said Ayako "it's starting to spin too. This looks good!"

"Ok, let's take it slow," said Fintan. "I'm going to increase the spin."

"Ok," said Ayako. "Nice and smooth."

But then something went wrong. "Fintan, stop the engines!" she screamed. The spin had become erratic, and the ship began to wobble like a buckled wheel. It caught on the ground, and under the force of the spin flipped over, hit the ground and rolled several times before coming to a stop, upside down.

"Fintan?" said Ayako. "Can you hear me? Are you ok?"

"Yes," he squeaked.

"What happened, are you hurt?"

"I'm ok," he squeaked again. "I got a bit bumped about, but I'm ok."

"Why are you speaking in such a squeaky voice?"

"You just don't know boys do you?"

A hatch opened at the bottom of the ship, which was now pointing skyward. Fintan climbed out holding his groin.

*

"It's a long message," said Zack "and we're almost out of time. I'll download it to your terminal, we'll head back to the barn, and we'll discuss tomorrow."

"Ok," she said. "The Barn?"

"I feel like a pilot now, and that's what pilots call home base."

"Zack," said Nizhoni. "You're twelve."

"And I'm flying a superfast flying saucer above the Mojave desert, dogfighting with the USAF. Your point?"

"Actually *I* was dogfighting them."

"Hmm. Good point, let's head back to the city and we'll discuss tomorrow."

"Roger Roger," she said, mocking his earlier tone.

*

It was night and the two boys were in their beds, staring at the ceiling.

"How's your project going?" said Fintan.

"I wish I could tell you" said Zack. "But I can't for so many reasons, one of which is we haven't done anything resembling a science project yet."

"Ten bucks says Nizhoni is telling Ayako what you guys are up to," said Fintan, joking. "It's ok. I understand that Trichallik wants you to keep it a secret."

"Wait a minute," said Zack, "how did you know Trichallik gave us the project?"

"Because Ayako told me," said Fintan. Zack could hear Fintan's bed shaking slightly. Fintan was laughing at him.

"I'm going to kill that girl," said Zack. "If she'll ever let me close."

He is smart and he is good too. His heart is so innocent, yet there is steel buried deep.

I know, but I am beginning to care for him, part of me wants to let him stay innocent.

It's too late for him to stop, and if we do it's likely too late for the rest of us.

Are things that bad?

I don't know, and whenever I try to find out, all I get are riddles.

"The library?" said Nizhoni. "Is that where you want to discuss this?"

"Yes," said Zack, "I think we'll need some of its resources."

"I read the decoded message," said Nizhoni "and it didn't make sense. It looked like a random stream of letters."

"The odds are we decoded it correctly," said Zack "but we just need to make sense of it. I think it's a skip-sequence grid."

"Explain."

"It's about laying all the letters out and then picking a skip sequence number that allows us to read the hidden message," said Zack.

He went on to demonstrate by drawing the following letters in the air on their shared terminal

```
aznasizoztehheoawnggi
```

"Now that's a string of letters that doesn't make sense, right?"

"Right," said Nizhoni.

"But look what happens if I take a skip sequence of '3', that is take every third letter," said Zack.

The letters changed to this:

```
az N as I zo Z te H he O aw N gg I
```

"My name," said Nizhoni.

"Exactly," said Zack. "No encryption, but encoding with a skip sequence of 3."

"Ok, I get it," she said, "but is that the case here?"

"Yes," said Zack. "I did some initial analysis, and tried many skip sequence numbers. I got plenty of results, but couldn't make sense of them. There might be some connections between them, but I can't find it."

"Show me the words," she said, and a long list of words appeared on the air in front of her.

"Oh," said Nizhoni. "That's a lot of words!"

"Yep" said Zack "so how do we figure out what they mean"

*

"Nizhoni told you what she and Zack are doing?" said Fintan, more of a question than a statement. He and Ayako were poking around the debris of various pieces of broken equipment.

"A little," she answered. "Trichallik has them flying around outside looking for stuff. It doesn't make much sense."

"How is that a science project?"

Ayako shrugged. "She has no idea, and frankly, neither do I."

Fintan sighed unhappily.

"They have no control over it," said Ayako, "so let's not hold it against them."

"Yeah," said Fintan, "I suppose you're right."

"I looked at the data from yesterday's test flight," she said "and was able to derive some useful information. I think I've figured out how we can change it so you won't crash again."

She paused for a moment.

"How are you feeling by the way?"

He laughed. "Just don't ask me to run for a little while, ok?"

She returned his laugh. "I bought you a gift in the rec store by the way."

"You did?"

"Yeah. It's for luck. You can wear it before today's test flight"

"Wow, thanks," said Fintan. "What is it?"

She held up an athletic cup.

*

"I keep seeing the same words repeated over and over again," said Zack

"Woman", "Third", "Dine", "Spider", "World" and "Rock" he listed out. "These words occur more than any others, it's like the messenger is trying to call attention to them."

Nizhoni looked over the words. Then something seemed to come alive in her eyes and she rearranged them in the air. She put 'Spider' and 'Rock' together, as well as 'Third' and 'World'.

"I was wondering about that" said Zack. "I remember you spoke about the 'Fifth' world once, but 'Fifth' isn't showing up here."

"Spider Rock," said Nizhoni. "I know this place."

"It's a place? I didn't know that."

"It's not just a place," said Nizhoni. "It's a *sacred* place. Our history tells us that it is where our people emerged from the Third World into this one."

" 'Third' and 'World' are on the list too," said Zack. "But what about Dine?"

"It's Diné," said Nizhoni, pronouncing it Din-Uh. "It means 'people' in my language. It's what we Navajo call ourselves."

"Hmm," said Zack. "You've given me an idea."

He called up the full string of letters again. "All these words came when I used a skip sequence of only 4. I expected it to be a much bigger number, with a harder to find sequence."

He animated taking every fourth letter and forming words from them.

"Is this number significant to you in any way?" said Zack

"Yes," she said. "It is."

She didn't elaborate, and Zack didn't force the issue. Instead he rearranged the words by taking every fourth one.

PROCEED TO SPIDER ROCK. THE DINÉ LEGEND OF SPIDER WOMAN AND THE LOST WARRIOR.

"I know that legend," said Nizhoni. "It's about a Navajo warrior who was being chased by his enemies. He got to Spider Rock, and Spider Woman lowered silk down to him. He climbed up and she fed him on eagles' eggs until he was satisfied. From there she lowered him down on a silk rope. From her he learned the art of weaving."

"And Navajo weaved rugs are so famous that even *I* have heard of them," said Zack. "But what does all this mean?"

"That we have to go to Spider Rock," said Nizhoni. "And maybe find our next clue."

*

"Are you ready Fintan?"

"Ready as I'll ever be," he answered. "And I'm wearing my good luck charm."

"Too much information, Fintan!" said Ayako.

He laughed. "Taking it up slowly now."

The ship lifted off slowly. It then started spinning.

"It's looking smoother," said Ayako. "Take the speed up a little."

The ship's spinning got a little faster. "Still stable," said Fintan. "Looking good."

"Ok," said Ayako "Let's try moving her a little forward."

The ship moved forward a few feet, stopped and continued to hover above the ground as it spun.

"How does it feel?" asked Ayako

"Good," said Fintan. "It's hard to control, but I think I can reprogram and tweak it a bit."

"Excellent," said Ayako. "And we still have a couple of days to spare, what ever will we do in our spare time?"

"I guess romantic dinners and walks by the river are out of the question?"

"Dream on."

*

As the saucer flew, from Area 51 to Spider rock was about 400 miles. They took it low and fast to avoid being chased by any more air force patrols.

"This route takes us past the Grand Canyon, doesn't it?" said Zack, checking his map.

"Yes," said Nizhoni.

"I've never seen it, can we take a look?"

"We'll do more than that, we'll fly straight through it. It will make a great hiding place."

"Oh sweet! This rocks. Ha. Rocks, get it. Rocks."

She didn't answer them, but continued to lead. They crossed over the Muddy mountains to reach Lake Mead where she lowered their altitude so they were flying just a few feet above the water.

From there she turned northwest to follow the lake.

"It's not a straight line," said Nizhoni, "but it will give us a lot of cover."

She dialed up the speed, and activated the collision avoidance system. Zack did likewise.

An outside observer would have seen two disks, flying at close to 800 miles per hour whispering across the water.

"No sonic boom," said Zack. "When a flying object crosses the speed of sound, about 740MPH if I remember, it creates a thunder-like boom."

"I guess nobody told the gods we're crossing that barrier," said Nizhoni.

Zack activated his heads-up camera and turned on the image enhancement. The canyon walls were growing either side of him as it got deeper. The passed the famous west rim in a blur.

"We're flying through the Hualapai reservation," said Nizhoni.

"They're related to us, but not as close as you might think."

"I'm learning more about your people every day," said Zack. "I can't believe how ignorant I was before."

Outside the view was stunning. The canyon was nearly a mile deep and several wide at this point. He could see lights along the rim on both sides.

"Campers," said Nizhoni "enjoying the stars"

"Wonder if any of them will report a UFO tonight?"

"I don't think so," said Nizhoni. "We're hard to spot."

"Makes you wonder how often saucers fly out of the city back into the real world, doesn't it?" said Zack. "Many people report UFOs around here."

They left the canyon and entered Navajo territory.

"Spider Rock is in a national park near the border with New Mexico," said Nizhoni. "My home."

She paused for a second.

"Zack," she said. "Spider Rock is sacred to my people. It would be best if we land a distance away and you let me go ahead there, alone."

He nodded. "Understood."

"Be careful," she said. "There are campgrounds there where tourists come to see the rock. It's beautiful. But they cannot be allowed to see us. "

"How will you know where to land?"

"I'm assuming what we're looking for is at or on Spider Rock itself, but I'm sure we'll have some sign when we get closer."

They crossed over another low mountain range, and approached the spot that Nizhoni had marked on the map.

A beacon started bleeping on their heads-up display.

"I guess that's it," said Nizhoni.

The beacon was right at Spider Rock itself, just as Nizhoni had guessed. "I know a place to land," she said "It's a short hike from the rock, but it's well hidden."

They hugged the landscape for a few more miles, and then a valley appeared seemingly out of nowhere. "It's more like a hole in the ground," said Zack, "than a valley or canyon."

Delicately she flew her ship down into the canyon, with Zack following. The gray landscape had given way to moonlit reds and yellows. Trees grew along the sides of the valley, and clusters of bushes dotted the landscape. Ahead of them, dark against the sky was a towering rock.

"Wow," said Zack "How tall is that thing?"

"It's about eight hundred feet," said Nizhoni

The rock was a tall, thin, straight tower, looking like a skyscraper from New York City had gotten lost in the desert. Because it was in the canyon, reaching from the floor of it, up to about ground level, it couldn't be seen from outside the canyon, unless you were on the rim looking down.

"It's beautiful," said Zack.

The rock stood where two valleys intersected, making the shape of a 'V'. Nizhoni took her ship to the left hand side of the rock, flying past it for a couple of miles before gently landing it in a small alcove.

Zack got out of his ship to see Nizhoni sitting at the edge of the alcove, legs dangling down. She turned to him and smiled. "I'm home."

He sat beside her. The sky was inky black and dotted with millions of stars. The moon was almost full and bathed the valley in a yellowish glow. He looked up at the rim of the canyon, almost a thousand feet above him. Campfires dotted a campsite near the rim, and Zack almost imagined he could hear people singing.

"Nice home," said Zack

"Well, I don't actually live *here*," said Nizhoni. "My village is a few miles from here, across the border into New Mexico but," she smiled again, "this is home."

She held up her bracelet and touched a button. A small display projected in front of her.

"Whatever the beacon is, it's at Spider Rock itself," she said, showing him the display. "I'll get going in a moment, but, beforehand, I'd better change. Wouldn't want to run into anyone in this uniform."

"Skirt too short?" said Zack, laughing.

She gave him her stern look, but her eyes were glistening in the darkness. "Try again. Wouldn't want anyone to have any questions about the uniform, right?"

"You mean like, where can I buy one of these for my girlfriend?"

She slapped him, playfully, on the arm. "You're hopeless! Now turn around when I change, and if I catch you peeping, I'll-"

"You'll what?" said Zack "Do a little dance?"

"I wouldn't want to spoil the surprise," she said. "But if you want a clue, think about Simon, ok?"

He heard the rustling of her changing and the zipping sound of her removing her uniform. He remembered her fearlessly taking on the air force planes. She was tough, that was for sure, but now she was just a little girl, changing in the darkness.

"Ok," she said. "I'm decent now, you can turn around."

She stood in front of him in cardigan, tee shirt and jeans. "How do I look?"

"Like a tourist?"

"Good enough," she answered. "Wish me luck."

She climbed down the entrance of the alcove, and jogged off into the darkness. Zack sat on the edge of the rock, dangling his feet watching her run. She was light on her feet and almost silent as she ran across the rocky ground. Before long she was gone in the darkness, and a moment of fear overcame him. He was surprised to find that he was more afraid for himself, alone in the darkness, than for her, running off into the unknown.

*

She had been gone for a couple of hours, but the time passed quickly. The night was beautiful and Zack spent it leaning back looking at the stars. Without city lights the sky was much clearer and the stars much sharper. Occasionally he'd hear the cry of a bird, maybe an eagle or an owl, out hunting at night, and the scurry of small desert creatures on the rocks beneath him. There was a faint sweet smell in the air. He felt that he could stay here forever.

"Wake up," said Nizhoni. "Some guard you are, a whole army could have come here and stolen the ships."

"A *Navajo* army maybe, if they're anything like you," said Zack. "You're quiet in how you run on this terrain."

She smiled. For once it seemed Zack had said the right thing. It felt good.

"I got it," she said. "But I am not sure what it is."

She held up a package. Inside was a piece of paper. On the paper was a picture of something that looked like a dome or a crater on a rocky floor.

"What's that?" said Zack

"I have no idea," said Nizhoni.

He thought about it a little more. "You know," he said. "This looks like it was taken from a satellite picture, right?"

She nodded agreement.

"But there are no domes or craters like our one on the Earth's surface, right?"

"What if it isn't a dome? What if it is something else? Could it be a volcano or something?"

"There's no spout, but…" he trailed off.

"What is it?"

"I have an idea" he said. "I've seen something like this before"

She waited.

"Underground weapons testing. Nuclear weapons. Back in the cold war, the government tested lots of nukes in Nevada, most of them underground. When I first got into the city, I figured that's how it had been built – they just blew great holes in the ground with nukes, but now I think they couldn't have."

"Why?"

"Because it would have to leave some kind of pimple on the surface that would look something like this."

"So you think this is in Nevada?"

"It might be. We'll have to search."

"Ok" she said. "But what's the point? Why did Trichallik have us flying these ships, getting used to them, and then send us on an errand to find something hidden here, only to go back to Nevada again?"

"There's something else," added Zack. "Back when you were dogfighting the USAF planes, a scanner on my ship picked up something hidden in the desert floor. It did a deep scan, and I haven't had time to analyze the data yet."

"So she sent us there for a reason?"

"They say God moves in mysterious ways," said Zack. "But I think he's a cheap con artist compared with the alien."

*

They had sufficient maps in the onboard computers within their saucers, so Zack decided that it would be better to stay where they were.

"Besides," he said, "don't want to encounter our USAF friends again, right?"

Nizhoni nodded. "You know we can do this the smart way, or we can do this the not so smart way," she said.

"The smart way would be to scan this image into the computer and have it do some pattern matching against maps. We can narrow it down by using the test ranges in Nevada."

"And the dumb way would be?"

"Looking over the maps manually!"

"You're right," he said. "I'm doing it the dumb way so I could spend more time here."

Nizhoni returned to her ship, carrying the paper. A few moments later she returned. "It's scanned," she said.

Zack called up some pattern matching algorithms and linked them to the mapping interface. The program started working through the maps of Nevada, looking for a match.

It only took a few seconds before the computer beeped. It was a match.

"98% accuracy," said Zack. "I think we have our pimple. And it's a crater, not a pimple. Darn it. I was hoping it would take longer."

They got into their saucers and took off, heading back westward across the Navajo land, entering the Grand Canyon at its eastern side, and meandering along it until they exited at Lake Mead. They cut northwest towards Papoose Mountain which towered over the south west corner of Area 51 and turned to head west.

"After we cross the next mountain range, we'll be at the north tip of a huge rift valley. It's full of craters from nuclear testing, and this one seems to be the biggest."

A few minutes later they were there. It was getting close to dawn and Nizhoni could see the sun beginning to add a yellow glow to the sky east of them.

"That's one heck of a crater," said Zack as they hovered over it.

"Sensors are showing it as over 300 feet deep"

"But why are we here?"

Zack headed south, slowly. There were many craters in the desert floor, none as large as the one they had just left.

"So many," she said.

He landed his ship and got out. The wind was blowing and sand stung his face. Everywhere was gray and barren. He shook his head.

"There's no life here."

"So sad," she replied.

"It's a complete contrast, isn't it?"

"What do you mean?"

"We came from a place of great natural beauty that your people have respected and preserved, to this place," he said. "It looks like *hell*, and it's made by *man*."

"Is she trying to teach us something?" said Nizhoni

"Maybe, there is something worth fighting for on this planet, but, that we have to be careful in how far we would go to fight for it?" he answered.

"Zack, that is deep. You surprise me."

"I'm full of surprises," he said. "Let's head for home."

Chapter 18: Show and Tell

You're preparing them for after, aren't you?
After?
Yes, after. They're coming aren't they?
We should always be prepared. Someday will be graduation day.

It was *Show and Tell* day at last. Some students were dreading it, but looking forward for it to be over. Others were proud of their projects, and had circled the date on their calendar so they could show off their work and get good grades.

Fintan was confident that his project was going to go well. He and Ayako had worked hard and were ready to 'wow' the audience. They had scheduled an outdoor exhibition so everyone could see not just how well they had repaired the crashed ship, but they had a few little surprises too.

Zack had been uncharacteristically quiet. He and Nizhoni had buried themselves in the library to prepare their presentation. When asked about it, Zack said "You probably think I'm lying, but I haven't prepared anything yet. We've spent the last few days chasing shadows, but, it was the journey that mattered, not the destination."

Fintan then pointed out that he sounded like the classic 'red indian' from cheap movies. "Be careful talking like that around Nizhoni," he said "or you might need a new dentist."

They both laughed.

In class Mister Singh gave them their presentation schedule. First, some indoor presentations would be given, and then around lunchtime they'd head outside to see the outdoor presentations. They'd then return to the classroom for the final presentations, including Zack and Nizhoni's.

Fintan was impressed by the quality of the projects. First up was Heather and Raj who, much to Raj's delight, had been paired up, despite looking like the typical odd couple.

They had done a good job though, explaining their desktop fusion reactor.

"Cold fusion," said Raj "is generally considered to be a hoax. However, it turns out that it isn't and the original inventors of cold fusion are graduates of this school. They went out into the University system, and leaked the technology too early, so it was discredited."

"There are a few potential pitfalls in generating energy with cold fusion," said Heather, "most notably contaminant radiation. When it's easy to build a self-sustaining nuclear reaction, and thus face meltdown or worse."

"How can it be a meltdown if it is cold?" heckled one student, a young African boy called Titus.

Singh shot him a dirty look, but Titus could hardly hide his grin behind his hand.

Heather was unflapped. "Should the reaction run away with itself, it would become hot, and could potentially lead to a meltdown or explosion."

Raj then started driving the details with presentations and photographs of he and Heather working together in the lab. In every picture he was smiling.

Heather again took over and explained their cold fusion experiment. After his fifth glass tube or palladium electrode, Fintan stopped paying attention and just wanted to see the results. She poured some water into the apparatus, telling how the hydrogen in the water would break down into deuterium, and that fusion would take place within these atoms.

Within a few seconds, a light bulb came on.

"Now a light bulb only requires a small amount of electricity," said Heather.

"So we wanted a much larger demonstration," said Raj. He turned on the projector again and showed one of the skyscrapers in the city center. "Using a device this size, we were able to provide power to this building!"

The lights in the building came on. Then they went out.

"For about 3 seconds," said Raj.

*

After several more demonstrations, all brilliant, Fintan was feeling nervous.

"You'll be fine," said Ayako. "I know you'll knock them dead."

They assembled in the field near where Ayako and Fintan had found the crashed ship. Ayako explained the ship systems end to end, identifying what was broken, what was missing and what was beyond repair. She was crisp, and clear and straight to the point, and showed her logical step-by-step disassembling of various noncritical systems, and how she and Fintan had cannibalized these to put together a working ship.

And then it was time for the flight demonstration.

"The task," said Ayako, "was to show that we could get the ship airborne, and fly it for a short distance. We were asked to do one mile, on the assumption that if you can do one, you can do fifty."

Fintan lifted the ship off the ground. It started to spin smoothly.

They had rigged a speaker on the ground, so Fintan's voice could be heard from the crowd. "Everything is green," said Fintan.

He then started moving slowly away from the group as Ayako explained the various setbacks that they had met and how they had gotten around them.

After a few moments, Fintan reached the landing point, one mile away.

They had timed their presentation perfectly.

Ayako thanked the crowd who clapped politely.

And then Fintan's ship exploded with a thud, and a huge black cloud started growing where his saucer had been.

Everyone gasped, and Singh turned pale. Heather screamed. Nizhoni looked stunned.

"I'm ok," came Fintan's voice from the speaker.

There were some cheers.

"And look behind you," he said. The crowd turned around.

Fintan's ship was hovering, impossibly quiet, right behind them. He waggled his wings and took to the air, trailing colored light behind him. Once he was about a hundred feet above them he used the skywriter to write 'Gothcha!' in the air.

Then he landed to tumultuous applause.

*

The class was buzzing from Fintan's prank as they returned to the classroom. Mister Singh eventually saw the funny side of it, but clearly wasn't impressed. "I won't mark you down for that nonsense," he said. "But if you ever do that again, I'll strangle you."

Finally it was time for Zack and Nizhoni's presentation.

They stood at the front of the class either side of the projection screen.

"What is Science?" asked Zack

"It is the effort to discover and increase our understanding of how the physical world works," answered Nizhoni

"And how do we increase our understanding?" asked Zack.

"Through controlled methods, we observe physical evidence, collect data, and analyze the information," she answered.

The screen began to show pictures. There was randomness to them. One minute it might be a mountain landscape, the next a river or a city scene.

"When we started this project, we had no idea what we were doing," said Zack

"And we thought about the definition of science," said Nizhoni.

"Whose understanding are we increasing?"

"Are we doing what we do for the benefit of all humanity?" asked Zack.

"Or just some of them?" answered Nizhoni.

The images on the screen changed now. Instead of scenes of beauty and modernity, they changed to images of poverty and suffering.

Zack and Nizhoni spoke through each of the scenes, linking them all back to science. They showed burned and charred bodies from the use of chemical weapons in Vietnam, and how they were caused by the science of effective weapons. They showed the effects of drought in regions of India, and how they were caused by global warming, a human effect. They showed animals that were extinct or near extinct and linked them. They showed the destruction of the rain forests, and how science made it all possible. Example after example of destruction, with linked, shocking images followed, stunning the class into silence.

Then he showed the image of a shadow on some stone steps.

Ayako gasped.

"This image," he said, "is from Hiroshima in Japan. This is a human being who was close to ground zero when we dropped an atomic bomb on their city. They were instantaneously vaporized, and this is all that remains. This is the result," he paused "of science."

"So science," he said "is more than a process of increasing our understanding. It is something that can easily and frequently be misused at the cost of great suffering."

He showed the pictures of the craters nearby. "Just a few miles from here is a canyon that looks like it comes straight out of hell. You can see the power of the destructive force that Science can give us. This one is called *Sedan Crater*."

He showed the picture that he had snapped from his saucer. "It's scale defies belief, and it is just one of hundreds. This is what we did to our world in the name of science,"

Nizhoni continued. "If this is what we would do to our world, what would others do? If this is how we treat our own people, how would outsiders treat us? "

Zack took over. "We are learning to go to the stars, but what will we find there? Are we ready for it? What does the evidence tell us?"

"And that was our project," said Nizhoni. "Our Science Project, where we decided to explore what Science was, we observed the physical evidence."

"We collected the data," said Zack

"And we analyzed the information," said Nizhoni.

Together they said. "And our conclusion was that while Science helps us to understand the Universe."

"It isn't enough," said Zack

"We must understand ourselves too," said Nizhoni.

They both sat. Mister Singh looked stunned. Then he slowly began to applaud. The rest of the class joined in and were soon cheering.

Fintan looked to Ayako, "Not bad, eh?"

Ayako nodded wiping the tears out of her own eyes with a tissue.

Chapter 19: Halloween.

Sunday.
Dance Day -5.
8:45PM

"Hey," said Zack. "There's going to be a Halloween dance". They were back in their dorms. Fintan was at his terminal working on his homework, and instant messaging with Nizhoni. A couple of weeks had passed since their science projects, and life was getting back to normal.

"What?" said Fintan.

"Look," said Zack, showing him a flyer that he'd gotten off one of the older kids. "This is going to be so cool!"

"It's not on Halloween, it's the day before," said Fintan.

"Close enough, so it's going to be so much fun. Let's get tickets and bring the girls along!"

Fintan looked in his wallet. The school gave them an allowance and being somewhat of a spendthrift, Fintan had some money left.

"I'm not going to buy a costume," he said. "I'm not even sure where you'd buy one in this city, something about its nature as an underground city, dedicated to the future of humanity's road to the stars, tells me that it doesn't have a costume shop."

"So you're going to be boring and go in dress uniform?"

"I'm afraid so."

"Argh! I have the most boring roommate in history!"

"It's a formal," said Fintan, reading the invitation card. "Meaning that guys buy the tickets and girls go with them. You're going to need a date."

"Ayako, of course," said Zack. "If I ever get around to asking her. Or maybe I'll ask Iara. Do you think they'd let a student take a teacher?"

*

Monday.
Dance Day -4.
10:22 AM.

Cosmic History class again and Sinclair's endless droning. Fintan was fighting to stay awake, but he knew that Sinclair was sneaky enough to wait for him to nod off and then ask him a question. So somehow he fought to stay awake.

Zack's eyes were glazed over. Fintan assumed he was running scenarios through his head in how he'd ask Ayako to the dance, and how he'd deal with rejection or acceptance.

He caught Nizhoni glancing his way. She smiled a little, embarrassed to be caught, and then turned her attention back to the lesson.

Class finished and they filed out into the corridor, complaining about the homework that Sinclair had given them. They had half an hour before their next class, so they went to the cafeteria for a drink and a sit down.

Zack elbowed Fintan, asking him to give him and Ayako a bit of 'lonely time'. Fintan shrugged, and asked Nizhoni to join him in the library for a few minutes – he had some questions.

As they climbed the stairs to the library, Nizhoni said. "So, are you taking me away from Ayako because you have to ask me something, or are you taking me away from Ayako because Zack wants to ask her something?"

She was grinning.

Fintan thought for a moment. "Yes," he said.

They got into the library and sat at a study desk. Suddenly Fintan found it hard to breathe. He was blushing from ear to ear. "Err," he said. "Umm."

Nizhoni just smiled.

He took a breath. "Willyougotothehalloweendancewithme?"

"Yes," she said. "I'd love to."

*

Monday.
Dance Day -4.
11:05 AM.

Fintan felt about a foot taller as he walked down the stairs. She said *yes.* They approached Zack and Ayako in the cafeteria. They were chatting about homework and drinking soda.

"Well?" said Fintan to Zack as the girls started chatting and giggling.

"Well, what?"

"What did she say?"

"I didn't ask her"

"Why not?"

"Err. Em," said Zack, fingering his collar. "I think I might ask Iara."

"Don't be silly," said Fintan. "Look at her! She's amazing. Why don't you just ask her?"

"I can hear everything you're saying, you know that?" said Ayako. She looked at Zack.

"Hi," he squeaked.

"We'll be late for our next lesson," said Ayako, coldly. She and Nizhoni walked ahead, arms linked, whispering and giggling.

*

Monday.

Dance Day -4.
10:44 PM

"She'll never say yes now," said Zack later that night as Fintan and he were ready to sleep.

"She won't say it if you don't ask her," Fintan responded. "And there's only three days to go."

"I'm going to work on my costume," he replied. "I'll ask her tomorrow."

"What is your costume anyway?"

"I'm not telling, you'll just have to wait and see. Oh, and Fintan?"

"Yeah?"

"Don't tell anybody about me making a costume, ok? I want it to be a big surprise."

"Ok."

*

Wednesday.
Dance Day -2.
12:30PM.

"So has he asked her yet?" whispered Nizhoni.

"I don't think so."

"Nobody else has asked her yet either, but, she's really beautiful, somebody is bound to," she replied.

"I know."

"What do you mean 'I know'?" said Nizhoni. "If you thought that, why didn't you ask her instead of me?"

"Err. That's not what I meant."

"Oh yeah, that's not what you meant. That's a weak excuse, Fintan, and I expected better of you."

"Sorry?"

She laughed, and pinched his arm.

"Girls," sighed Fintan.

*

Wednesday.
Dance Day -2.
10:22 PM.

"So, Zack, what's going on? Have you asked her yet."

"Yes," said Zack

"And?"

"Well, yes, I have asked her a thousand times in my head."

"That doesn't count."

"I know."

"So go there. Now."

"I can't."

"Why not?"

"I'm working on my costume."

"Your costume? There's no point in having a costume if you don't have a date!"

"There's no point in having a date if you don't have a costume."

"Well I have a date," said Fintan.

"Nizhoni?"

"Of course."

"Heh. Well done man."

*

Thursday.
Dance Day -1.
6:32 PM.

All through classes there was an air of anticipation. If folks were inviting others to the dance, nobody was telling. Fintan was sitting at dinner with Zack, Ayako and Nizhoni.

"So, who do you think asked Heather?" said Ayako.

"I heard some fifth-year did," answered Nizhoni.

"A fifth year? Wow!" answered Ayako. She glanced over to the table with fifth years. "Maybe I can go over there and see if one asks me?"

"Are you kidding?" said Nizhoni. Zack started nodding to agree. "They'd be lining up to ask you," she continued. Zack stopped nodding and looked morosely into his food.

Fintan elbowed him.

"Err. Ayako?" said Zack.

"Yes?"

"Is it more proper to call you Katsuragi-san?"

"Yes it is. Your point?"

"Nothing. Just wondering."

Fintan and Nizhoni rolled their eyes.

*

Thursday.
Dance Day – 1.
10:11 PM.

"Yes!" said Zack from his side of the bedroom. He had been working behind his partition not allowing Fintan to see.

"Did you ask her on e-mail?"

"No. But that's not a bad idea," said Zack. "I was saying 'Yes' because I've finished my costume. And it looks awesome. "

Fintan sighed.

"Ok, that's it," said Fintan. "We're going over there now, and you are going to ask her, or God help me I will burn the costume."

"You wouldn't do that!"

"Watch me," said Fintan. He strode to the other side of the partition, grabbed Zack's arm and walked out the door.

"Let go!"

"Not on your life," said Fintan.

They walked down the connecting corridor and into the boy's common room. They continued through it towards the dining area.

Two second-year boys saw the commotion, and Fintan heard one of them say "What's going on?"

The other answered "He's finally getting Zack to ask that Japanese girl out".

"Oh."

*

"Is she waiting for us there?" said Zack, breathlessly from being dragged.

"It would be nice if she was," said Fintan.

"You mean you haven't arranged anything?"

"Nope. This is spur of the moment."

"What?"

They entered the dining room, and there was no sign of Ayako or Nizhoni.

"Well that's it then," said Zack. "You can let go now."

Fintan didn't let go, and in fact tightened his grip as he led Zack towards the entrance to the girl's common room.

"We're not allowed to go there," said Zack

"I'll take the punishment instead of putting up with you another minute," said Fintan.

"What does that mean?"

"You know exactly what that means!"

The doors slid open to the girl's dorms. Some girls were lounging around in casual wear and pajamas.

One of them looked up and screamed.

"Sorry," said Fintan. He closed his eyes. He whispered to Zack. "Close your eyes darn it!"

Zack obeyed.

"Sorry," repeated Fintan. "Can you ask Ayako Katsuragi to come out here? If she isn't already here?"

One girl answered. "Is that Zack?"

"I'm Fintan," said Fintan. He shook Zack a little. "This is Zack."

"Oh I get it," said the girl. "Hang on."

There were a lot of giggles.

"I'm going to kill you Fintan," said Zack.

"Good. Make it quick, better than this slow torture."

They could hear hushed whispers and giggles. One girl stood almost nose to nose with Fintan. He could feel her breathing.

"If you open your eyes you'll wish you'd never been born," she said.

"I already wish that," said Fintan. "So maybe I should just open them."

She screamed and ran. There was a shuffling noise. Fintan assumed she was hiding behind something. More giggles.

Then there was a hush. Fintan assumed that Ayako and Nizhoni had arrived.

"I've got a bad feeling about this," said Fintan

"You've got a bad feeling about this?" said Zack. "What do you think I feel?"

"What's going on here?" said a voice. It was an adult voice.

"Uh-oh," said Fintan.

"Uh-oh Uh-oh," said Zack

"Sorry Miss, we got lost," said Fintan.

"Well of course you got lost if you are walking around with your eyes shut," she said.

Fintan recognized the voice. "Miss Parmour, is that you?"

Miss Parmour was their astronomy teacher. Their *really scary* astronomy teacher.

"Yes it is, Mister Reilly," she said. "And you'd better stop lying to me. Why are you here?"

Suddenly the bizarreness of their situation, and Zack's image of the blob from the planet Mungo came back to him.

He laughed. Long and hard.

*

Friday.
06:55AM.
12 hours and 5 minutes to go.

"Ayako" said Zack. "Will you please come to the dance with me tonight?"

He held up two tickets.

"Yes."

"Really?"

"Yes."

"Really really?"

"Yes," said Fintan. "You see, it isn't hard!"

They were in their room, getting ready for breakfast. Fintan was helping Zack practice asking Ayako. He tore the black wig off and threw it to the ground. "I can't believe I did that," he said to Zack, referring to the wig.

"Actually you looked good. Maybe I'll ask you instead" said Zack.

"I'm going with Nizhoni, remember?" said Fintan. "You know she's always there at 7 sharp. I emailed Nizhoni last night and asked her to make up an excuse for why she'll be a few minutes late. I will be too, so you have 5 minutes. Now go!"

Zack wandered out the door. He was dragging his feet as he made his way towards the boy's common room.

"I can see you," said Fintan. "Now hurry up!"

He turned back to his terminal. It was an e-mail from Nizhoni.

```
Target Alpha gone ahead to breakfast. I'll be
down in a few minutes. Is Target Dumbhead on the
way? He better, or else…
```

Fintan replied to her mail.

```
Roger Roger. Dumbhead is inbound and weapons are
hot. Over.
```

He sat back, sighed and rubbed his forehead. This had better work.

*

Friday.

07:05 AM.

11 hours and 55 minutes to go.

At 7:05 Fintan innocently strolled into breakfast. He saw Nizhoni entering from the opposite side – the way from the girl's common room – and nodded to her. She returned his nod.

With butterflies in his stomach, worse than those when he had asked Nizhoni out, Fintan tried to remain calm. He got his breakfast and sat beside Zack and Ayako. Nizhoni arrived at the same time.

"Sorry I'm late," said Fintan. "Couldn't find my socks."

There was silence over the table.

"Did Zack find his socks?" asked Nizhoni innocently. "You know. He's a man, and a real man has a pair of, you know, socks."

Fintan nearly choked.

Zack finally spoke. "Tonight is going to be the best night of my life," he said. He looked to Ayako and turned to them. "She said *yes!*"

*

Friday.
Dance Day. 6:45 PM.
15 minutes to go.

"I've asked the girls to meet us there," said Zack, "I want to make a grand entrance with my costume, and have everyone see it at the same time."

"Ok," said Fintan. "But let's not be too late. I'd hate to keep Nizhoni waiting."

They returned to their room to get changed. Fintan had dry cleaned and pressed his dress uniform and quickly put it on. He glanced at himself in the mirror.

He looked *good*. It wasn't that anything physical had changed about him, but he realized that his weeks here had built his confidence, and when he thought of Nizhoni he walked with a spring in his step and a smile on his face. He was *ready*.

"So how do I look?" said Zack.

Fintan walked out of the room and gasped.

Zack was dressed from head to toe in brilliant green, and had a huge bulbous head, also shining green, on his shoulders. Its eyes were large and black, and it had a tiny mouth. The top of the head was scraping the ceiling.

"Are you supposed to be Trichallik?" said Fintan, trying not to laugh.

"Yeah," said Zack. "Or at least a caricature of her."

"It's creative," said Fintan, snickering.

"It's pretty cool, because her mouth is a one way visor that I can see out of. The only problem is the head is a bit top-heavy, so it wobbles a lot when I walk."

Fintan couldn't help himself now. He flat-out laughed. Tears were streaming down his face.

"We'd better go," said Zack.

"Ok," said Fintan as he guided Zack through the corridors towards the dining hall. They passed some students who stopped and stared, mouth wide open as the odd couple passed. Fintan just shrugged with a 'What can you do?' attitude.

"Do they like it?" said Zack.

"Err, I think so," said Fintan.

It was a short train ride to the ball, so the stares that they got from the other passengers were easy to ignore.

*

Friday.
Dance Day.
Dance Hour.

They finally made it to the hall.

"Sorry," said Zack. "I thought I could walk a bit quicker, but this head is killing me."

"You ready?" said Fintan

"Yep," said Zack.

Fintan opened the doors and they walked into the hall. It was the most beautiful room he had ever seen. Long and rectangular with floating lights lining it, and beautiful silks and fabrics decorating the walls. A band played in one corner. Their music was otherworldly and soothing.

"Da daaaa," said Zack, spreading his arms wide in a 'look at me!' gesture.

In the distance, someone dropped a glass and it shattered on the ground.

"Oh crap," said Fintan.

"What is it?"

"I don't think it's a fancy dress dance," said Fintan.

"What?"

Fintan looked over the crowd. All the men, like him, were in dress uniform. The girls were in dresses.

He saw Ayako and Nizhoni standing near the entrance.

Ayako was wearing a lilac colored Kimono with Japanese platform shoes. She carried a parasol, her face was painted white, and her hair was long and straight. Fintan smiled as he saw her. She looked *great*.

"I said I don't think it's a fancy dress dance," said Fintan.

"Uh oh," said Zack.

Nizhoni stood beside Ayako. She wore a simple light brown dress, with shawl weaved in the four Navajo colors draped over her shoulders. She had a band with the same colors woven through her hair, which was tied up in a bun behind her head. Sharp jade-colored earrings that looked like arrowheads hung down from her ears. Fintan realized that she was simply the most beautiful thing he had ever seen

"Can Ayako see me?" said Zack as he slowly inched backwards towards the door.

"*Everyone* can see you," said Fintan.

Zack turned and broke into a run, the head bouncing comically as he got faster.

Fintan's eyes met Nizhoni's. He shrugged with a look that said "I'll be back," and followed Zack, torn between wanting to laugh and wanting to cry.

*

When Zack and Fintan entered, this time nearly fifteen minutes late, a few people laughed, and Ayako looked ready to kill Zack.

"Let's get a drink," said Nizhoni to Fintan.

"Don't you think we should hang out a little first?"

"Let's get a drink," repeated Nizhoni, more firmly this time. "Ayako needs to talk to Zack."

"Ah," said Fintan, and he joined her at the drinks buffet. She offered him a yellow liquid. "Desert Tea" she said. "It's delicious".

She was right. The warm, sweet liquid flowed down his throat most delightfully.

Despite the strange beginning, Fintan was entranced. It quickly became a magical night.

Chapter 20: Study Party

You are watching him closely aren't you?
Yes. His family relationship interests me.

November seemed to pass in a flash. Every day was filled with work, more work and then homework. Despite that Fintan was happier than he had ever been in his life.

He loved what he was doing. He even loved *Cosmic History*.

But a dark shadow was looming over them. Christmas Exams in the second week of December.

"It's snowing back home by now," said Ayako, one morning at breakfast. "It is so pretty in Japan when it snows."

"Everybody in my neighborhood is putting up their Christmas lights," said Zack. "They like to compete with each other, and each year they up the ante. I think it's brighter at night than it is during the day".

"I don't understand Christmas," said Nizhoni. "But that doesn't stop me loving it. I'm looking forward to seeing my family again after the Christmas tests."

"Now she said it," said Zack. "The dreaded words. Christmas tests. Thanks Nizhoni!"

Nizhoni smiled. She looked to Fintan. "What about you?"

"I don't know," said Fintan. "I don't really like Christmas."

"Why not?" asked Ayako. "It's a wonderful holiday."

"Yeah, you'd think," said Fintan. He didn't really want to talk about his family, but these were his friends. It would be a load off his chest if he did. But then something blocked him.

"My family," said Fintan, starting, but then stopping again. "My family is not very good at celebrating Christmas properly."

"Properly?" said Zack. "What's properly? Isn't it just a time to be together and have joy?"

"It is," said Fintan. "That's the problem."

"There is no joy in your life, is there Fintan?" asked Nizhoni.

"Wrong," said Fintan. "There is joy in my life. Here. With you." She blushed.

"And Zack, and Ayako, and everything," he continued. "I guess I just don't want to go home. I'm probably going to stay over the holidays."

The clock ticked forward. They had to get up to go to class. As they left the dining hall, Nizhoni touched his hand gently. It felt good, and he could forget about home for a little longer.

*

"We should have a study party," said Zack later that night from his side of the bedroom.

"A what?" said Fintan.

"A study party. You, me, the girls, maybe Raj and Heather, we get together to study for the exams. It'll be much more fun than this."

"I don't think it's supposed to be fun," said Fintan.

"Why not?" said Zack. "As long as we're doing the work we may as well be having a good time. I mean, this isn't exactly fun, and I bet you're too bored to work now, right?"

Fintan thought about it for a bit. "You're right," he said. "How do we do it?"

*

"You're kidding," said Ayako.

"For once I'm not," said Zack. "Think about it. We work much better together in teams, right? Nizhoni and I did a far better job than anybody expected in the science project, and we got first place didn't we? Nobody saw that coming."

"Speak for yourself," said Nizhoni. "You were the one expected to flunk."

Zack made a face at her. "But still-"

"And what do you think Fintan?" said Ayako.

"Why not?" said Fintan. "We've revised everything already, so we can continue doing it until we are sick of it and demoralized, or, we can at least have fun working a couple of times a week as we count down to the tests, right?"

Ayako pursed her lips. Nizhoni raised her eyebrows.

"Ok," said Ayako. "Let's do it."

*

"That's a great idea!" said Heather. "I'll bring the drinks."

"The drinks?" said Zack

"Of course," said Heather. "It's a party, right? Someone brings food, someone brings drinks, someone brings dessert. You guys host and decorate."

"We host?" said Zack.

"Of course, it's your idea."

"Oh, yeah, I suppose," said Zack.

"Afraid we'll see that you have a messy room?" said Heather. "Of course you have a messy room. You're a boy!"

*

"I think I've given birth to a monster," said Zack. He and Fintan were back in their room. The party was only a day away.

"Meaning?" said Fintan.

"Look at this place, it's a pigsty!" said Zack. "I think I smell my underwear from back in September."

"That's because they're still in your closet, unwashed," said Fintan. "And something is probably growing on them. And besides, look at my side of the room. You could eat your dinner off the floor here."

"Only if you wanted to die of something horrible."

They laughed.

"Fintan," said Zack.

"Yeah?"

"Do you mind going and rustling up some decorations. I've some tidying to do."

Fintan sighed.

*

Just like it didn't have a Halloween costume shop, a city designed to build humanity's readiness to go to the stars also wouldn't have a Christmas store.

Or so Fintan thought.

"Of course we have a Christmas store!" the worker said. "We're still human you know, or at least most of us are! Speaking of which, have you seen our new Alien decoration?"

"Err no." said Fintan.

"Oh you've got to see it, it's delightful!" she said. She went to a shelf and took down a small box. Out of it she took a plump and rubbery character. It was an alien, wearing a Christmas hat.

"Yeah. Pretty." said Fintan, unconvinced.

"Oh you haven't seen the best part yet!" said the woman. She flipped a switch at the bottom of the figure. Nothing happened.

She clapped her hands and the figure started dancing and singing 'Jingle Bells' in a very loud, very shrill, headache-inducing voice. When it started he nearly jumped out of his skin. Then he laughed.

"I'll take it" said Fintan. "Scratch that, I'll take two."

*

He made it back to the dorms overladen with tinsel, holly, paper stars, real stars, lights and the two singing aliens.

He got into his room and dropped them all on the floor.

"You carried all that yourself?" asked Zack.

"Yeah," said Fintan. "Not sure how"

"And now look!" said Zack. "Your side of the room is so messy and mine is so tidy"

"I was wondering what the smell wasn't." said Fintan.

"Oh ha ha."

*

They finished decorating the room in the nick of time. Fintan had been careful in finding decorations that would appeal to everyone. He guessed that Ayako would like the pale pinks, and whites, which would remind her of Cherry Blossoms and the snows of Japan. For Nizhoni, he had taken white, blue, yellow and black papers and fashioned Christmas tree murals on the walls. For Zack and Heather, as well as the usual red and green, he had some American red, white and blue. Finally for Raj, he had bought some small candles, having read that Indian celebrations use little candles that they called 'diya'.

The aliens would be for everyone. He set them to flank either side of the door, and cranked up the volume so they were as loud as he could get them. The idea was that when people walked in, they would trigger the songs.

Ayako was first, carrying a plate of Sushi. She didn't flinch, just laughing as she entered. "They sound like Japanese Opera," she said. "Except not as bad."

Nizhoni was next. When the aliens started singing, she moved in a blur, kicking one across the room with her right leg. It zipped past Zack's ear. In a blur she turned and kicked the other into the door. All this without spilling a single one of the Tacos she carried.

The statue behind her continued singing, but its singing slowed, grew deeper and stopped with a painful cry.

"Whoah!" said Zack, checking his ear to see if it was still there.

"Sorry," said Nizhoni. "Reflexes, you know?"

Ayako was doubled up laughing.

Fintan took the broken one, picked it up and shook it. "She's dead," he said.

"We still have one" said Zack, placing it beside the door. "And Raj and Heather aren't here yet!"

"They're coming?" asked Ayako.

"Yeah," said Zack

"*They* are coming?" emphasized Ayako. "*They*"

"Yes," said Zack. "There's more than one of them, so you use the word 'they'"

"That's not what she means," said Nizhoni. "Are you saying they're an item?"

"Oh," said Zack. "Yes. I believe they are."

"But-" said Nizhoni.

Immediately the door chimed and Zack answered it. Raj and Heather were at the door. Raj, stood in front, afraid to be hidden behind Heather. Fintan noted that he barely reached his girlfriend's shoulder, and that he was standing as straight as he could. Both were beaming.

As he stepped through the door, the statue started singing. Raj squealed and jumped into Heather's arms.

*

The dorm rule was that no girls were allowed in the boy's rooms after 9PM. So they had a few hours to study. Fintan had figured that they'd try for a little while before breaking down into a general hang out time.

But, like him, these guys were different. They put their heads down and collaborated in study in a way that made him proud. By 8PM they'd worked hard for a couple of hours, and realized that it was probably time to relax.

"Nice decorations," said Ayako, admiring the colors.

"Yeah," said Nizhoni. "They're amazing. I can't even smell Zack. You guys have outdone yourselves."

She touched the multicolored trees tenderly, turned and beamed at Fintan.

Raj was clearly enjoying himself. He was hand in hand with Heather walking around inspecting everything.

"Sorry about the Jingle Bells," said Fintan.

"Don't be sorry," the Indian boy replied. "Heather caught me and hasn't let me go since."

Heather laughed.

"Let's do this more often," said Zack. "It'll make the last few weeks a lot more fun to have Friday nights like this."

"And let's do a big party after the exams are done!" said Ayako. "Before we all go home."

Fintan's stomach sank almost to his feet. But he smiled along with the others and said "Great idea!"

Chapter 21: Tests and Dreams

I'm walking through the valley, and I'm an animal, maybe a bear, sometimes a mountain lion. I always hear a voice calling me, calling me. I turn to look for it, but I cannot see it, I can only just hear it. Or maybe I'm in the ocean, swimming. I'm an insect like a locust or a grasshopper. There's nothing around me, just the vastness of the ocean. I see nothing, except, a huge monster always comes out of the ocean, it looks to me, expecting something of me, I don't know what it wants, and then it devours me.

Fintan woke up, screaming.

Sweat was running down his brow into his eyes, they stung.

He could hear Zack on the other side of the room. "Nightmare again?"

"Yeah," said Fintan.

"You were crying out her name, do you know that?" said Fintan

"Whose?"

"My mother's," said Zack, sarcastically. Then, more softly he added "Nizhoni's name of course."

"Really, I don't remember that."

"Well you did," said Zack "she could probably hear it all the way from her room."

"Sorry," said Fintan.

"It's ok," said Zack. "I'm your friend and I'm worried about you."

"It's just the pressure of the exams," said Fintan.

"Yeah, that's probably it."

They both went quiet. Within a few moments Fintan could hear Zack snoring gently.

He slipped back into sleep himself.

And I'm walking through the valley, through the trees and the grass. I can hear a voice. It's calling me. And I can see the rock. The rock! It's there. I approach it, I touch it and I-

*

December came fast. Anxiety gave way to frenzied preparation, with the Friday night parties being a great release valve.

Exams were here, and Fintan was ready.

Cosmic History as a test was like its teacher: boring and old-school. They had exam booklets and questionnaires that they had to write essays on. Fintan figured that Sinclair would expect them to use standard pencils too.

But he had been working hard at this subject. The American kids had an edge, but Fintan had been working his way up the rankings. He was confident of a top ten finish, which he hoped would keep Sinclair off his back until summer.

He finished his paper early, and, as was his habit, he didn't leave the exam room right away. His strategy was to do something else while waiting, and not think of the exam. It amazed him how often things that he couldn't remember during the exam would come back to him when he was doing something else.

He found a piece of blotting paper and started doodling. He just let his mind wander and drew whatever came to mind.

Before long, what he was drawing was gradually taking shape. It was tall and thin, and had many layers, like strata. It reminded him of the desert mesa that he had seen on TV many times, but was slightly different in that it did not jut up from the surface like they did, but was more recessed, like it was in a valley.

In a valley.

He stopped for a moment, and then drew in the walls of a valley, with some trees lining the edges, and the tall, thin mesa in the center. He was never good at art, but this looked pretty good to him.

He stopped for a moment, drew his breath and tried to remember where he could possibly have seen this image before.

He noticed Zack, head down, frantically scribbling answers on his paper. The American boy stopped, and rubbed his eyes, steeling himself for the next question. He looked over to Fintan, ready to give him a nod, as if to say 'almost there!' His eyes flicked downward at what Fintan was drawing. He looked away, to go back to his paper, before a moment of realization turned him back. He looked again at Fintan's doodling and his eyes went wide with shock.

*

"What were you drawing in there?" asked Zack. Everyone was filing out of the exam hall, talking about the questions and how they approached them. Students were slapping themselves on the head saying 'why didn't I think of that' or gleefully teasing their friends.

Zack's question caught Fintan by surprise. He stopped. "Huh?"

"The thing you were drawing or doodling. What was it?"

"It was nothing," said Fintan. "What's come over you?"

"Do you still have it?" Zack had a worried look on his face that was beginning to bother Fintan.

"Err, I'm not sure, hang on," said Fintan, who began to fumble in his bag. He pulled out several pieces of paper, and started to inspect them.

Zack snatched one and looked at it closely.

"This is it," he said. "Wow!"

"What is getting into you? It's not *that* good."

"Do you know what this is? Have you ever been there?"

"I don't know what you are talking about."

"I know this place," said Zack. "I've been there, with Nizhoni."

It felt like something stabbed Fintan in the stomach. He tried not to sound too jealous. "Nizhoni?"

"When we did our Science Project, we flew here. It's in her reservation; it's a special place to her people."

"You visited her reservation?"

"Sort-of, we were guided to this location by an encrypted signal that we found in Nevada."

"You're losing me," said Fintan.

"Sorry, I'll explain the fine details later. For now, you should show this to her."

"Why?"

"Because this place is special to Navajo. It's *sacred* to them. She made me wait by the ships while she went there alone."

Fintan could feel his stomach churning and the hair standing up on the back of his neck. Why was he feeling so angry? He snatched the paper back from Zack. "You let her go alone, at night, in the desert? Alone?"

"It's her home," said Zack. "She knew what she was doing there. Actually when she's there, you see a different side of her," he paused. "Well I did anyway."

"What?" said Fintan, anger growing like a waking beast. "I thought you were my friend, I thought you were-"

"What's going on here?" said Nizhoni. She had walked up behind them. Fintan was so angry he didn't hear her coming.

"That's what I'd like to know!" said Fintan, sounding angrier than he wanted.

"Fintan's jealous about the time we spent together on the project," said Zack. "And, in my usual manner I said all the wrong things, and I think he has the wrong end of the stick."

Before Fintan could say anything, Zack continued. "Anyway, what is more important now is this!"

He grabbed the paper from Fintan and showed it to Nizhoni.

She looked at it, not recognizing anything for a moment, and then Fintan saw realization dawn on her face. Her mouth dropped open, and she seemed to stop breathing. She put her hand to her mouth.

"See?" said Zack. "I told you it was important."

"Shut up, Zack," said Nizhoni. "I need to talk to Fintan."

He shrugged, as if to say 'ok'.

Nizhoni looked him in the eye. Firmly she said "Alone!"

*

She pulled Fintan aside, pinned him to the wall and looked him right in the eye.

"Fintan," she said. "This is serious. Where did you see this?"

"I don't know," said Fintan. "Really."

"Think," said Nizhoni. "This is really important."

Fintan breathed deep, released it. He pursed his eyebrows.

"I really don't," he paused.

"What is it?" asked Nizhoni. She was a little softer now.

"It's silly," said Fintan. "Please don't get upset with me?"

"Just tell me, please" said Nizhoni. Her voice quivered a little.

"It was in a dream," said Fintan. "A dream."

Her face went still. She smiled a little, and to Fintan's surprise a tear burst out of her left eye and ran down her cheek. She put her hand, tenderly to his face.

"Tell me about your dreams Fintan," she said. "All of them"

*

Fintan started to tell her, but couldn't. There were many, and he was embarrassed to tell them all. He told her of the valley, but she was always hungry for more. But there were tests to be done, and she would have to wait.

He promised to tell her everything when the tests were all done.

"I'll hold you to that," she told him, warmly. Fintan's chest puffed out, and he felt ten feet taller.

The rest of the testing went by in a blur. Thankfully Fintan was well prepared for all of them, and was happy with their progress.

If anything, Nizhoni seemed much closer to Fintan now, almost protective. He wasn't sure what to make of it, but held his tongue.

The final test was in *basic flight*. Iara had drilled them heavily, and was openly expecting them not just to pass, but to excel. The biggest surprise of the day was Zack, who literally flew rings around everyone, even Nizhoni and Fintan, who were considered the best pilots.

As he landed and exited his ship, even Iara was impressed. Zack winked at her and strode past proudly.

Heather giggled. Raj gave her a stern look. Fintan shook his head and Ayako and Nizhoni looked like twins as they rolled their eyes.

But testing was done, and Christmas was on the way.

*

The Friday night study group had agreed on a big party to celebrate the end of the Christmas tests. All first-years were invited as were the other members of the Starball team, on Zack's request.

"Are you sure?" Fintan had asked him.

"Yeah," said Zack. "I'm going to the tryouts next term to get on the team. It would help to have some friends."

"You're certainly good enough," Fintan said. "I'm sure you'll get in"

*

They had rented a conference room in the exam halls, and together Fintan, Zack, Raj, Heather, Ayako and Nizhoni decorated it. They had piled the tables high with food and drinks. Everything was ready to go.

The party was a massive success. Even Simon turned up and gorged himself on Ayako's sushi. A gracious host, it was clear that she melted his heart, and he was extremely polite to everyone, even Fintan, although he gave Nizhoni a wide berth.

After time the party dwindled, and Fintan's anxiety grew. In a few hours everyone would be leaving to go home for the Christmas break, and there were lots of emotional 'goodbyes' at the party.

Zack, Ayako and Nizhoni would be going tomorrow, and while Fintan had told them that he probably would not go home, he hadn't confirmed. He didn't want to be a dark cloud over the party, so he had pinned a smile on his face all night.

His false cheer was wearing off now, and as they began to clean up, he sat in a corner, morosely watching them.

Zack, Ayako and Nizhoni looked at each other, wordlessly. Finally, Nizhoni approached him and kneeled in front of his chair. She was smiling. Fintan figured it was for his benefit, but he found it difficult not to smile back.

"You owe me some stories about dreams, remember?" she said. "You didn't think I was going to let you forget, did you?"

*

She had told him to tell her everything, and to leave nothing out. So he did. He started with a dream that he had had when he was a child. He was only six years old, but he had dreamt that he was walking down a street. There was a girl on the other side of the street. He couldn't remember her face, but she had long dark hair and a big smile. She was smiling at him. He crossed the street to find her, but when he got there, she was further away. Then he was standing at the edge of the ocean, and she was among the waves. She was reaching for him, he walked out to find her, but he grew scared. The surf was too rough and it was throwing him around like a toy. She was still smiling, but now he could see tears on her face. She vanished below the waves.

Throughout his recounting of this dream, Nizhoni's face was impassive, not wanting to distract him.

"I remember waking up from that dream," said Fintan. "In my back yard."

Suddenly, Nizhoni stirred to life. "Your back yard?" she said, looking worried.

"Yeah," said Fintan. "I guess I had sleep walked."

He paused for a moment. "Funny thing is, I changed overnight. I suddenly became the brightest kid in the class, which made me a target for bullies. Ireland can be a rough place if you stand out. But I couldn't help but be the best and brightest in my class. I always wondered what caused it, but figure that it was my helplessness to save the girl in my dream gave me motivation to use what I had up here," he pointed to his forehead, "as much as possible."

"Did you also become obsessed with the stars?" asked Nizhoni.

"Strange that you should say that," said Fintan. "But yes. My first memory is of the stars, but only after that did I realize that. Pretty odd, huh?"

"Not really," said Nizhoni. "Don't discount it, if it had real effects on you."

He continued with the rest of his dreams, including the dreams of being an insect in the ocean, and a bear in the valley.

"They've been much more intense since I came here," said Fintan. "I can't explain it, other than the fact that I'm under pressure here."

She knit her eyebrows and nodded. "Maybe."

"So," said Fintan. "What do you think?"

"I think that dreams are messages. Sometimes from our ancestors, sometimes from the spirits, sometimes from our subconscious about lost memories. You should not dismiss them, but I cannot interpret them for you."

"What was the place that I drew?" said Fintan.

"You've never been there," said Nizhoni, "but maybe an ancestor was, or a spirit is trying to tell you something."

"I don't believe in spirits," said Fintan. "Or at least I don't think I do."

"It's ok," said Nizhoni. "Few people outside my people do. My family are great believers in the old ways of the Navajo, indeed my clan is at the heart of a resurgence in our beliefs."

She stopped for a moment, before continuing. "Because of this place," she said. "Something important is happening here. Something that we've been preparing for for a long time."

"You mentioned a fifth world before," said Fintan.

"Yes," she said. "But not now. I will tell you another time. For now, I want to tell you that I believe that you are somehow connected to what is happening. That you are here for a reason. And that reason is connected to the Navajo. That's why the spirits showed you Spider Rock."

"Zack mentioned that it's a sacred place to you."

"Yes, and it is hard to explain. Maybe in time you will understand us better, and then you will understand, in your heart, why it is sacred, and why it is important that you are dreaming it."

Fintan looked at the clock. It was nearly 2AM and well past their curfew.

"You'd better go back to your dorm," said Nizhoni. "Don't want to get the important dreamer in trouble!"

*

The next day Zack and Ayako left early in the morning. Fintan saw them briefly at breakfast and they gave their goodbyes as they hustled for the transports back to Las Vegas. Nizhoni was nowhere to be seen.

He spent the rest of the morning in the flight simulator room that Nizhoni had shown him. It wasn't nearly as much fun by himself, and he was already missing her greatly. He returned to the dining hall for lunch.

Nizhoni was waiting for him in street clothes at their usual table.

"You'd better hurry and pack," she said. "Or you'll be late."

She paused and smiled.

"You're spending Christmas with the Navajo."

Chapter 22: The Rez

Fintan was shocked, but happy to see her, not to mention a little nervous at spending some time with her and her family over the Christmas holidays.

But it felt good to be wanted. He really didn't want to go home, and he didn't want to stay here alone, he'd miss her terribly. And, it would be a great adventure to go and spend some time with her people.

"But," he said. "How?"

"Oh don't worry about that. I have my ways," she said, winking at him.

Delirious with happiness, Fintan made his way back to his room, and quickly packed his bag. He was grateful to have some chocolates that he could bring as a gift, as well as some US Dollars in case he had a chance to go shopping. However, he knew that Nizhoni lived on a reservation. And it dawned on him that she never spoke about it, so he had no idea what to expect. The comical image of him sleeping for the next few days in a wigwam made him smile again. This really was an adventure into the unknown.

He made his way back to her, and she led him out of the dorms onto a train into the city. Fintan couldn't contain himself – he just couldn't stop smiling, and that brought a happy smile to Nizhoni's face too.

"I don't know what to say," said Fintan. "Other than 'Thank you!' you don't know how much this means to me."

"It's our way," said Nizhoni. "We can't let others suffer if there is something in our power to stop it. I could see how much the thoughts of Christmas were tearing you up."

The train went a little further, and she continued.

"Besides, it'll be really nice to spend some time together without worrying about lessons, projects, or what Zack and Ayako are saying about us behind our backs!"

Fintan laughed.

They got off at a stop in the city center, and Nizhoni led him through an array of streets towards an unknown destination.

"It's around here somewhere," she said, standing on a street corner, looking up and down the side streets.

"This isn't a typical city, is it?" said Fintan. "Not a lot of traffic. Not even that many people."

"There's usually more than this" she said. "But a lot of them go home for Christmas too. That being said, there's plenty of room to expand. They thought of this place with the future in mind."

Nizhoni then grunted in a way that could only be positive, and made her way towards a small building at the end of a long and narrow street. As they got closer, Fintan realized that it, too was a train station, but for some reason it wasn't connected to the rest of the grid. It was the terminus for a single line that led towards the rim wall.

Despite her cheerfulness, Fintan noticed that as they got closer, Nizhoni was not really at one hundred percent. She stopped a few times, for just a moment, holding her abdomen. Whatever was bothering her, she was hiding behind a smile, but at one point she stopped for a moment, wrapped her arms around herself, grimacing, before going onwards.

Fintan reached out and took her backpack.

"That's not necessary," said Nizhoni. "I'm fine."

"Ok," said Fintan. "But I'm not doing it because it's necessary."

She tried to pull it back from him, but he strode ahead.

"There's really no need," she said, but he didn't answer.

They got to the train station just before a train departed. This time, instead of sitting opposite him on the train, she sat beside him, and leaned on him a little. She felt hot.

"Are you sick?" said Fintan. "You seem to have a temperature."

"No," she said. "I'm ok. Don't worry about it," she smiled and continued the small talk. Whenever Fintan would try to ask where they were going, or what they were going to do on the reservation, she widened her eyes slightly, and changed the topic. He soon got the message. It wasn't something that they should speak about in public.

The train didn't make any stops until it reached its terminus. It looked like it was in the middle of nowhere, but as they climbed off the train and got off the platform; they realized that ahead of them was an enormous causeway leading to the rim wall. On all sides they were surrounded by earth, some of which had given away to weeds, some of which looked like it had been tilled once upon a time.

"It looks wider than a highway," said Fintan, pointing at the causeway.

"Wider than two highways," said Nizhoni, who walked towards it, clearly following it towards the rim wall.

As they approached the rim wall, Fintan noticed that there was something built into the wall. It reminded him somewhat of the place Simon had taken them during their hazing. "Yeah," said Nizhoni, reading his expression. "It's similar."

"Do you know what it is?" asked Fintan, figuring it would be safe to talk now.

"Not yet," she said, probably not answering his spoken question. "But we'll see in a minute."

They walked on in silence because Nizhoni was clearly having some kind of difficulty. Fintan decided not to ask her about it further, but she didn't protest this time as he carried her bag.

As they got closer to the wall, Fintan again was awed by the scale of the place. From this vantage point it really looked like they weren't in a dome at all, as the wall just seemed to go straight up. The last time he was close to the wall it was at night, but now, in the full artificial sunlight he could see it. It was painted a pale blue, and looked just like the sky.

Except the sky didn't come to a sudden stop about 150 feet off the ground on a sand colored wall. He turned and walked backwards, and smiled at the beauty of the city.

"Look," he said to Nizhoni, and she joined him in walking backwards.

The city was relatively small by most standards, maybe twenty or thirty tall buildings, surrounded by smaller ones and domes like an army of foothills. But it was beautiful, and the buildings gleamed in the false sunlight. The pale blue dome on the far side accentuated the beauty and the slight shimmering haze from the artificial sun above them gave it a dream-like feel.

"I hope I never have to leave here," said Fintan. "I'd love to spend the rest of my life in this place."

"Really?" said Nizhoni. "It's impressive and all, but, I look at it as a stepping stone towards finding my real place in the universe."

"And where might that be?" said Fintan, half in jest.

"Someday I'll learn," she said very seriously. "And then I'll know. Until then, I have no idea."

*

They reached the building. It was big and thick and looked like it could withstand several nuclear explosions. Low down, near the ground at one side was a door. It was locked, but there was a combination lock beside it.

Nizhoni typed something into the lock and the door yawned open. She smiled and walked through it, with Fintan following. Beyond it was a narrow corridor with an elevator that they entered. There were no buttons in the elevator, but as it started moving, Fintan felt his stomach fall towards his knees, and realized they were going up.

It didn't take long before the doors opened, and they exited. Beyond lay another short corridor and they took it. Fintan glanced behind to see windows flanking the elevator. Through them he could see the city, but could also see the top of the rim wall. They were at the same level as the top of the wall, but moving away from the city into the bedrock beyond the dome.

At the end of the corridor was a hatch which Nizhoni pushed open and they both stepped through. They were in a large cavern with rough walls and ceiling illuminated by floodlights at the sides.

Its purpose was unknown, but it had been hastily converted into a hangar. A few saucers were parked at one side, as well as a larger yellow ship that Fintan didn't recognize.

In front of them stood a huge man, with folded arms the size of clubs. His etched face bore an expression of shock and surprise, mixed with hostility. He towered over Fintan and Nizhoni and looked like he could tear them apart with just one of his hands.

Fintan gulped as the man stared at him. His gaze turned to Nizhoni and softened a little.

"Hello Nizhoni," he said in a soft, but strong voice.

"Hello Standing Bear," said Nizhoni. "It's good to see you again."

*

Standing Bear's gaze returned to hostility as he looked at Fintan

"Who is this?" he said.

"His name is Fintan," said Nizhoni. "He's my friend."

"Your *friend*? Do you know what I'm risking by being here?"

"Yes," said Nizhoni. "And he can be trusted."

Standing Bear grunted and walked towards Fintan, his glare never breaking from Fintan who felt like he was being studied like a bug.

"How do you know?" said Standing Bear.

"He has saved me more than once. He has my trust, that's all you need to know."

"Is it?" said Standing Bear. "What if you are deceived?"

"It was him in the Starball game," said Nizhoni.

"The one that stopped the other team from ramming you?"

"Yes. He took the hit for me. And that wasn't the only time. He's proved himself time and time again. He is a friend, and he can be trusted."

"We agreed Diné only," said Standing Bear, looking a little annoyed, but rubbing his stubbled chin in thought.

"Then we'll just have to make him one of us, won't we?" said Nizhoni, smiling.

Her smile was disarming, and the big man's face broke into a smile too.

"Well you can tell your father, because I certainly am not!" he laughed and opened his arms. She rushed to him and he gave her a bear hug, which looked like it might crush her, but must have been gentle enough not to even hurt her. She was beaming as he let her down.

"And you, my young white boy," he said, looking to Fintan. "I guess you are coming with us to the reservation, so I say welcome to the rez."

He clapped Fintan on the shoulder with a blow that felt like it would dislocate his arm.

"And I think my name of 'Standing bear' probably sounds silly to you, so you can call me what the other *Bilagaana* all call me."

"And what's that?" asked Fintan.

"Bob."

*

It turned out that Bob worked in the records department and was able to falsify the records so that it looked like Fintan had left and had travelled to Ireland for the holidays. Similarly, he was able to make it look like Nizhoni had flown to Las Vegas and from there on to Albuquerque where her parents would meet her.

"Bob's a very useful man," said Nizhoni. "He helps us to come and go as we please. That's why secrecy is very important. You might be the first non-Navajo that knows about him and what he can do. So please, forgive his hostility, he's risking a lot to help us."

"Not the first," said Bob, "and the others have all been good investments. I hope you will be too."

He didn't explain further, instead leading them to some of the saucers that were parked at the side of the makeshift hangar.

"Nobody knows about these," said Bob. "We've cobbled them together out of spare parts and broken, crashed saucers, so they may not handle quite as smoothly as the training ships you're used to flying."

As Bob and Nizhoni entered their craft, Fintan climbed into his. Bob was right – it clearly wasn't in prime condition, but compared to the one that he and Ayako had gotten flying, it was in pretty good shape.

Under Bob's lead they took off and flew towards the back of the cavern. It was dark, but when Bob turned on his search beams he illuminated a long, dark, tunnel.

"What is this place?" asked Fintan.

Bob's head appeared on Fintan's heads up display. "Best we know," said Bob "Is that it was used when they were building the city. We figure that there had to be a staging area somewhere to remove debris and dirt, and this must be it."

It made sense when Fintan thought about it.

"I figured the city was built in a natural cavern, or something," said Fintan.

"It's possible," said Bob, "but I think we'll never know."

Something about Bob's voice made Fintan a little uneasy. "Just how old is the city?" asked Fintan.

"Nobody knows," said Bob. "Or if they do, they're not telling."

"How long have you lived here, Bob?"

"Over twenty years."

The tunnel they were flying down was darker than Fintan could have possibly imagined. Their lights were swallowed by the darkness and shadows danced at every turn.

"A little further," said Bob, "and then we'll have to go up a vertical shaft."

"Good," said Fintan. "This place is pretty scary."

The tunnel narrowed, and Bob led the way into a vertical shaft. Looking up, Fintan could see stars far above.

"Turn off your searchlights" said Bob. "We don't want to be seen from the surface. On most maps this is listed as an unused mine shaft. But there are always UFO spotters who'd be very excited to see saucers emerging from it."

"But nobody believes most people when they say they saw a UFO," said Fintan.

"Nobody in the outside world," said Bob "but if the folks inside heard about UFOs being spotted exiting a mine shaft near the city, then our cover might be blown."

"Got it," said Fintan. "Thanks."

Slowly they moved up the shaft. It was narrow, so they had to be careful. Finally they made it to the top, and Bob led them up to a high altitude. "It's not as pretty," he said "but we can travel much faster at this height. There are flight lanes in and out of Las Vegas airport that we'll be crossing, not to mention there are air force bases and bombing ranges around here, so we need to make sure we're not spotted."

Nizhoni nodded and Fintan agreed as Bob led them towards the south-east. While it had been mid-morning inside the city, here it was the small hours, not long before dawn. "We should make it to the borders of the reservation quickly," said Bob "and once we're there, we can fly more easily without worrying about being spotted."

"Why's that?" asked Fintan

"Because it's mostly deserted," came the reply.

It was black dark outside, but Fintan could turn on image enhancement equipment so that he could see the landscape they were flying over. Dark, rocky, mountains gave way to long stretches of desert scrub, occasionally punctuated by a highway or a small town.

They crossed the I-15 over the Moapa River Reservation, and ahead Fintan could see a small town at the edge of a lake. "That's Overton," said Bob. "Nice place". They avoided the town and turned more eastward, crossing the Virgin Mountains. This took them across the border into Arizona, and Fintan noticed the land rising to meet them.

"This is Grand Canyon country," said Bob. "We're climbing as there are many plateaus here. You'll also notice that the ground is getting wetter."

Fintan nodded. Beneath him the rocky desert was giving way to patches of green. Ahead he could see trees getting gradually thicker.

They dropped their altitude as dawn approached, and flew low and fast along the treetops. To the South, the landscape was spectacular. "That's the Grand Canyon itself," said Bob.

"Bob," said Nizhoni. "I remember when I was younger, you'd come to visit my family every Christmas."

"Yeah," he said. "I'd take a break from the city, and enjoy your good company."

"I remember that you'd sing to us," said Nizhoni

Fintan smiled. He couldn't imagine the big guy singing. But then Bob started to sing, and his voice was shrill and beautiful.

Silent night

They flow south, and entered the Grand Canyon.

Holy night

The canyon was a mile deep, and Fintan felt awe at its scale. It made him realize just how big and beautiful the world he lived in was.

All is calm. All is bright.

Outside all was silent and calm, just like Bob was singing. This terrain had been here, unchanged, untouched for millions of years.

Round yon virgin, mother and child.

It really was *Mother* Earth thought Fintan. And he had seen so little of it. His chest felt ready to burst with happiness, only a few months ago he figured that the rest of his life would follow in his father's footsteps, with the next drink being his only ambition.

Holy infant, so tender and mild

He thought of Nizhoni, and could see her face on his display. She was reliving some of her happiest memories, and Bob had been a part of them. Fintan longed to be a part of them himself, to have that kind of connection. Who knows? Maybe in the future she would look back on her time with him with the same fondness. Maybe they would share those memories together.

Sleep in heavenly peace.

Fintan was in a bigger world now. He was part of something wonderful. And he would use his gifts and his knowledge for the betterment of all. Ireland was such a place of conflict for such a long time. And peace was something often spoken about, but rarely experienced.

Sleep in heavenly peace.

*

They left the Canyon and changed their heading to almost directly eastward. "You're now in Navajo country, Fintan," said Bob. "Welcome."

They were flying really low now, maybe only a hundred feet above the ground. "Don't have to worry about bumping into skyscrapers here," said Bob, with a little chuckle. Despite that, on the horizon, Fintan could see Mesas like the buildings of a vast and spread-out city.

They crossed over a narrow roadway and gradually turned towards the north east. Fintan could see another highway to his left. Bob was leading them parallel to it. The sun was peeking over the eastern horizon ahead of them, and bathing the scene in a warm, reddish light.

They crossed over several Mesas that jutted out of the landscape. The colors were simply beautiful, with many deep shades of yellow, brown and red.

"I always thought the desert was just plain sand," said Fintan. "I never thought it could be this beautiful."

"Ok," said Bob, directing at Nizhoni. "You can keep him."

"Just a little further," said Nizhoni. "We're almost at the border with New Mexico."

"We'll be landing in a hiding spot of mine near Teac Nos Pos," said Bob. "I'll pick up my truck and we'll drive the rest of the way."

"It's not far to my home," said Nizhoni, excitement building musically in her voice. "Only about 30 miles."

*

They landed on a shelf of a rocky mesa, overlooking a road that bent round sharply to the north towards the town that Bob had mentioned. From this position, they could only be spotted by someone who happened to be driving along that patch of road as they landed.

"We don't get much traffic here," said Bob "so it's easy to hide."

After covering the ships with sand-colored tarps, they climbed off the shelf, and stepped down through sandy rocks to level ground.

"Wait here," said Bob. "I'll be back soon."

Nizhoni was breathing heavily and holding her abdomen now. It seemed that she was waiting for Bob to leave before doing so.

"What is it?" said Fintan. "And why are you hiding it from Bob?"

She looked at him with a gaze that said 'Can't you guess?' before giving up and just saying "Girl stuff."

It took a moment before Fintan realized what she meant.

"Oh," he said, embarrassed. "Sorry"

"It's ok," she said. "No, it's not ok. This hurts."

Fintan shrugged. "Sorry," he repeated.

"Is that all you can say?" snapped Nizhoni. "Better to just say nothing, ok?"

Fintan nodded. "Ok." He started to apologize for it again, but stopped and said nothing.

"Hey," said Fintan, "I know a joke about this; maybe it will cheer you up?"

"It better be good," said Nizhoni.

"What's the difference between a girl with, you know, what you have, and a hungry attack dog?" said Fintan.

She shrugged.

"Lipstick," said Fintan, laughing.

Nizhoni punched him, hard, on the arm.

"Ow," said Fintan. "That hurts"

"Good."

"Maybe it's not a joke at all. Maybe it's the truth."

She hit him again. Not so hard this time. She smiled a little.

"Good thing I didn't tell you the other joke about why girls get that," said Fintan. "Because they deserve it!"

At that moment Bob rounded the corner as Nizhoni grabbed a branch and swung it at Fintan's head.

He leaned out the window of his truck. "Am I interrupting something?"

*

The ride was bumpy and dusty, but filled with cheer. "We're heading to a town called Shiprock," said Bob. "Nizhoni's family lives just outside it."

"What's it like?" asked Fintan.

"Depends on what you're looking for," said Bob. "If you are into bright lights and pretty buildings, you'll have to look somewhere else. But, if you're looking for a place where people build a community and really look out for each other, it's hard to find a more beautiful place on Earth."

To the south a tall, dim tower stood on the horizon.

"That's the Shiprock itself, but it's an ugly name given to it by the Spanish. We prefer to call it *Tse Bit'a'i*." said Bob.

"We've realized that we want to use our own names for things now," said Nizhoni. "It's important for us to keep our own culture."

Fintan nodded. "I can appreciate that" he said. "In Ireland, except for some small areas, we've pretty much become that same as the English. It's a shame."

"You're Irish?" said Bob. "I didn't know that. I knew an Irish man once. Good man."

He turned to Nizhoni. "He had a clan too, can you believe that?"

"So, Fintan," said Bob. "Do you have a clan?"

"Funny you should ask that," said Fintan. "My mother's maiden name is O'Carroll, and she's big into the family clan. They meet once a year to trace ancestry and all that. They claim to be from the Laigin clan."

Bob was silent for a while.

"I guess that means you aren't a *Bilagaana* after all," he said.

"I've heard that word a couple of times now," said Fintan. "What does it mean?"

"Literally," said Nizhoni. "It means someone without a clan. It's usually derogatory."

"Oh thanks," said Fintan.

"Sorry," said Bob "but we're used to calling white people by that term. Maybe when you know us better you'll understand. No offense intended."

"I think I understand a little," said Fintan. "There's a derogatory word in my language too. We can sometimes call someone a *Sasanach*."

"What does that mean?" asked Nizhoni.

"It's pretty bad," said Fintan. "And you're a girl and all that. Don't want to hurt your delicate ears."

She punched him again, and Fintan could see Bob smiling in the rear view mirror.

"So?" said Bob. "What's a *Sasanach*? I like the sound of it, and know some people who are not very nice that it might suit."

Fintan smiled. "It means English man."

Bob laughed, long and hard.

*

They finally arrived at Nizhoni's house. Bob pulled the truck up the dirt drive, and Fintan saw an old and run-down one-story house.

Nizhoni read Fintan's expression.

"It's not much to look at," she said. "But it's full of love."

"And that's what truly matters," said Fintan.

Bob stopped the truck and wrestled the door open. He stepped around the side to let Nizhoni out. By then, the front door of the house had opened, and a man came out, followed by a woman and a younger girl.

"Father!" cried Nizhoni and ran to embrace him. He held her for a long time, closly. "Mother!" said Nizhoni as she hugged her mother too.

"Nanabah!" cried Nizhoni, hugging the younger girl. She looked just like Nizhoni, except smaller.

Fintan got out, and walked around the car to stand beside Bob, as a respectable distance to allow the family to enjoy their reunion.

Nizhoni's father was the first to spot him. Like Nizhoni his hair and eyes were dark, and he looked almost Asian. His long hair had steely grey in it, his eyes were wrinkled, and his skin looked tough and weathered.

"Who is that?" he said in a gravelly voice.

"Nizhoni's boyfriend," said Bob, smirking. "Reilly, Fintan of the Laigin clan."

"What?" said Nizhoni's father. "I send my little girl to school and she comes home with a *boyfriend*. Hold him while I go get my gun."

Bob's powerful arms wrapped themselves around Fintan while Nizhoni's father went into the house. He came back out holding something covered with a cloth.

"Dad!" said Nizhoni. "Stop!"

Fintan wanted to run, but he had nowhere to go. Bob's grip held him like a rock.

Her father approached him. "You know what I like to do to outsiders," he said to Bob. "Particularly white men who come here with my daughter."

Fintan had visions of being scalped by the red-skinned warriors of old cowboy movies.

The man looked Fintan in the eye and removed the cloth.

"I like to welcome them to my humble home," he said, and handed Fintan a cold drink. Nizhoni rolled her eyes.

"You must be thirsty from a long journey," he said with a slight smile.

A light lunch welcomed them inside Nizhoni's house. Like the house itself, it was modest, and everything was homemade, from the taco-like fry bread, to stews made of dried corn and chili.

"Sorry," said Nizhoni. "I forgot to tell you that my father is a bit of a joker."

Her father laughed and clapped Fintan on the shoulder. "For a white boy, you are already pale," he said through a mouth full of food. "But you got even paler. I figured you were ready to chew Standing Bear's arm off to get away!"

"And Dad," said Nizhoni. "He's not my boyfriend, ok!"

The only answer from her father was a laugh.

"Sir," said Fintan. "She's right, and I'm sorry to impose. Nizhoni and I have become good friends, and I wasn't going back home for Christmas, so she asked me to come here instead of being alone."

Nizhoni's father looked at her. She met his gaze, unblinking. "So you do remember what I taught you?" he said. "Good."

He turned back to Fintan. "Sir, eh? I like the sound of that. Reilly, Fintan of the Laigin clan, while in this house you are a friend of my family and you may call me *Sir*."

Nizhoni and her sister rolled their eyes and looked down into their food. Nizhoni's mother discretely went to the kitchen to get some more food. Bob kept eating, seemingly oblivious.

She returned with some more fried bread and chilli. She offered some to Fintan and smiled, genuinely happy when he took some. "You can call me Mrs Benally," she said. "And my husband Mister Benally. Don't worry about what he says."

Nizhoni raised her eyebrows at her father to say 'now we know who the boss is'. Bob kept eating.

"It's nearly Christmas," she said "and while we don't really celebrate it, we do like to buy little gifts for each other. We were waiting for Nizhoni to come back, so would you mind if we went down to the trading post later?"

"I'd love to!" said Fintan. "And I almost forgot!"

He left the table and reached into his bag. "There's something small I brought from Ireland that I'd love to share with you, as a thank you for opening your house to me."

Fintan took out the box. "I'm sorry," he said. "It's only small."

Nizhoni's mother took it gratefully and unwrapped it.

"Chocolate!" cried Nanabah. It was the first thing Fintan had heard her say.

"Chocolate?" said Nizhoni. She looked at the package in her mother's hands. "Chocolate!" she repeated.

Mr Benally smiled. "I live in a house full of girls."

"Oh," said Nizhoni. "I've been so excited I almost forgot!". She took her mother into the kitchen to tell her something. Nanabah followed. Inside there was some whooping and cheering.

"Ah," Mister Benally said to Bob. "I guess that means it is time for her *Kinaalda*."

*

Bob left them after lunch and they drove a rickety station wagon to the local trading post. Fintan was doing his best to unlearn everything about his old life as he tried to look at life through their eyes. His mother had always taught him that they were better than most of the people around them, and that his family was the one that most others looked up to. She'd be upset by him associating with such obviously poor people, but Fintan realized that he'd grown up quickly in the last few months. Now he was looking at them with different values, and he was impressed.

Nanabah didn't say much with her mouth, but her eyes danced as she and Nizhoni glanced around the jewelry in the trading store. Occasionally they'd glance over at Mrs Benally who was looking at dresses with the store clerk.

Fintan looked in his wallet. He had some money from the school stipend, and other than the Christmas party, he hadn't spent a lot. He was more worried about what he could pick up for them than by how much it would cost.

For Mister Benally, Fintan figured that a leather wallet would suit. Nizhoni's mother would get a small glass charm that would look pretty in the house. Nanabah would get a simple blue bracelet that looked like it would suit her. For Bob he found a nice pen, and he still had plenty of money left over.

And then he blanked out a little. His heart fluttered and he laughed at himself. He blushed a little, even though nobody was looking.

Nizhoni and her sister had moved on to looking at shoes, so he creeped into the jewelry section. And then he saw it, a simple chain with a carved eagle's feather. It was stained in the four colors of the Navajo that were so precious to her. It was perfect.

Discretely he paid for it, and tucked it into his pocket.

*

"The Kinaalda," said Mister Benally "is a pretty sacred ceremony to the Diné. We celebrate it when the girl comes of age. It's special." He paused a little, smiling. "My little girl is going to become a woman."

The ceremony started after they returned from the trading post. Nizhoni and her mother withdrew to the family hogan, which was in the yard behind the house. When they emerged, Nizhoni looked radiant. She was wearing a traditional, woven dress in the four colors of turquoise, white, yellow and black. It was wrapped around her waist with a thick black woven belt. Her hair was tied up in a bun, and around her neck was an array of necklaces of silver and turquoise.

Other family members, various aunts, uncles and cousins as well as family members started to show up. They all went into the hogan, but Fintan stayed outside, part shy, part unsure if he would be welcome or not.

A few moments later Nanabah's chubby face peeked out of the flap covering the entrance into the hogan. "Come on in," she said. "We don't smell."

She smiled that same smile that Nizhoni had when she was playing with him.

He gently moved the flap aside and entered the hogan. It was pretty big, holding maybe twenty people with room to spare. Inside it reminded him a little of a miniature circus top, having eight walls and a high, angular roof. It was lit and heated by a fire in the center. A hole in the roof above served as a chimney.

Nizhoni was sitting on a mat near the center, and an old man was chanting over her. Her mother was waiting eagerly beside her. Bob was a little to Fintan's left, and he gestured to Fintan to come and sit with him. Fintan joined him, sitting cross legged, and watching the ceremony.

"Nizhoni's grandfather is a medicine man," said Bob. "It's a great honor for her to have him perform her Kinaalda."

The old man stepped away from Nizhoni and muttered something to her mother. Smiling, Mrs Benally kneeled in front of her and started massaging her shoulders and head. She started softly and then got steadily harder with her massaging.

"She's molding her," said Bob. "It is what will shape her into a beautiful and strong woman."

Soon it was Nizhoni's turn. She left the hogan and stood outside while everyone lined up to be molded by her. Fintan wasn't sure whether he should join or not, but Bob urged him on, pushing him into the line near the back. He felt a little awkward as the other family members looked at him and smiled at his uneasiness.

He watched as Nizhoni spent a lot of time with each person, rubbing her hands over their shoulders, their head, their face. It was beautiful to see her interact with them. Some of them spoke the Navajo language to her, and she answered in kind.

"They are pointing out their ailments," said Bob. "And she's paying special attention to them so that the blessings that she has received are shared and they may be healed."

Finally it was Fintan's turn. He blushed. A few of the family members laughed good-heartedly.

"I don't know what to say," he whispered.

"You don't have to say anything," Nizhoni answered. "I know your heart. I have seen your dreams." Her hands were on his arms pressing him hard. She moved up his shoulders to his neck and squeezed so hard that he gasped.

"You have the seeds of greatness within you," she said. "You will grow to be a wonderful man. I am blessed to share even a little time with you."

Tears were welling in Fintan's eyes now. It was hard to see her.

Her hands were on his head now, moving over his head, through his hair, pressing hard.

"Don't ever surrender your dreams, Fintan," she said. "They are what make you special."

*

After Nizhoni's blessing, Fintan was stunned --her words and touch were so powerful. He needed a moment to catch his breath and clear the tears from his eyes.

"There aren't many people that my daughter would speak to like that," said Mister Benally. "You both may be young, but I believe that you are wise beyond your years."

"There is a bond between them," said Bob. "Something more than just friends or boy and girl. Something special."

Fintan looked at both men. The tears returned to his eyes once more, this time running down his cheeks.

Mister Benally crouched down beside him, looking him in the eye. "Whatever the pain," he said. "You are part of our family now. You no longer have to be alone in your pain."

Fintan nodded.

"Clear your tears my friend," said Bob. "It's almost time to run."

At that moment there was a scream, a blood curdling cry, and Nizhoni began running away from the hogan, eastwards. Everyone cried and ran with her, both young and old, but all followed her, none overtaking.

Bob grabbed Fintan's arm and pulled him along. Fintan, at first half running, and half being dragged by the giant man, shook himself free and followed her. It felt good to run.

*

Having finished the run, Mister Benally went into his house and returned with several shovels. He handed one to Bob, and another to Fintan.

"Now," he said. "We dig."

They spend some time digging in the hard ground. It might be desert, but it got cold in the winter and the ground was icy. Bob carved out a perimeter using the length of a shovel, and instructed Fintan to dig about as deep as his elbow.

It was hard work, but it gave them a chance to talk as they dug. Nizhoni's relatives looked approvingly as the sweat stains on Fintan's shirt as he worked.

"They like you," said Bob.

Then, out of the blue, Mister Benally said. "Did you know that my daughter was once abducted by aliens?"

*

Fintan was stunned. He knew from Nizhoni that the Navajo knew about the city, and figured that they knew about the aliens there, but, from the tone in Mister Benally's voice it seemed that he didn't know anything about them. He looked to Bob, but couldn't read the older man's gaze.

"I can tell from the expression on your face," said Mister Benally "that you know something about it."

"And so do you," he said to Bob.

Bob said nothing. Mister Benally looked back to Fintan.

"I long suspected that your school is somehow connected with this. Why else would they take so many Navajo into it? "

He looked long and hard into Fintan's eyes. Fintan didn't know what to say.

"I'll take your silence as guilt," he said evenly.

"No," said Bob, putting his hand on his friends shoulder. "He didn't know."

Mister Benally looked back to Bob.

"I'm sorry," said Bob "that I didn't tell you sooner."

"No," said Mister Benally. "It's ok. We Navajo are trustworthy, right, so we can't tell everybody everything. We have to compartmentalize, so the secret doesn't get out."

His words were neutral, but his tone was bitter.

"I will tell you everything when I can," said Bob. "But rest assured, your daughter is in no danger."

"She is close to those things that took her before, how can you say that?" said Mister Benally.

"I don't believe that they are the ones that took her," said Bob

"Oh, so there's two breeds of alien?" said Mister Benally.

"I don't know," said Bob. "But I do know my brother is not there, and he was the one that was taken and not returned."

The big man's voice was starting to break.

Mister Benally looked down and continued digging. He looked up again.

"I am sorry," he said "seeing my daughter like this brings back those memories. I am sorry I got angry at you." He looked to Fintan. "Both of you."

They finished digging in silence.

*

When the hole was complete, they filled it with wood and set fire to it. "To bake the edges of the hole" said Bob. "Nizhoni is making a cake that we will bake here. If we seal the hole with fire first, it will not collapse nor leak sand into the batter."

Mister Benally returned to the house, and Fintan sat with Bob as they stoked the fire.

"Six years ago," said Bob. "My brother. My twin brother went missing. At the same time some children vanished too, including Nizhoni."

He paused before continuing. "Three days later, the children were found, wandering in the desert, distressed and crying. They had no memory of who there were and where they had been. My brother was never heard of again. There were stories that he did it, that he took them, and then suddenly got guilty and left them, while he ran and hid. It brought shame on my family."

He breathed deep. "My brother would never do anything like that."

Mister Benally had joined them, they didn't hear him walking up with the crackling of the fire. He was carrying a ragged notepad.

"In the days after that," he said "the children started getting their memory back, with Nizhoni more slowly than the others."

He placed his hand on Bob's shoulder and sat beside him. There was a clear and close bond between the two men, one that would not be broken by a secret or a disagreement.

"Nizhoni would dream at night," said Mister Benally. "Crazy dreams, nightmares that would make her scream. Over and over again she said that the 'insect people' had come for her."

"The insect people are from our ancient beliefs," said Bob. "It is said that they came from other worlds to this one. On each of the other worlds they did something wrong or evil and were kicked out. They settled on this world, and blended into the human race. They are our ancestors."

*

"She would wake up in a cold sweat," said Mister Benally "terrified from what she had seen. I would stand by her at night to be there when she woke. I listened to her talking in her dreams."

He lifted the notepad and flipped through it. He had a lot of notes. He showed Fintan one of the pages, something was circled on it several times.

"It's written in Navajo," said Fintan. "I can't read it."

"Then I'll read it for you," he said. "It appeared to be a name, but not one that I had ever heard before." He ran his finger under the characters as he read them out. "It says 'Fintan'"

Chapter 24: Christmas

The Kinaalda was due to go on for four days, ending on Christmas morning. Each morning and afternoon, Nizhoni would take a run to the east, each one longer and faster than before. On the afternoon of the third day, Christmas Eve, the women emerged from the hogan, carrying buckets of batter and circular sheets sown from corn husks.

The women lined the hole with one of the corn husks and Nizhoni proceeded to pour the batter into the hole. When she was done, a basket with corn flour was passed around, and each person sprinkled some on the cake, while muttering a blessing.

Nizhoni offered some to Fintan and he took it and murmured 'I wish you the best, you deserve it' as he sprinkled it onto the cake. When all was done, Nizhoni uttered her blessing and they placed another corn husk sheet on top of the cake.

Night was falling, so the men quickly laid wood over the cake and lit it. "The heat will bake the cake," said Mister Benally. "Someone must watch over it to make sure that it doesn't burn too hot, or it doesn't go out while we pray."

It was an all-night prayer, so Fintan took responsibility for the fire. They handed him a shovel and entered the hogan.

*

All night, Fintan could hear the prayers coming out the door of the hogan. Occasionally the fire would begin to die, so he piled more wood on it. If it looked to be too hot, he would spread the wood around with his shovel.

He thought he might have trouble staying awake, but that didn't turn out to be the case. There was so much to think about. There were so many unanswered questions.

Nizhoni had been abducted by aliens, or so Mister Benally thought.

When she returned she had had nightmares about the 'insect people'.

When Trichallik had visited him in hospital, Fintan had had a panic attack. Her eyes were like those of an insect.

In her dreams she called out his name. His name wasn't common, even in Ireland.

When he first met Nizhoni, he knew that she was Navajo, but how?

He came to realize that she knew that she had said his name in her dreams all those years ago. That would explain her interest in his dreams. That would explain her interest in *him*. But it was more than curiosity. There was a genuine affection in everything that she did. How could he forget her Kinaalda blessing for him?

Beyond all that, how did this fit in with the school? Why were they really hiding under the Nevada desert in Area 51? What was the point? He heard the story about not wanting to cause mass panic due to the presence of the aliens, but, was that the truth? Or was something else going on? How was it connected? Or was it connected at all?

"Lost in thought young Reilly?"

Fintan looked up to see Nizhoni's grandfather, the medicine man. "I thought you were praying," he said.

The old man smiled and chuckled a little. "Need to pee," he said and went into the house.

*

As dawn approached, Fintan was beginning to feel a bit sleepy, but he had come this far, he wasn't going to pass out now. Of course, the closer it came, the further away it seemed, and the harder it was to stay awake.

So it was a blessed relief as other relatives started to filter in for the last morning of Nizhoni's Kinaalda.

Fintan was so tired he could barely lift the shovel. An uncle took it off him with a kind smile and started moving around the near extinguished logs.

Mercifully the sun made an appearance over the horizon. The flap opened on the hogan, and Nizhoni emerged running. She passed Fintan with a smile and a 'Hi' and Fintan suddenly woke up. He lept up and ran after her along with the rest of her family.

After the run, it was time to go back into the hogan to eat the cake. Fintan sat with Nizhoni's family who she served last. They each took a bite from the cake, and it was delicious.

"I'm not a child anymore," said Nizhoni. "Now I'm a woman."

She smiled and touched Fintan lightly on the arm before going to talk with the rest of her relatives.

I'm family now thought Fintan. *These people have made me one of them.*

*

They slept in for the rest of the morning, and Nanabah, who never seemed to sleep woke Fintan in the afternoon.

"We're opening presents," she said excitedly. "Come!"

Fintan felt cheap thinking about the Christmas that he had always celebrated. He felt disappointed in himself when thinking of Christmas being all about the presents. With *this* family, presents were almost an afterthought. A hearty meal was waiting on the table as he came down, and a sleepy Nizhoni was waiting for him.

There was no Christmas tree, but in the center of the room on a small plastic table, a nativity scene had been set. To Fintan's surprise Mister Benally told the Christmas story, with sincerity and more feeling and heart than he had ever heard it told.

"We're not Christian," said Nizhoni's mother. "But we understand a story of sacrifice for the greater good, and the hope that it brings. So we like this story."

When he had finished the story, it was time for presents. Again, Fintan felt ashamed at his previous Christmases where the focus was on tearing presents open and screaming at whatever toy was within.

Nizhoni's family took it slowly, enjoying the moment. First they gave a gift to Nanabah who opened it and hugged her parents when she saw a new pair of shoes. "Now my feet won't be cold in the winter when I walk to school," Fintan heard her say.

Nizhoni received a new blouse. She held it up against herself modeling it. "Red is your color," said Mister Benally. "Watch out for the boys in your school when you wear it!" He winked at Fintan, and now it was Nizhoni's turn to blush as bright as the red in her blouse.

They then handed a package to Fintan. "You don't have to," he protested.

"But we do," they said. Fintan opened it. It was a silver bracelet, with a turquoise stone in its center. "This is too much," he said. A pang of guilt hit him. This was a much bigger present than what they had bought for their own children. Again he was humbled by the Navajo way.

It was his turn now. He handed the package containing the wallet to Mister Benally who took it and unwrapped it with glee. "Wow!" he said. "It's amazing. Thank you!"

Fintan noticed him take his old wallet, which was beaten and torn, and take the very little he had in it to put into the new wallet. Most treasured were pictures of Nizhoni, Nanabah and Mrs Benally. He passed it around the family, and all admired it. Fintan felt embarrassed that he had bought such a small and cheap gift.

Next he gave the glass charm to Mrs Benally. She unwrapped it, and ran to a window in the far corner of the room. She lifted the dusty shade, and he saw how the sunlight came through the window, throwing a spectrum of light through the charm.

Nanabah cheered and clapped. Mrs Benally hugged Fintan and kissed him on the head. He blushed again.

"You white guys blush a lot, don't you?" said Nizhoni.

Nanabah was next, and she gasped in delight at the bracelet. Fintan was right. It did suit her.

Finally it was time for Nizhoni. Fintan's stomach fluttered as she opened it. Her eyes lit up when she saw the necklace, and she smiled broadly. Mrs Benally took it in her hands and examined the handiwork. "Beautiful," she said. "Such nice quality."

She took it and closed the chain behind Nizhoni's head. The feather hung down around her neck, catching the light.

"Thank you Fintan," she said. "I'm never going to take it off."

Without a doubt Fintan thought it was the best Christmas ever.

Chapter 25: Tryouts

Bob was returning to the city a couple of days after Christmas, so Fintan decided to join him. Nizhoni would return early in the new year with the rest of the kids.

Bob arrived after dinner to pick Fintan up. He was surprised how emotional he was at leaving. Nizhoni's father shook his hand and clapped him on the shoulder. Her mother gave him an enormous hug, and even Nanabah embraced him.

Nizhoni hugged him too. Shyly at first, but then more tightly. "I'll see you in January," she said.

They left, and the drive back to where they had hidden the saucers seemed much further than it had when they were arriving. They drove mostly in silence, but not long before arrival, Bob slapped himself on the forehead.

"Oh I forgot!" he said. "Thanks for the wonderful pen. I have something for you too!"

He handled Fintan a ragged bundle. Fintan unwrapped it to see a beat up pair of binoculars.

"Sure, they're old," said Bob. "But, they're really good. I don't think they make 'em like this anymore."

Fintan used them to look through the front of the car. Bob was right. They *were* good.

"Bob," said Fintan. "There's something I've been meaning to ask you."

"Sure," said Bob. "Anything."

"Did you teach Nizhoni how to fight?"

"Yes. And she's a good learner."

"I want to learn how to fight. Can you teach me?"

"Are you sure?" asked Bob, curiously.

"Yes," said Fintan. "Back home I was constantly bullied. If you do anything that makes you stand out, you get picked on. If you're smart, dumb, short, tall, fat, skinny, whatever."

Bob said nothing.

"I got bullied a lot," said Fintan. "A lot."

"And they call us savages," said Bob. "Yes, my friend, of course I will teach you to fight."

*

They flew back to the city under cover of darkness, with Bob towing Nizhoni's ship. Fintan memorized the map so he could figure out where Bob's 'secret' entrance to the city was located. They landed and Fintan took the train back to the school, alone.

It was strange walking back into the dormitory by himself, but it was also good to have the place to himself for a while. He had some thinking to do.

The days passed quicker than Fintan expected. Between working on the unsolved questions that kept peppering him, and his afternoon sessions with Bob that both invigorated and exhausted him, the time flew by.

And then, one evening there was a clattering at the door of his dorm. He had been used to having things quiet when Zack poked his head around the door.

"Yo," said Zack. "Did you miss me?"

*

It was great to get back into the swing of things. That evening Ayako turned up, and then later so did Nizhoni. The first thing Ayako noticed was her new necklace which she greatly admired, embarrassing Nizhoni a little.

Zack, noticing this, decided to admire it loudly too and continue her discomfort. He kept looking sidelong at Fintan as he made a fuss over her necklace, an action which made Fintan uncomfortable too.

"Ok, that's enough!" said Fintan, irritated.

"A-ha!" said Zack. "I knew it, you bought it for her didn't you?" he laughed.

"He did?" asked Ayako

Nizhoni nodded.

The Japanese girl turned to Fintan with a big smile and a thumbs up. Zack started making kissing motions, only to find himself being hit from three sides.

Things were back to normal.

*

The highlight of the first couple of weeks of school for everyone, regardless of their year was the tryout for Starball. In the first game of the season, the team had to make up its shortcomings with a draft, and it could only play the players that it had, with no reserves or backups.

Now, there were a number of spots up for grabs. Simon made it clear that despite their performance in the first game, Nizhoni and Fintan would have to try out if they wanted to get on the team.

"You've got it easy," Fintan told her. "There's no way he's going to turn you down, you can fly rings around most of us."

"You'll be fine too," she told him, but he wasn't sure that he agreed.

"So what do you think he'll be looking for in the tryouts?" asked Zack. "I'd give my back teeth to get on the team. Of course, that's a pretty good deal for me as my back teeth are pretty rotten. Look!"

He opened his mouth and stretched it with his fingers to say 'Aaah' to let them see.

Ayako put some butter in it.

*

The morning of the tryouts came. Each of the prospective team members from Red Squadron lined up at the appointed place, an outdoor hangar close to where Fintan and Ayako had had to repair the ship for their science project. Ayako had decided not to try out, Starball not being her thing. But Fintan, Nizhoni and Zack all showed up.

"Run!" said Simon. "And don't stop until I tell you to."

A few began to protest, Zack included, but Nizhoni shut him up with an elbow to the ribs. Those that complained were kicked out of the team already, without a tryout.

"You can't do that!" said one girl, angered almost to tears.

"I can and I have," said Simon. "Now get out."

So they ran. And ran.

"Good thing we got practice at your Kinaalda," said Fintan to Nizhoni as she ran past him. "Hey, hang on!"

After almost thirty minutes of running, Simon finally stopped them. Most fell to the ground, exhausted and breathing heavily.

"Flying in a Starball match is physically demanding," said Simon. "It's not like playing a video game. If you want to play, you have to be at peak condition. Look at you! Most of you can barely breathe after a simple run. How do you expect to be able to play?"

Faces fell.

"Situps!" said Simon. "Give me fifty!"

This time they all tried without protest. Most of them couldn't handle it.

"Don't worry this time," said Simon. "Obedience is what I was looking for, and you all passed."

He stopped, and then, voice dripping with sarcasm: "For now."

Next he led them into the hangar. A number of saucers were waiting for them. "A few of you," said Simon "have probably never flown a real saucer before. And you think you can fly them in a game? Let's put that little dream back where it belongs, right?"

He divided them into groups of two. "What you'll do is very simple," said Simon. "The two of you will fly against Red Two and Red Three. If you can last more than thirty seconds without getting zapped, you can stay in the trials. If you can't then you don't belong here. Got it? Oh and don't worry, you can't get hurt by the shots, it's just a simple tagging."

The first pair, a couple of third-years that Fintan had seen around the dorms got into their saucers and took off. They hovered over the hangar as Red Two and Red Three took off. As soon as they were in the air Red Two and Three started shooting, and the prospectees were out in less than a second.

"Tsk. Tsk," said Simon. "They had a chance at least to run, but they sat around and made themselves targets. Too dumb for the game."

He stroked a red line through their names on his sheet. "Gone."

Next up were Jo-Jo and Monica, a pair of French Canadian first years. Fintan didn't really know them well, as they mostly kept to themselves. Red Two and Three's saucers were still hovering over the hangar, and it was clear to Fintan that it was likely that they'd start shooting as soon as the first years left the ground.

Fintan noticed them play a game of rock-paper-scissors before getting into their saucers. It was clear that they had a strategy planned out. This would be interesting to see. They started their saucers, but remained motionless on the ground, spinning.

Simon raised an eyebrow. What were they up to?

They kept spinning, but not moving. Red Two and Red Three were getting impatient and began to drop closer to the hangar before pulling away. Then, without warning, Jo-Jo's saucer bolted straight at Red Two in a head-on collision course. Red Two barely dodged, but instead of escaping, Jo-Jo changed course to aim at Red Three. She also dodged, and Jo-Jo attempted to escape. They both attempted to follow before realizing that they'd been had. While distracted, Monica's ship had slipped away and was heading for the far side of the dome and gathering speed. Jo-Jo was dodging like crazy, and it took several well placed shots before the hunters got a hit.

Twenty Five seconds. So close. By now, Monica was at the far side of the city. There was no way that they would be able to catch her. She passed.

The next pair ran for their saucers and tried to escape while Red Two and Three were distracted. It didn't work, and they were tagged before they got to a hundred feet. Two by two everyone else fell, except for a couple of lucky exceptions.

And then it came down to just Zack, Nizhoni and Fintan left. Simon was smiling. He was going to enjoy this.

"I'll go by myself," said Zack. "I can take them on easily."

Simon raised an eyebrow and opened his hands towards the saucer.

"What's he up to?" asked Nizhoni.

"Dunno," said Fintan. "But I know it's going to be good."

Red Two and Three hovered above the hangar waiting for him. Two was close to the front entrance, and Three close to the back, covering his exits.

Zack started his ship spinning on the ground. The spinning got faster and faster.

"He's going too fast," said Nizhoni.

The ship was spinning so fast that it was humming now. The whole hanger seemed to be vibrating. Fintan's ears began to hurt. And then Zack shot straight up, through the roof of the hanger, throwing a huge amount of debris upwards. The shards of wood from the hangar roof exploded into Reds Two and Three, knocking them off course. Red Two crashed into the ground at the front of the hangar, while Red Three got stuck momentarily. In the cloud of dust, Zack was nowhere to be seen.

"No!" said Fintan, looking up at the 'sun'. "That clever git!"

In the glare of the sun he thought he could see a saucer darting around.

But the thirty seconds expired before Red Three could gather himself up and chase Zack.

"He's in," said Simon, smiling.

And now it was Fintan and Nizhoni's turn. Fintan had no idea how they could top what Zack had done, but Nizhoni strolled confidently into her saucer.

Her face came on his heads-up display. She was smiling.

"I have an idea," she said.

As earlier, the two saucers were orbiting the hangar. Now they had three holes to cover, the front and back doors and the huge one Zack had left in the roof.

Nizhoni started her ship spinning. She hadn't said a word, perhaps afraid that Red Two and Red Three had tapped into their communications. Instead of launching she gently angled her ship so that it was hovering about ten feet above the ground, but at a forty five degree angle.

Red Two and Red Three weren't dumb – they realized that she was getting ready to exit the hangar at an angle, so making her harder to hit, so they changed their orbits to get the best possible shot at her as she exited.

Then it Fintan realized what she was planning. He hovered his ship and angled it in an identical way to how Nizhoni had done it. He then moved his ship so that he was at the opposite end of the hangar from her, and started to move upwards towards the hole in the roof.

They moved to intercept him, which meant that they were in range of an edge shot from Nizhoni.

She shot twice, in quick succession. Both were direct hits. Then she made a run for it through the hangar doors as Fintan launched through the roof.

They were long gone before the others could react.

Simon's voice came over their intercom. "Come back," he said. "You passed."

*

That night it was hard to get Zack to do anything but celebrate.

"I'm a Starball player!" he exclaimed. "And I'm only a first year! Woo Hoo!"

"So are Nizhoni and I," said Fintan. "But we're not quite so loud about it."

"Party poopers," said Zack. "This is huge. This is awesome! You hear me man? This is awesome!"

Fintan thought that Zack simply wasn't going to sleep that night. Luckily it was Saturday so they could sleep in.

In the middle of the night, in the middle of a deep dreamless sleep, Fintan began to hear a voice.

Fintan it said *wake up.*

It was quiet, almost whispering. He grunted, turned in the bed. Then he felt small hands on his shoulder, shaking him gently. *Wake up.*

He opened his eyes. Nizhoni was looking down on him out of the darkness.

"Nizhoni?" he whispered. "What are you doing here?"

"Wake up" she said. "And get Zack up too. Hurry!"

Fintan looked at his clock. It was a little after 4AM.

"What's going on?" whispered Fintan.

"I'll explain on the way," she said.

Fintan clambered over to Zack's side of the room and shook him.

"Wake up, Zack!" said Fintan. "Something's going on."

"What?" said Zack. "Go away, I'm sleeping."

"Come on," said Fintan. "It's important!"

"Oh wake up!" said Nizhoni, louder than she intended. Fintan shushed her.

"Nizhoni's here?" said Zack. "Huh?"

"Just get up and follow me you idiots," said Nizhoni. "Quickly!"

Fintan didn't argue and quickly dressed. He grabbed the binoculars that Bob had given him while Zack dressed. They scurried out of the dorms to the common area. Ayako was waiting for them.

"You have to see this," she said.

They left the dorms, but didn't go to the train station. Instead they walked out, past the dome into the fields behind it. A service ladder led up the dome towards its roof. Ayako led them up towards the roof, and pointed at a scene taking place near the center of the city, some quarter of a mile from them.

The roof and observation platform were open and saucers were coming and going. Several larger ships were also landing.

"What's that?" said Fintan. "What's going on?"

"That's the question, isn't it?" said Ayako. "It's been going on for over a half an hour."

Fintan took out his binoculars and focused on the scene. He watched a saucer land and a soldier get out of it. He was wearing reddish camouflage fatigues.

"Looks pretty serious," he said and handed the binoculars to Ayako.

Her eyes squinted as she looked through them. "It's pretty busy," she said. "Whatever it is."

Nizhoni took the binoculars. "I see a transport ship," she said. "It's landing."

She paused for a moment. "Oh my God!" she said.

"What is it?" asked Fintan.

"Take a look."

"I don't need the binoculars to see what's going on," said Zack.

Fintan looked and could see some ambulances lining up near the transport.

"They've been in a war," said Zack. "And they lost."

Chapter 26: Puzzles

They returned to their rooms for a sleepless night. The following morning all were bleary-eyed at breakfast.

"Something is clearly happening," said Zack.

"I wonder where we fit into it," said Fintan. "Or indeed *if* we fit into it"

"Well they are teaching us to fly saucers that are pretty similar to the combat ones," said Nizhoni. "Are we being trained to be soldiers in this war?"

"We don't even know what this war is," said Ayako. "And there's no point talking to the teachers about it. We're on our own."

"Not on our own," said Fintan. "There are other students."

"What are you suggesting?" asked Nizhoni.

"A conspiracy," said Fintan. "A conspiracy of light. Let them assume we don't know anything, but let's reach out to the other students; some of them may have other pieces to the puzzle. Let's all work together. Let's not be ignorant recruits in a war we don't know about."

"Not a bad idea," said Zack. "But who can we trust?"

"Most," said Fintan. "We've got nothing to lose right now. But let's just approach them carefully so we don't look foolish. We can start with Raj and Heather."

"Not just Red Squadron," said Ayako. "We should reach out to the other squadrons too."

"And there's an ideal opportunity," said Zack. "The Starball games."

"I know a Japanese boy in Yellow squadron," said Ayako. "And they are our first game."

"Conspiracy of light," said Zack. "I like the sound of that. Let's do it."

He put his hand out, palm down in front of him. Ayako placed her hand on his, followed by Nizhoni. Then Fintan joined in. "Shine the light!" said Zack.

*

They were supposed to be concentrating on their schoolwork, but as with everyone else, it was hard for them to think about anything other than the upcoming Starball game against Yellow squadron.

As expected, Simon was driving them hard, but his urgency appeared to be surprising even to the older kids who had been on his team for several years. "He's really desperate to win this year," said Melanie, a tall, dark haired New Yorker who was a fifth year, and had been on the team for three years. "He's really driven."

When pressed, nobody wanted to talk about it further than that.

The teachers were still teaching as usual, but it was getting harder to concentrate on lessons. One day, after a particularly boring Cosmic History lesson, Raj just threw his hands up in the air.

"I'm not coming back," he said. "It's boring and pointless!"

Heather tried to calm him down, but he wasn't about to be appeased.

"I gave up my family to come here," said Raj. "And they told us that nobody fails, nobody drops out, so why bother working? What's the point?"

"Good grades now will help us later," said Heather. "They'll help us choose what we specialize in."

"Maybe that was true once upon a time," said Raj "but look at the older kids. What are they doing? Do you see them following different careers? They are all either pilots or kids who want to be pilots. Is that all that is waiting for us in our future? Where are the scientists? Where are the researchers?"

He paused before continuing.

"Heck," he said. "What about diplomats? Politicians? Artists? We're supposed to be training to go to the stars, but what about when we meet someone when we get there? We're training to be combat pilots! Doesn't that tell you something about what they are expecting us to meet out there in space?"

His words rang true in the light of what Fintan had seen a few nights before.

"So to heck with classes," said Raj. "If they want pilots, let's quit the pretense and just be pilots."

"We should talk," said Zack. "But not here."

"Before the Christmas break," said Ayako. "We used to have Friday night study parties. We should continue them."

"Haven't you heard a word I said?" said Raj. "I'm done!"

"*You* aren't listening," said Ayako. "We should continue our Friday night study parties."

Heather understood. "Good idea," she said. "Raj and I will be there."

He looked at her angrily, but she stared back, impassively.

Something passed between them and Raj looked downwards, nodded at Ayako, and he turned and wandered off. Heather followed him a short distance behind.

*

Friday came, the night before the first Starball game. It was easy for the Conspiracy of Light to meet up without being noticed, as parties were breaking out all over the dorms.

Raj entered, looked at Zack and Ayako. "So," he said. "Let's get down to business."

They told him about the 'Conspiracy of Light' and welcomed him and Heather as the newest members. Sitting them down, they took turns explaining everything that they had encountered and everything that they had seen.

Fintan spoke passionately about his dreams. Nizhoni explained about her abduction and Ayako about the activities that they had seen a few nights before.

Heather and Raj looked to each other.

"And I thought it was just us," said Heather. "We didn't want to talk to anybody else about it, but something odd happened to us too."

"And what is that?" said Zack

"I am from Seattle," said Heather. "And Raj is from Mumbai, but we were recruited by the same person. A tall, thin white guy called-"

"Mister Smith," said Fintan and Zack at the same time.

"So you were too." she said.

"Not that unusual, he just gets around," said Zack.

"Maybe," she said. "But, think about the test. That's a lot of equipment for the first part of the tests and a real and space-worthy saucer for the second part. Are you telling me that they have a setup for that in Seattle, another in Mumbai, another in Tokyo, another in Fresno, another in Dublin and another on the Navajo reservation?"

"You're right," said Ayako. "That *doesn't* make sense."

"But that's not all," said Heather. "When we tried to discretely enquire with some of the others about where they came from, and how they were enrolled, their stories were different."

"They were?" said Fintan.

"Yes. They didn't say much, and we weren't able to piece much of a story together, so we kept it to ourselves."

"So Smith is recruiting some, and somebody else is recruiting some. That's not a big deal, right?" said Zack. "I mean they must have a few recruiters?"

"True," said Heather. "And that's what we thought too. But, what was different was that none of the others would even talk about their recruitment. They just completely shut up when we mentioned it. Until now, we thought that we were the only two Smith-recruits."

"I only knew you were recruited with a flight test, when I saw you on the plane," said Ayako to Fintan. "And I just assumed that we were all recruited like that."

"And that's odd too, right?" said Heather. "That Zack from California, you from Japan and Fintan from Ireland just happened to be on the same plane at the same time?"

"So what is your conclusion?" asked Nizhoni.

"I don't have one," said Heather. "But, if you think about the resources that Smith must have to be able to travel the world and cherry pick us, he must be military. Who else would be able to do it?"

"And if he is," said Raj. "Then surely he's recruiting some people to be in the city that are the type that the military want."

"And," Heather continued. "He made an educated guess that we'd find each other."

"So how many more are there?" asked Fintan. "And if we are a group that he's trying to foster, the question is why and for what?"

*

"Military." Zack paused for a moment and slapped his head. "I had forgotten about that!"

"What?" asked Fintan.

"The science project," he said. "The one that Nizhoni and I did last term."

"What about it?"

"At one point we were chased by USAF fighters, and my scanners picked up something buried in the desert not far from here. I can't believe I forgot all about it. "

"Show us," said Ayako.

Zack went to his terminal and downloaded something to a data crystal. He came back and used the projector to project it into the air.

"I wasn't able to do a full analysis," he said. "I'm just not that good with computers."

"But I am," said Raj. "And so is Ayako."

They projected his findings into the air. A three dimensional mound hovered above their table.

Raj and Ayako plugged heir bracelets into the projector. Virtual keyboards were projected on the screen and they went to work.

Zack watched, a little jealously as Raj and Ayako made a perfect team. They were like a well- oiled machine, working smoothly to piece together the data from Zack's scan.

Slowly the picture began to take shape. The mound was hollow, and inside was something big.

"How can you get all this data?" asked Fintan.

"Zack's scanners provided X-Ray, Ultrasound and a lot of other readings," said Raj. "We're piecing them all together to create a visual."

"Trichallik sent us on that errand," said Zack. "Maybe it was more than just a science project."

"We thought that all along," said Nizhoni. "But we couldn't figure out what."

The image was clearer again. Ayako zoomed in, and within the dome was clearly a huge hangar with a massive, triangular shaped object.

"It's still fuzzy," said Fintan.

Zack continued. "What if she did it so that we'd discover this and this is something that the military are working on? They chased us after all. And what if she knew that we were taken in by Smith for whatever nefarious scheme he is working on, and what if she wanted us to see this and put two and two together? We weren't recruited here because we're dumb. What if Trichallik and Smith are rivals, and that either he is trying to undermine what she and her people are doing here, or-"

"Or she is trying to undermine the progress of the human race?" said Nizhoni.

"That's a lot of 'what ifs'," said Fintan.

The image cleared once more. Now they had a beautiful, clear, three dimensional model of the inside of the mound.

It was a hangar and a factory at the same time. Fintan could see the outlines of people working on building something. It was large, and black and triangular. Measurements showed it as being close to one thousand yards long. On its underside bristled weapons and saucers.

"That's a warship," said Zack. "A bloody great big warship."

"It's worse than that," said Ayako. "I'm getting radiological readings."

"Radiowhatchama whatsits?"

"Radiological readings," repeated Ayako. "That thing is equipped with nukes."

Chapter 27: First Game

The morning of the first Starball game of the season had arrived. The whole dome seemed to be in the mood for a party. Colored banners, holographic decorations and loud music seemed to be on every corner in the city.

In the first match of the day, Blue and Green squadrons would match up. Zack wanted to watch the game, so he could get a feel for these teams before they would play, but Simon barred the team from watching. Their focus would have to be on Yellow.

"Yellow are the weakest team," said Simon. "Traditionally, anyway, but they have been known to have some surprises up their sleeve. We must not let our guard down."

Fintan looked around. The full squad of 22 players was assembled, and looked to be an interesting mix of unproven players as well as cynical veterans. There was clearly an air of disappointment amongst the older pilots – they were used to dominating, but now had a lot of new players, so they couldn't be sure if they'd continue to.

Simon named his starting 11, and naturally there were no new pilots amongst them.

"This is a long and hard game," he said. "We can substitute at will, so the rest of you will have to be on a moment's notice to give us relief. Stay sharp."

Fintan was a little upset, Nizhoni didn't seem to care, but Zack was devastated. When Simon had dismissed them, he looked ready to blow.

"Come on!" he whispered angrily. "I'm clearly one of the better flyers. I've worked hard, I'm ready. And he won't let me start!"

"Be patient," said Fintan. "You'll get in, and then you'll just have to be at your best, and you'll earn a spot."

"Are you sure?" said Zack. "You and Nizhoni were brilliant in the last game, and he passed you over, again."

Nizhoni changed the subject. "I wonder if Ayako had any trouble reaching out to the guy from Yellow that she mentioned."

*

They caught the end of the first game, and it was no contest. Blue had dominated Green since the beginning, winning by four goals to zero.

"Pretty impressive," said Zack. "Of course I'm probably not going to get a chance to play them."

"Stop sulking," said Nizhoni. "You'll get on the field today, don't worry!"

Fintan elbowed her and gestured to the far end of the hangar. Ayako was happily approaching a Japanese boy whose uniform showed him to be from Yellow squadron. Smiling she bowed to him and then started talking. His face was impassive. She cocked her head to the side and continued talking. He didn't answer. She reached up her hand to touch his left arm as they spoke. He brushed her off and walked away without another word.

*

Butterflies danced in Fintan's stomach as the kickoff approached. He and the rest of the reserves had a special holding area off to the side of the cube in which the game was played. At ten minutes before kickoff, they had to launch their saucers and hover within it.

Kickoff time was met with fireworks and music. Yellow entered first to a huge cheer from the on-looking Yellow Squadron supporters.

"I wonder what happened with Ayako earlier," said Zack, for about the tenth time. "That guy really disrespected her."

"She's a big girl," said Nizhoni. "She can handle it."

"You don't know what boys can be like," said Zack

"I don't?" said Nizhoni.

"Err. I didn't mean it like that," said Zack.

"Like what?"

"Nothing."

"Really?"

"Err. Yeah."

"Cut the chatter you two," said Melanie. Her face appeared on their screens, looking stern.

"Sorry Red 7," said Zack.

Fintan snickered.

"Something to say Red Sixteen?" asked Melanie. Fintan suddenly realized why people found New York accents to be aggressive.

He gulped. "Err no ma'am. I mean Miss. I mean Mel-"

"Radio silence *now*!" said Simon cutting into their conversation.

It was time for Red Squadron's starting eleven to enter the arena. Inspiring music began to play over the speakers. Red fireworks and smoke started to blow around the dome.

"Ladies and gentlemen," came the booming voice of a P.A. announcer. "Please welcome your reigning Spaceball champions, Red Squadron!"

Simon led the rest of the first eleven into the arena. They entered in a straight line but then broke apart and spread around the arena, making elaborate formations and stunts, before lining up in the center of the field opposite Yellow squadron.

The crowd went crazy.

The referee blew the whistle and it was game on.

Simon instantly caught the ball and drove at the yellow line. He was swarmed by three fighters and quickly passed to Red Two who was also triple teamed. Yellow intercepted the ball and drove on goal, scoring easily.

Only a few seconds had passed, and Yellow squadron were leading 1-0.

The reserves watched in shock as the clock kept ticking and Red simply could not penetrate Yellow's defences. It seemed that every time they got the ball, Yellow ships would swarm the player, and would instinctively know what he was going to do with it.

Half time came, and the team assembled in their hangar for a fifteen minute break.

"What the heck is going on out there?" yelled Simon at the team, breaking their stunned silence.

"We have no room to play," said Melanie. Simon shot her an angry look, and she didn't meet his gaze.

"No room?" said Simon. "They triple team whoever has the ball, so all you have to do is pass it!"

"We are passing," said Red Seven.

"Yes," said Simon. "Straight to them."

"Have you considered making substitutions?" said Zack. "You guys are getting exhausted out there, but we're fresh and ready to go."

"You will speak when spoken to, nugget, and I will not repeat myself. You got that?"

And then it was time for the second half. Simon kept the starting eleven, making no substitutions.

The second half went just like the first had done. Yellow continued to swarm whoever had the ball, and continued to know exactly what Red were going to do.

"If we had a strategy, you'd think they were stealing it," said Zack to Nizhoni and Fintan on a private channel.

Simon continued to push hard, and with deft flying, he and Red Two were running rings around Yellow, but unable to penetrate the goal.

"Come on," said Zack. "Substitute us. Bring in someone fresh and confuse them!"

But the clock ticked down and no substitute was forthcoming.

Whatever ideas Red had had, they were running out, and their reflexes were slowing. Yellow began to press the game again.

"This doesn't look good," said Nizhoni. "I don't think we can equalize at this rate."

And then it happened, Simon again had the ball and drove at the Yellow goal. This time, only one Yellow defender tracked him, but tracked him close. Fintan could see the sparks as their saucers span against each other.

Sensing a chance, Simon pressed forward, pulling Red Two and Seven into formation with him. Then, as he was about to pass, the Yellow defender dropped off him, directly into the passing lane and intercepted the ball.

Six yellow players had broken forward, expecting the move. The defender lobbed the ball forward and they caught it. Outnumbering the defense, they were able to pass the ball around and score easily.

It was 2-0 to Yellow, and there were less than two minutes left on the clock.

"Ok," said Zack. "In the comic books now is when the rookie comes in and pulls out a miraculous victory!"

"I don't think Simon reads comics," said Nizhoni.

She was right. In despair they watched as the clock ticked down to a stunned finale. It seemed to be a futile eternity, but finally the clock reached zero and the game was over.

It would go down as the biggest surprise victory in years. But Yellow had won.

*

Back at the dorms the mood was somber. Red hadn't lost a game in years, and now lost their opening game against the weakest team. Simon hadn't even given them a debrief

As first years, Zack, Fintan and Nizhoni got a lot of dirty looks off the older kids, as if it was somehow their fault.

They sat for dinner at their usual table; Fintan and Nizhoni were disappointed and morose, while Zack brimmed with anger. Several times he made to stand up and approach Simon's table for a confrontation. Several times Nizhoni and Fintan had to cool him down.

"Haven't you noticed that something is wrong?" said Nizhoni.

"What?" said Zack, angrily.

"Where's Ayako?"

Chapter 28: Jousting.

Zack's anger didn't abate for days. He wasn't a lot of fun to live with, and answered most questions with gruff monosyllables. Even Ayako couldn't cheer him up.

Several days after the defeat to Yellow squadron they had a flight class.

"We're going to do something different today," said Iara. "We're going to try a little competition."

There was a nervous, but excited shuffle amongst the students.

"We'll be pairing you up one-on-one to do some jousting," she said. "After that terrible exhibition against Yellow, it's pretty clear that our skills in one-on-one are totally deficient, so today we're going to joust."

"But Ma'am," said Zack. "None of us got to take the field, so how can you say our skills are deficient?"

"Save your petulance for Simon, Zack," she snapped back. "And for that comment, you'll be matched up with me."

There were thirty-one students in the class, so by adding herself to the mix, Iara was able to turn it into a knockout championship. Everyone put their names into a hat, except Zack who would be matched up with her in the first round.

Iara started pulling names out of the hat and writing them on a display.

The first pair of names out of the hat were Raj and Heather's. "Just because she's beautiful and you're in love with her, don't go easy on her, ok?" said Iara to Raj as the whole class laughed.

"You're beautiful and Zack's in love with you, so should he go easy on you?" said someone from the back to Iara. Zack growled, and started to lunge, but Fintan held him back.

Iara just laughed. "Surely, *everyone* is in love with me, but I won't go easy on *them*," she responded.

As she pulled more names out of the hat, Fintan got matched up with Willis, a quiet American boy that he seldom spoke with. Ayako with a French boy called Laurent and Nizhoni with a young Indian girl called Lakini. Fintan didn't really know her much either, other than from her dislike of Heather, presumably because she was jealous of her relationship with Raj.

Iara and Zack went up first, so that she could demonstrate how the jousting would work. As they entered the hangars, Fintan could see how the saucers had been augmented with a shield towards the left and front and a long pole towards the right and front.

"You've probably seen ancient jousting where knights would prove their mettle. They'd charge headlong at each other on horseback, trying to knock the other knight off their horse by hitting their shield with their lance."

She stopped while the class took in the saucers.

"For us it will be a little different," she said. "Once you knock your opponents shield off, or, if you force them out of the arena, you win."

"Everybody to their ships," she said. "And Zack, you're with me." She winked.

They launched, and Iara set up force fields to create a jousting arena. It was long and tubular. She divided the class in two, according to their matchups, and they were to wait at either side of the arena.

She entered at one end, and waited while Zack entered at the other.

She indicated a countdown display that counted from three down to one. "When that hits green," she said, "Charge!"

The others could see the competition on their heads up displays.

Fintan opened windows that showed Zack's and Iara's faces, as well as another that showed a close up from the front camera of their saucer.

Zack was looking uneasy, but Iara was smiling confidently.

As the light turned green, Iara's face changed drastically as she screamed a rousing battle cry and accelerated headlong towards Zack.

Zack, taken aback by her scream started more slowly. He barely dodged her attack in time, bouncing off the wall of the arena as he did so.

"Good!" said Iara. "Now let's see if you can do it again!"

They flew to the end of the arena, turned and charged again. This time Zack was more ready for her and charged forward first, aiming his lance low. Just before they passed each other he turned and twisted, hoping to surprise her, but she was onto him. She lifted and twisted her saucer as she passed him, coming in at an angle at his exposed shield, knocking it cleanly off.

"Hit," she said. "You're out Zack!"

The jousting continued, with Nizhoni and Fintan winning their first round easily. Ayako struggled a little more, taking six passes before she edged past her opponent.

Surprisingly, their second round matchups were pretty easy, with Nizhoni and Fintan knocking their opponents shields off at the first pass. Ayako knocked her opponent out with the second pass to set up a quarter-final against Iara.

Fintan was happy to see that he avoided Nizhoni in the quarter finals, getting what he figured would be an easy matchup against an American girl called Melissa who had struggled through her first two games.

Iara and Ayako were up first, and everyone was expecting an easy and quick victory for the teacher. But Ayako proved to be slippery.

Iara was trying different moves, spinning, lifting, sinking and more. "She's really digging into her bag of tricks, isn't she?" said Zack.

But Ayako seemed to be ready for them all. On the screens Fintan could see her face, impassive and concentrating. Iara was beginning to lose her confident edge, and growing a little more desperate in their moves.

She tried a feint, opening her shield for Ayako to attack.

"It's a trap," said Fintan to himself, wishing Ayako could hear, but, for safety the competitors couldn't hear any incoming comms.

He could see what Iara was up to. If she could draw Ayako into turning enough to aim at her shield, then she could corkscrew her ship and hit Ayako from the side.

"No!" he said as he could see Ayako falling for the trap. Ayako lunged at Iara, and Iara started to corkscrew. But at the last moment, Ayako changed her lunge, flipping her ship through ninety degrees so that her lance pointed straight up, catching Iara's shield and neatly clipping it off.

Zack's face appeared on Fintan's screen. "Whooo!" he said. "Did you see that? That was hot!"

Ayako's expression hadn't even changed.

"Nice move," said Iara, impressed and stunned at the same time.

Nizhoni won her match easily, attacking her opponent so fast that it appeared impossible to control the lance, but she hit the shield dead center, knocking it flying across the arena.

Fintan's match was up third, and he confidently entered the arena. When he got the green light he dipped his nose and angled his ship to protect the shield, with the intent of turning at the last moment and clipping Melissa. She was heading right into his trap. This would be easy. But, at the last moment she turned drastically, catching Fintan's ship with her lance. The momentum flipped Fintan's ship upwards and he lost his orientation for a moment.

In that moment, his shield was exposed and Melissa knocked it off using the edge of her saucer.

The lights came on. Fintan had lost.

"Can she do that?" he asked Iara.

"She can, and she did," said Iara. "Nice job Melissa!"

Heather, who had beaten Raj in the first round, won her match too, leading to an all-girl final four.

Iara pulled their names out of a hat. First out was Melissa.

"Come on, be either Ayako or Nizhoni next!" said Zack, wanting his friends to be kept apart, hoping they'd meet in the final.

Next name out of the hat was Heather, making the other semifinal Ayako versus Nizhoni.

"Dang it!" said Zack.

"At least one of them will be sure of being in the final, right?" said Fintan.

"Yeah. But wouldn't you love to see them go head to head in the final?" said Zack.

The first match was ready to begin. The victory was surprisingly easy for Melissa who seemed to get stronger with each passing game. On the second pass she did a simple feint that caught Heather off guard and knocked her shield off.

Finally it was time for Nizhoni and Ayako to square off. In the end it turned out to be an anticlimax. On the first pass, Nizhoni went in hard and fast, ready for a last second feint, but Ayako was ready. She lifted her ship, turned it, and clipped Nizhoni's shield as she passed. The shield wobbled a little, but as Nizhoni decelerated at the end of the arena, it fell off. Victory to Ayako.

Nizhoni was upset, but took defeat well. "Nicely done," she said to Ayako. She left the arena to watch the final match-up. Before the match, Fintan opened a com channel with her and gave her a thumbs up. "Nice job!" he said to her. Nizhoni smiled back but said nothing.

"Let's wish Ayako some luck," said Zack.

Nizhoni nodded. "I don't think she'll need it!"

It was an intriguing matchup. Melissa had looked useless until she beat Fintan in the quarters and blew past Heather in the semis. Ayako was the clear favorite having taken out both Iara and Nizhoni.

"Don't count Melissa out though," said Zack. "She's better than she looks."

The first few passes were cautious, with neither attacking aggressively and thus risking defeat. After the sixth pass, Iara made a big show of yawning and shrank the dimensions of the arena a little. This spurred Melissa.

At the next pass the American girl screamed a battle cry and charged so fast that Fintan thought she would not be able to stop once she reached the end of the arena. But Ayako wasn't fazed, and in response she decelerated.

"Clever," said Fintan. "She's staying back from Melissa, so that Melissa has to decelerate before they contact, or she'll overshoot and lose."

Ayako's move played off. Melissa was occupied with decelerating, and lost her concentration long enough for Ayako to accelerate, corkscrew and clip Melissa's shield off.

Ayako had won the jousting tournament.

*

They assembled back in the classroom later.

"So," said Iara. "What have we learned from this?"

"Never joust with your teacher?" said Zack.

"Ha," said Iara, not really laughing.

"It's simple," said Iara. She held up her arm and flexed. For a woman as slender as she was, she had an impressive bicep.

She pointed at it. "While sometimes you can win with *this*," she said, and then pointed at her head. "When you use *this* you will always win. It wasn't the strongest, the fastest or the most skillful that won this game. It was the one that used her head better than any of us."

She bowed to Ayako, who bowed back.

"Nice job, Ayako Katsuragi."

She gracefully accepted the praise, but modestly added. "It's just math. I figured out what you were doing and programmed my ship to counter."

Chapter 29: Green Squadron.

Zack was to get his chance at playing in a game sooner than he expected. The game with Green started well: early on, Simon performed a brilliant move to split the green defense, and leave Red Two wide open to score. From then on they were able to try and catch Green squadron as they tried to break. Before half time, Green pushed forward, but Red Two intercepted and pitched a long ball forward to Red Seven (Melanie) who scored easily.

Half time was two-zero. Simon's half time talk was much more cheerful than the last game, but still he kept with his starting eleven, to Zack's disappointment. The second half started hard and fast, with Green being much more aggressive, and going for broke. Red Five lost her concentration, and dropped the ball, and green were able to capitalize by scooping up the loose ball and scoring.

Tension began to set in as Green chased the equalizer. The momentum was turning again, as they seemed to be first to every loose ball, and Red seemed to be getting slower with each play.

"They need a break for heaven's sake," said Zack. "Why won't he trust us?"

Then, as Simon got ready to call a time out, Green were able to break through and score again, tying up the game.

Simon got his timeout and the team had a 'huddle' where comms were open and they could all see each other's faces on their heads-up displays.

"What is going on out there?" yelled Simon. "What's wrong with you guys? You are playing like pansies!"

"They're tired," said Zack.

"What did you say, nugget?"

"I said they're *tired*," said Zack. "You are insisting on playing the same eleven without any substitutions and Green are taking advantage of that. Your team is tired."

"Oh and you think you could do better?" said Simon

Zack didn't respond.

"Yeah, that's what I thought, so shut up, you got that?"

"Sir," said Red Two

"What is it?"

"We need to substitute. Give the nuggets a chance."

Simon glared on his monitor.

"Ok," he said. "Thirteen, Fifteen, Sixteen and Seventeen, you're in. Three through Six, you're out"

That meant that Zack, Fintan and Nizhoni were in. There were only four minutes left.

"Don't screw this up," said Simon.

As they were the freshest, they spread out across the center of the park. Melanie played up front along with Red Seven.

Fintan watched closely, monitoring how Green was adjusting to the situation. At first they were cautious, feeling out the new Red players, but when Nizhoni grabbed the ball and made a run for goal, they quickly double teamed her and intercepted her pass towards Zack. Green now rushed downfield, trying to carry the ball through the hole that Nizhoni and Zack had left behind.

Simon moved to intercept, with Red two dragging behind him blocking the goal. But something didn't seem right, and Fintan then noticed a Green ship breaking down the right hand side. As the ball holders were moving leftward, the wingers move was discrete and isolated. Fintan couldn't reach in time to block him. It was clear that they were going to engage Simon and Red two, and they'd spin the ball out to the wing player who'd likely have an open goal.

"Simon!" said Fintan. "Disengage!"

"What, nugget?" said Simon. "What are you talking about?"

"Do it! Look right."

Credit to Simon, he saw the plan, so he quickly turned and moved to intercept.

"Nizhoni, Zack, break forward!" said Fintan. They didn't ask why, and they charged forward into the gap left by the Green attack.

Green passed the ball right, before they saw Simon's move and he was able to intercept. He launched the ball forward to Zack who charged the goalkeeper, passing to Nizhoni at the last second. She had an easy drop into the open goal. Red had taken the lead 3-2.

Fintan looked at the clock. There were only a few seconds left. Simon ordered a full press, one-on-one with Green, making sure that they couldn't put any kind of move together. It seemed like an eternity before the buzzer rang. Red had beaten Green!

*

After the game, during the celebration, a member of Green Squadron approached Fintan.

"You're the Irish one, aren't ya?" he said in a thick Irish accent.

"Aye," said Fintan, smiling.

"A little birdie tells us that some of you guys in Red have a study group goin' on Friday nights," the boy said. "Except you don't really study anymore, you do somethin' more interesting. Is that right?"

"It might be," said Fintan, a little more guarded.

"Well, we have somethin' a little more interesting for you. Can some of us come to your next meeting? You're not the only ones who are keepin' an eye on things, y'know?"

Fintan nodded.

"Let's meet in the game halls in the city center. You know how to get there, don't you?" the boy said.

"Yes,"

"So it's a deal. See ya there, next Friday, seven o'clock."

As he walked off, Fintan realized he didn't even know his name.

*

On Friday night Fintan and the others made their way to the game hall. He didn't realize that only he and Nizhoni had been there before, so the others were a little taken aback.

"Here's where we practiced before the fresher's game," said Nizhoni. "It's a cool place."

They entered and looked around. Fintan wasn't sure he would even recognize the guy again. A girl with Green squadron uniform bumped into him roughly as she walked past.

"Huh?" said Fintan. He put his hand in his hip pocket and there was a note there.

He read it out. "Tube station. Five minutes."

"Maybe she likes you," said Zack.

"Feel free!" said Nizhoni.

"They want to meet somewhere else, obviously," said Heather.

Fintan shrugged and led them out, back across the road towards the train station. The girl was waiting on the platform, alone.

"I was right," said Zack, smiling.

"Wait," said Fintan.

A train arrived and she got on, meeting their eye as she did so.

"That was a look," said Zack. "More than a glance, less than a stare. We're traipsing around here for you to go on a blind date."

Nizhoni glowered at him.

"Hey, I'm not the one she's ogling," said Zack.

Two stops later the train stopped, and the girl got off. They followed her.

Zack started to speak but Fintan just said "Shut up!" quietly. Zack shrugged. Ayako smiled.

They were in an unknown part of city now, near some buildings that looked like they were offices. The girl went into one, and took an elevator upwards.

"You know," said Raj. "They could just be out for revenge for us beating Green in the last game. They're taking us somewhere to beat us up."

"You know," said a voice from behind them. "I'm surprised that it took the brilliant Red squadron that long to think that up as our plan. Actually, I'm disappointed more than I'm surprised."

They turned, and the Irish boy was standing in the hallway behind them with about ten other members of Green squadron.

He laughed at their scared expressions. "Don't worry," he said. "We're not interested in pounding on nuggets."

He gestured to a room behind them. "Please?"

*

They sat in the room, and the Green group joined them. Their faces were grim and hard to read.

"My name is Seamus," said the boy. "And I'm here to welcome your Conspiracy of Light to the real world."

"How did you know?" said Ayako.

"We didn't until now," he said. "Thanks for confirming!"

Zack stood up and slapped his hand to the table. "That's enough!" he said. "What is going on here?"

The boy turned and looked at him calmly. He ignored the question and asked one of his own.

"Tell me," he said. "How do they divide the squadrons? What makes me Green, and what makes you Red. Have you figured that out yet?"

They looked at each other in silence.

"We never really thought about it," said Fintan.

"If you did, it might tell you a lot about this school," said Seamus.

"Yellow are the brains," he said. "We're all smart, or we wouldn't be here, but they are the brains of the brains. They know stuff, they do stuff most of the rest of us can't even begin to understand."

He continued. "Green, us, are the brave. We're built to be fearless, and that gives us an edge."

"How?" said Zack.

"Well how do you think we knew so much about you?" he said.

"Simple," he continued without waiting. "We spy. It's amazing how simple it is to break into your laundry and steal some uniforms. Then we'll have our guys wander around your dining halls listening carefully. You'd be amazed what we hear."

Fintan looked at Zack, who was dumbfounded.

"That's pretty brave, right? Not just to spy on you, but to hide in plain sight. Not like sneaking around for information, which of course brings us to our dear friends in Blue."

"Blue?" said Ayako.

"Yes" said Seamus. "They are the type that will do whatever it takes to succeed whether honorable or not. 'Sneaky' some might say. 'Ambitious' others may say. And of course there's you noble folks from Red. Can you guess what you're selected for?"

"We're all-rounders," said Ayako. "We're generalists, pretty good at everything, but not masters of any."

"Very good," said Seamus. "But, ultimately it doesn't matter!"

"Why not?" asked Zack.

"Because," said one of the girls from Green. Her name badge read 'Wilson'. "Because it doesn't matter what our differences are. What matters is why the school divides us this way."

"And I bet you have a theory," said Ayako.

"No," said the girl. "That's where you come in."

"Us?" said Fintan.

"Yes," she said. "You guys have connections with Trichallik and with another man, one that they call 'Smith'"

Fintan nodded. "Yes, a little."

"Much more than any of us," she said. "And we have to put our foot down and say 'enough is enough'. We need to know what's going on."

"Why?" said Fintan. "Why is it so important to you?"

"The oldest of our group is a third year," said Seamus, cocking his head at a tough looking girl who nodded back at him.

"Because Green tend to graduate very early," continued Wilson. "And they never come back."

"Where do they go?" said Zack

"Military graveyard, most likely." said Seamus

Chapter 30: Fintan's Strategy

Her words weighed on Fintan for the rest of the week. Simon had them meeting regularly to strategize for their showdown with Blue. The way the chips had fallen, the winner would square off against Yellow for the championship.

He couldn't concentrate – it was just too hard to get Wilson's words out of his mind. Green students had been graduating very early, usually in third year, so they were only fifteen years old, and never being seen again.

Was there a war going on? Where did they go?

No wonder Green's Starball team hadn't been doing well. They were young and inexperienced.

"We only have their word for it," said Zack. "They might be deliberately misleading us."

"Why?" said Ayako. "Why would they do that?"

"Do what? Why would Green mislead us? Or why would the school send them out to fight and die?"

Nizhoni rested her head in her hands. "That explains it," she said.

"What?" said Ayako.

"Only Fintan knows this," she said. "Please don't tell anyone else, ok?"

They nodded. "We Navajo have known about the city for some time," she said. "We've known about the aliens, about everything. Or almost everything."

"Almost?" said Ayako.

"Almost," she said. "No matter how hard we tried, we could never get anyone into Green. The Navajo inside have helped the Navajo outside to get them into good places within the city, so that, should the city bring mankind to the stars, we'd be well placed to break free of mankind and go out on our own."

"Anyway," she continued. "We could never get anyone into Green, nor could we find anything out about them. We never knew why."

She breathed deep, closing her eyes, clearly troubled.

"That would mean that they know what you know," said Ayako. "They know that the Navajo are coming and going as you please, and they're keeping Navajo out so you don't find out about Green."

"Who are *they*?" asked Fintan. "The ones who are running the city, or someone operating under their noses?"

"My brain hurts," said Zack.

"Kinda makes tomorrow's game unimportant doesn't it?" said Nizhoni.

"Maybe not," said Ayako. "Maybe by winning this tournament, we're showing that we can be a good replacement for Green."

"More cannon fodder for the war?" said Zack.

"We don't even know that there *is* a war," said Ayako. "Let's not jump to conclusions."

She continued: "Maybe by winning, we're showing that we're too valuable to graduate early. Red has won the last few tournaments, and I see lots of older Red squadron students around."

"So by winning, we save ourselves, and condemn Green to be 'graduated early'?" said Zack. "That sucks."

"The fact of the matter is we don't really know anything," said Ayako. "We should take this new information under advisement and continue on trying to figure this out. And the best way we have of doing this is to be more involved in the school."

"And how do we do that?" said Zack.

"We win the tournament for starters," said Ayako. "Those 'field trips' they send us on might be important. And we need to know what's going on out there."

Zack shook his head. "I didn't sign up for this."

"None of us did," said Ayako. "What a nice surprise."

*

The game with Blue went surprisingly well. Simon yielded somewhat and had a rotating squad, with one surprise -- Fintan was on the field for the entire game.

Under Red Two's advisement, Fintan took the very center of the park, and took a strategic role. It was clear that he was gifted at this, and under his guidance, and the skill of flyers like Simon and Zack, they quickly tore Blue squadron apart, winning by three goals to zero.

"Not bad for a nugget," grinned Simon after the game. "But, I'm clipping your wings."

"What?" said Fintan. "I can't fly anymore?"

"Yep!" said Simon with mock cheer. "Actually it was Red Two's idea. You should talk to him."

He smiled sarcastically and walked off

Red Two was waiting for Fintan as they left the stadium. "Come with me," he said. He led him to a room that overlooked the arena. "We don't use this much," he said. "Perhaps we should."

In front of the large picture windows that overlooked the Starball arena, was a number of large monitors. "From here," said Red Two "you can co-ordinate the whole team."

"What?" said Fintan.

"I've been watching you," said Red Two. "I've barely even seen you touch the ball, but when you're on the field and talking to us, we play much better. We owe the fact that we're in the final to you, despite what Simon says."

"Thanks," said Fintan. "I think."

"As you know, with one exception, we can only communicate when we are on the field, so we either have you on the field, with ten other players, or, we have you up here."

"With one exception?" said Fintan.

"Yes. Here," said Red Two. "From here you can talk to the whole team."

"But Simon is Captain," said Fintan.

"Yes, but he wants to win, so I convinced him that you'd work better up here than down there."

"So it was your fault," said Fintan. "Thanks."

"You might not like it now," said Red Two. "But think about it. Those of us in the ships are learning to be pilots. Fighters. Your gift is elsewhere – in command. Simon sees that now, and we can all do better with you up here."

"Thanks," said Fintan, more sincerely this time.

Red Two nodded and started to leave.

"One more thing," said Fintan. "What's your name? Everyone calls you Red Two, and even your badge reads it."

"That's the way I like it," said Red Two, and he left.

*

"*Commander* Fintan," said Zack with a mock salute over dinner.

"I like the sound of that," said Ayako. Zack's smile turned into a scowl.

"Me too," said Nizhoni.

"And me," said Heather.

Raj hit Fintan with a bread roll.

"Now we're really going to kick some Yellow butt," said Zack.

Ayako shot him a glare.

"I mean we're going to kick some Yellow *Squadron* butt," he said. "I think?"

Ayako smiled. "Gotcha!"

*

For the rest of the week, Fintan spent every spare moment looking at tapes of their first game with Yellow. They had played a perfect game. In fact it was too perfect. The more Fintan looked at Red's maneuvers and the brilliant piloting of Simon and Red Two, he just couldn't understand how Yellow had always known exactly what they were planning, and what they were doing, and how they could instantly react and take advantage of Red's strategy, and easily use it against them.

And then he realized. The booth that Red Two had shown him. Maybe Yellow had one too, and maybe they had somebody brilliant in there. After all Green had told them that the exceptionally smart kids were taken in to Yellow.

He sighed. This would be quite the task - - figuring out how to defeat someone much smarter than him.

He buried himself even further in watching the old games. The more he watched the more he realized that there was simply no way he could be smart enough to beat them.

He laid his head down on his desk, ready to sleep.

"I don't think you'll figure out their strategy in the wood grains," said Simon.

Fintan lifted his head. His eyes were red from staring at too many screens.

"Aww, no need to cry!" said Simon. "Little baby needs some milk?"

"What did you say?" said Fintan.

"I called you a little Baby and asked if you need some milk, you want to do something about that?"

"Yes," said Fintan. Something was forming in his mind. "I think you've given me an idea, now get out and let me think."

Simon saluted. "Yes ma'am," he said sarcastically. "Enjoy the milk"

*

The brain was a funny thing. Simon's words made a connection with Fintan. He remembered his mother always telling him that the connection between a mother and a baby was special. It was almost like the mother could read the baby's mind, and that Fintan rarely cried as a baby. She just knew when it was time to feed him, and he'd always eat then. She just knew when his diaper needed to be changed, so she could do it before he became uncomfortable.

Could it be that Yellow are somehow reading our minds?

He looked at the tapes again in a new light. Now he could see it. There was one ship that did little in the game but followed Simon everywhere. There were even times when it could have engaged or tried to block Simon's ship but it did nothing.

Very interesting thought Fintan.

*

The day of the final game came, and the entire dome was decorated in yellow and red. Lasers lit the sky, flags flew from every building and the ceiling of the dome was lit up in red and yellow instead of the usual projection of a blue sky.

Before the game, Fintan took Simon aside and whispered in his ear. "You don't like me, and you don't like what I am doing, but if you want to win, you will do exactly what I say, when I say it without question or argument. Do what you do best and just *fly*."

He pushed Simon off and glared at him when he tried to answer. Understanding filled Simon's eyes and he nodded.

The game started to the same fanfare as the opening game. It had been just a few short weeks since they had played the opening game, but Fintan felt years older. Inside he was squirming, and he mentally crossed his fingers and toes hoping that he was right.

*

"Simon," said Fintan over the intercom as the game kicked off. "Take Red Two and Three out of your plans. They're mine. Red Two take a look at Yellow seven. You job is to get on top of that ship and keep it busy whether we have the ball or not. Don't be afraid to be physical.

Bump it, push it, do whatever you can to keep it busy. Red Three, you are going to fly and hover in front of their booth. It's opposite mine, and your job is to simply keep them blind. Got it? Now go!"

He could see the other squadron members looking at each other, aghast at Fintan's orders. "Have you gone crazy?" said Red Two.

"Do what he says," said Simon. "Now!"

And then the strangest thing happened. Yellow squadron just fell apart. Red scored easily within a minute, and then again, and again. By half time, they were up by eight goals to zero.

For the second half, Yellow began to press themselves again. Fintan was ready for them – they had swapped pilots, and he quickly figured out which one was the one he needed to block. He sent Red Two to harass that pilot instead, and again Yellow fell apart.

It was mercy for Yellow when the referees blew the final whistle. Red had won by fifteen goals to zero, and had completely destroyed the previously dominant Yellow.

*

Fintan was in no mood to celebrate, so he returned to his dorms alone, allowing everyone else to party.

The dining hall was deserted, but he was able to get a dessert, and sit and quietly eat it. Someone sat opposite him. He looked up to see a girl in Yellow squadron uniform. She was Asian, but her features weren't as soft as Ayako's. Her nametag said 'Ling'. Behind her stood several other members of Yellow. Fintan was surprised that he didn't hear them coming in.

"Fintan," she said. "We need to talk."

Chapter 31: Yellow's Secret.

Fintan used his bracelet to call Zack who could barely hear him above the noise of the celebrations.

"Zack," he said. "Get back here!"

Fintan could hear loud music and cheers through the speaker. Zack's voice barely registered above it all. "What?" he said.

"Zack. I think you should get back here now."

"Really? What's up?"

"I'm with Yellow Squadron."

"I'm on my way."

*

He led the Yellow members into a conference room.

"What's this about?" he said. Ling said nothing in response, and just sat quietly. Fintan recognized Toshi, the boy that Ayako had been trying to speak with all those weeks ago, but who had brushed her off.

The door banged open and Zack entered, with Nizhoni, Raj, Heather and finally Ayako.

At the moment Ayako entered, Toshi stood up. He had fire in his eyes.

Ling looked at him. He looked back. No words passed between them and he sat, but if looks could kill, they would.

The exchange wasn't lost on Ayako, who sat, quiet but alert.

Fintan looked at Ling. "You can read minds, can't you?" he said.

"Yes," she replied.

"Oh come on!" said Zack. "Reading minds?"

He stopped. Then he said "Sorry. And sure I will sit down."

"Stop that!" said Fintan. "Zack. She didn't say anything, she just made you think she did."

"Get out of my head," said Zack.

"You are easy," said Ling. "Your thoughts are so loud that it is easy to hear and change them. And no, Zack I will not do what you're thinking. That's rude. And not anatomically possible."

Zack stayed quiet.

"Explain," said Fintan.

"Have you ever been in a room with really thin walls?" said Ling.

"And you can just hear what is being said next door? It's not clear, and it's blurry. But when you strain and concentrate, you can make out words."

They all nodded.

"It's like that," she continued. "So with a lot of people, if I am near them and I really concentrate, I can hear their thoughts."

"That's how you won in Starball, isn't it?" said Raj. "You were reading our thoughts, and predicting our moves."

"I didn't have to read everyone's, just the leaders. We knew well that Simon wanted to control everything on your team, so I just got close to him, and it was easy to predict what you'd do. That is until *he* figured it out." She pointed at Fintan.

"So that was those odd orders you gave before the game," said Zack. "You were harassing her ship."

"Yes," said Fintan, nodding. "I noticed from the tapes that she didn't always, instantly, predict our moves. Sometimes she was a bit delayed, and that happened when she was otherwise occupied, flying her ship, avoiding collisions and the like. So by keeping her busy I was able to cancel out her gift."

"Nicely done," she said. "But this goes beyond Starball. I wasn't always this way. It started about six years ago."

"You were there too, weren't you?" said Nizhoni. "You were abducted. Six years ago."

Ling nodded. "Yes," she said. "And they did this to me. It sounds like a gift, but it's a curse. Sometimes I just want there to be some peace and quiet, but your thoughts are in my head all the time. Like whispers."

She paused.

"There's something else isn't there?" asked Fintan.

"Yes," said Ling. "Do you know that there's a traitor amongst you?"

"A traitor?" said Zack. "Who?"

Ling pointed to Ayako.

*

Ayako had been sitting with her head down. She looked up at Ling, and silently stared. Her gaze was scaring Fintan. It was like something had moved within her, and her eyes were darker than before.

Ling stared back wordlessly. Zack started to speak, but Nizhoni stopped him with a hand on his arm.

The staring match continued. Fintan noticed abject hostility on Toshi's face.

A bead of sweat formed on Ling's forehead and ran down her face. She was reddening. She gasped and then gasped again.

Fintan stood and started to walk around the table towards her, but she stood and backed off the table. She gasped once more.

"She can't breathe," said Fintan. "Ayako, stop!"

But Ayako wasn't listening. Nizhoni shook her, but she didn't respond.

Ling backed to a wall and slumped to the floor. Her hands were at her neck, trying to loosen her uniform.

"Ayako. Stop!" yelled Fintan.

Nizhoni pulled Ayako with all her might, but the smaller Japanese girl didn't move.

"It's not her," said Raj. "It's something else."

"Nizhoni! Do something!" said Fintan. Ling was turning blue now.

So Nizhoni drew back and punched Ayako square on the jaw. Ayako hit the ground, out cold, and instantly Ling started breathing again.

Toshi stood up. "She's with them!" he shouted. "The ones that abducted Ling. Her family is behind it all."

"That's ridiculous," said Zack.

"No it isn't," said a voice from the far side of the room. "But it's not the whole truth either."

They turned to see who had spoken.

It was Mister Smith.

*

"Do you want to explain something?" said Zack.

"Not really, but I'm going to anyway," said Smith. "What you just saw was a defensive impulse that we planted in her head should anybody try to do a deep scan. And Miss Ling, I have one too, so if you try to scan me, you might start turning blue again, and I don't believe Nizhoni can knock me out with a single punch."

"I'm willing to try," said Nizhoni.

Smith smiled. "I know you all want to know what is going on, what is really going on, but I can't tell you it all. Rest assured though, I'm keeping it from you for your own protection. However, if you're looking for someone who has been pulling the strings from the beginning, someone who has been building you all into the group you are, then look no further. It's me. And if you're looking for a purpose, I aim to give it to you."

"You clearly know something is going on, something more than just an innocent school that is training the future space farers, and you'd be right. So, in order to learn about the future, it's good to think about history."

He pointed at Nizhoni. "Miss Benally here is a Navajo. What happened to her and the other indigenous Americans when the Europeans arrived?"

"They were conquered," said Zack.

"Oh it's a lot more than that," said Smith. "They were almost made extinct. And the first part of that was when the first Europeans landed and shook hands with them, passing bugs and bacteria that the natives had no resistance to. Nobody knows exactly how many people were killed by the bugs, but it was probably 90% or more of the population. They make a big deal about the white men with their guns, but it was our bugs, and not our guns that mostly wiped them out."

"And it gets worse," said Smith. "Those that survived were physically and culturally overwhelmed by the invaders. They were all but extinct by the turn of the twentieth century. Even today, while the various tribes and nations are boasting large populations, for example the Navajo nation has over a quarter of a million people, not many of them are pure Navajo. Even Nizhoni, who has the appearance, is probably no more than 30% Navajo."

"They were wiped out," said Smith. "Pure and simple."

"And you think that will happen to us?" said Zack.

"Yes," said Smith. "And no."

"Let me ask you," he continued. "What would have happened had the Navajo, the Apache, the Comanche and the other tribes been a seafaring, gun toting civilization that met the Europeans on the ocean, instead of a group that could be deemed 'savages' by the European governments and churches, and thus butchered without guilt?"

"They would have treated us with more respect," said Nizhoni.

"Maybe," said Smith. "Or maybe instead of an easy target, they would have seen you as a threat. And how would they respond?"

"With war," she replied.

"Probably," said Smith. "So either way, it would have ended badly for you. This pattern has happened throughout history. When one civilization meets another, conflict ensues, and the weaker one gets wiped out."

"So are there other civilizations out *there*?" asked Fintan.

Smith nodded slowly. "There are. And there are many. Some good, some not so good. Either way, we aren't yet ready to meet them. And we'll probably never *be* ready."

"Never?" said Zack. "So what's the point of all this?" he spread his arms to take in their surroundings.

"That's the other part of our story," said Smith. "Remember, we have already made contact with another civilization."

"Trichallik's people," said Ling. "The abductors."

Smith smiled, but said nothing.

"Something doesn't make sense in your story," said Zack. "If things will always work out as you say, why aren't we at war with them?"

"There are several reasons why that could be so, but let's cut through the academic, and go for the truth." said Smith.

"Because they are hiding here, aren't they?" said Nizhoni.

Smith nodded slowly. "Yes," he said. "Because their world was destroyed, so they came to a galactic backwater to hide amongst us savages."

"Who destroyed their world?" asked Fintan.

"Does it matter?" said Smith. "The better question is why their world was destroyed."

"And why was that?" asked Zack.

"Because they did things like what they did to Ling," said Smith. "And Nizhoni, and you too Fintan."

"What did they do to us?" asked Fintan.

"I don't know what they did or why they did it," said Smith. "Though I have theories."

"Wait a second," said Nizhoni. "Trichallik is one of them, why is she in charge of the school if her people are doing that kind of thing."

"Because I want her to think that we're happy dumb slaves that are co-operating with them, swallowing their story of uplifting us and getting us ready for the stars, hook line and sinker. I don't want her to suspect that we're secretly building our forces against her. There's an old proverb: 'Keep your friends close, but keep your enemies closer'."

Smith looked to Toshi. "And Ayako has been working for *me*, since the beginning. I recruited her and convinced her to be a part of this school so she can get to know all of you, and start working on building you into mankind's future army. Because we *will* go to the stars. And when that happens, *you* will be the humans that other civilizations will meet, and hopefully they will treat us with respect and dignity, based on their experience with *you*."

He smiled. "Hopefully."

Ayako was waking up now. "Don't hold what just happened against her," said Smith. "As I said earlier, that's a block that we programmed into her. Some of the aliens are telepathic, and we didn't want them to know what she knows."

"So what happened to us?" said Ling. "Why did they...augment us?"

"We have a number of theories for that," said Smith. "But they are just theories."

"They're building us as an army to get revenge on whoever destroyed their world." said Nizhoni.

"That's one of the theories," said Smith. "What's important now is that we continue building our forces. That we continue gathering strength, so that when the time comes, we'll cast off the aliens, and take our own place amongst the stars."

He looked around the room. "Your job is to be good students in this school. Learn and grow. Yellow – you will become the key to our research. We've been stealing their technology for years, and we need your brains to figure out how it works. Ling, bury your gift. Don't use it again, for we fear if the aliens see your ability, they'll take you away from us for their own nefarious ends. They did it once before – six years ago to you, and they'll do it again if given the chance."

Ling nodded and looked to Toshi. He put his head down and said nothing.

"And to Red, you guys did well this time. Trichallik is sending you to Mars on your 'field trip'. Be on your guard. We don't know what she might be planning."

"But what about Green Squadron?" said Fintan. "Are they really going to war?"

"No" said Smith. "But we realize that we need to accelerate their military training. We've spread them out all over the world, training them in Trichallik's technology, so they'll be ready as a fighting force when the time comes."

Fintan looked to Ayako. "So the *war* was a fake? That night when you woke us to see what looked like an army?"

"Was a simple training exercise," said Smith. "We figured you might over-read it, and we needed to nudge you in the right direction. It led you to form your little conspiracy. Nice job. But let's get down to the real business of saving the world, ok?"

Chapter 32: Field Trip

The weeks that followed were a blur for Fintan. He did his duty and did his best to learn at school, but his mind was on what Smith had said.

It was clear that life wasn't cut and dry, and life in times like this was always going to be confusing. He could not hope to understand it – he could only hope to survive it.

But a burden was also being placed on him, despite what Smith had said. The air felt darker and thicker. It was harder to sleep, harder to eat, harder to think about anything other than the bigger world he was now beginning to see.

Aliens amongst us, not as friends, but as manipulators he thought. He remembered that day in the hospital when he looked in Trichallik's eyes. His *panic*.

Zack was cheerful as always, but Fintan could see that he was being eaten up inside too. Everything that he had believed in and lived for was turned upside down. He couldn't let go of his theory that his country – the country that he was so proud of was being played like a puppet by the aliens. The United States was building a war machine, providing soldiers and who knows what else for the aliens to use for *their* purposes.

*

The day of the Field trip finally came. The atmosphere was like carnival-like, so it lightened their mood somewhat. The Starball flyers had the honor of flying escort to the transport ships that carried the rest of the squadron. At noon they launched, and they flew straight up, into orbit.

"There's gotta be some nutcases watching Area 51 tonight. They'll get a show that they can tell each other for years to come!" said Simon as they shot upwards.

Fintan figured that they would make quite a sight. Half a dozen large transport ships, affectionately known as 'school buses' and nearly two dozen flying saucers in formation, heading straight towards the Moon.

Once in orbit, Zack squealed in delight. "Check this out," he said, beaming co-ordinates to the rest of the squadron.

Fintan checked it out on his display. "It's the Space Shuttle!" he said.

And indeed, in the distance was a tiny white dot, which under magnification resolved into the airplane-like shape of the Space Shuttle.

"Seems like a toy now, doesn't it?" said Red Two. The others nodded.

"Do you think they can see us?" said Zack.

"No," said Red Two. "It would be like looking for a piece of hay in a big stack of needles."

"Ok, Ok, cut the chatter," said Simon. "We have to change course. Plot a course following mine, let's stay tight."

Having broken orbit, the principles of flying changed a lot. They didn't think about gravity or air drag any more, it was all about momentum and acceleration. Simon took them in a looping path towards the far side of the moon.

"The far side of the moon," said Fintan. "*The far side of the moon.* This is so cool."

"It took the Apollo mission days to get to the moon," said Zack. "And we'll be there in just a couple of hours."

"The star base is on the far side of the moon," said Simon, "to keep it from prying eyes on Earth. As you may know, the same side of the moon always faces the Earth, so we can build stuff on the far side and nobody can see. It's a lot easier than burying it under Nevada."

As they flew, there was a gradual change from flying *towards* the moon to flying *over* the moon. Simon's orbit was so smooth and so precise that Fintan was only a few thousand feet above the surface before he noticed any difference.

"It helps that there's no atmosphere on the moon," said Simon, answering Fintan's unspoken thought.

The landscape beneath was sparse, but beautiful. Fintan could make out mountains, valleys, dust rivers and everywhere were craters, both large and small. Some craters were so large that they had shock lines reaching out from them like rays from the sun.

Despite the lack of color, it was beautiful.

"Like someone took a picture in black and white," said Zack. There were murmurs of approval. They were losing altitude now, moving towards a blip on their radar.

"The moonbase," said Simon "is inside a crater between two of the largest seas or *mare* on this side of the moon. It's called *Taruntius* and it's an ideal location because it is close to the lunar equator as well as surrounded by mare. We found permafrost, thus water, in these mare, so we could build the base there."

Their altitude had dropped to only a few hundred feet as they approached the crater. They climbed to move over the crater wall, and Fintan gasped as he saw inside. The crater had smooth, curved walls that they followed downwards. The impact that had created this crater left a small, circular ridge within the crater, and on this ridge Fintan could see a cluster of domes.

To one side of the cluster stood a tall, cigar shaped silver craft, and to the other, a set of scaffolding with something being constructed underneath. The convoy moved towards the silver ship. Simon held the saucers back as the school buses docked with the ship. They connected near the bottom of the ship, evenly spaced around its circumference.

Simon pointed out small dimples near the nose of the craft, and showed how a saucer could dock with it. The skin of the ship grew around his saucer in an almost liquid way. It was a surprise to Fintan who expected it to be made of hard, cold metal.

Red Two followed, along with the rest of Red squadron, in order. When it came to be Fintan's turn, he landed his ship, smoother than he expected to, and there was a strange noise and feeling as the ship enveloped him. Shrugging it off, he left the ship to find a ready room, with the rest of the pilots within.

"Come on," said Simon. "There's an observation lounge aft of here. We don't want to miss the launch!"

*

Nizhoni was waiting for Fintan in the observation lounge. It was at the 'bottom' of the ship, but instead of looking downwards at the moon, they were looking outwards at the moon.

"Some form of artificial gravity?" said Fintan.

"Yep," said Nizhoni. "And it's earth-normal gravity. I fancied being one sixth my normal weight on the moon, but I'm just my usual fat self."

"You're not fat," said Fintan.

She smiled.

"A little chubby maybe, but not fat," he smiled. He dodged as she swung a punch his way.

"I see Standing Bear's lessons are working," she said.

"Wanted to try them out," said Fintan. "And you're not chubby. You're perfect," he said, feeling his face flush.

"Better," she said. "Watch what you say in future!"

Zack was nowhere to be seen.

"I think he went to the docking area to look for Ayako," she said.

"Makes sense," said Fintan. "You'd want to share this view with someone you love."

It was a strange view. They were at the bottom of the ship, and thanks to the artificial gravity on the ship, the 'ground' wasn't beneath them, but directly out the window. It gave the eerie feeling of being in a cave, looking at a colossal grey wall

"Yeah," said Nizhoni, straining to see something other than grey dust. "So *romantic*."

There was a rocking and a groaning sound, and then the wall began to recede. The ship was taking off.

"I was expecting a big rocket or something," said Fintan.

"Water," said a voice beside him. "To launch from the surface of the moon, you only need water. Steam blows from the bottom of the rocket, and it's enough to get us into space."

Fintan looked to see the source of the voice. It was Trichallik, and another alien was standing with her.

"Meet Tricnollak," she said. "My life mate."

The other alien bowed. It was a little taller than Trichallik, and its skin was a little darker. Its eyes were also slightly narrower and something about it made Fintan think it was a more hostile that it's mate.

"This," said Trichallik, "is a pair of our finest new students. Fintan Reilly of the Irish and Nizhoni Benally of the Navajo Americans."

Tricnollak gazed at Fintan, meeting his eyes. His expression was unreadable. He then turned to Nizhoni, and looked deeply at her in the same way. Fintan felt Nizhoni's hand slip into his and grip him. He gripped her back.

Tricnollak didn't say a word, and returned his gaze to the windows.

The moon was receding away now as they lifted off slowly. The mountains, craters, dust seas and plains were showing in stark contrast.

"We can see them better, now that we're not flying ourselves," whispered Nizhoni.

Fintan nodded.

The dusty grey color of the moon provided great contrast in the sunlight. The shadows were a deep black and the mountains, while grey, went through thousands of shades of grey.

"It's breathtaking!" said Fintan.

Then everyone gasped. As the ship moved further away from the moon, they could see the horizon. A blue crescent showed above it. The crescent resolved further into the edge of the Earth.

"Earthrise," said Nizhoni. "Like sunrise except – it's *home*!"

Her voice broke, and a tear crawled down her cheek. She released her hand from Fintan's to wipe it away. The Earth was rising over the horizon. Fintan could make out North America, partially hiding under a swirl of clouds.

"From here you don't see any borders," he said. "Lines on a map. Amazing that we pay them so much attention."

She nodded, wiping a tear away once more.

"It is beautiful," said Fintan. "And worth fighting for."

The ship rose up above the curve of the moon and started moving towards the Earth, picking up speed to pass the planet.

"Get ready to see the jump," said Trichallik. "It's quite spectacular and never the same twice."

"The jump?" asked Fintan. He noticed that Nizhoni hadn't returned her hand to his. He wondered if he should try to hold hers instead.

"At this speed, it would take months to reach Mars," said Trichallik. "Our jump technology opens a wormhole between here and there, and we pass through in just a few moments. On the other side we'll be maybe twenty minutes flight from Mars."

"Why not jump straight to the surface? Why do we need a space ship at all?" asked Fintan.

Trichallik nodded. "Good question. It's simple really, a wormhole has to be calculated for the precise mass of our ship. In a gravity-well like a moon or a planet, debris may get dragged into the hole, and the consequences would be unfortunate."

"How?" said Fintan.

"Boom." said Tricnollak. His voice still made Fintan squirm inside. He was glad the alien didn't speak much. "Really *big* boom," he repeated, meeting Fintan's eye, almost smiling.

They watched in awe as they approached and then passed the Earth. Fintan reached out to take Nizhoni's hand and this time, she held him back. It felt good.

The Earth passed beneath them and to their right. For a few minutes they watched the stars.

"They don't twinkle," said Nizhoni. "No atmosphere to diffract their light."

Fintan nodded and squeezed her hand a little. She squeezed back.

"It's starting," said Trichallik.

At first Fintan didn't notice, but then could hear a low hum emanating from behind him. Its intensity was building.

Directly ahead of them a point of light appeared out of nowhere. It was brilliantly intense and soon expanded into a ring with what looked like multicolored lighting reaching from its center to its rim. The lighting flickered and sparked like an angry animal before winking out suddenly.

The ship moved towards the ring, picking up speed.

"We're opening a hole in the sky," said Tricnollak "and travelling to another world."

Nizhoni's grip tightened further on Fintan's. She gasped, and turned to Tricnollak looking shocked. The little alien gave her a strange smile and walked off.

Then a feeling like having his guts wrenched through his ears hit Fintan. He wanted to scream, but nothing came out. He tried to breathe, but nothing would come in.

And then, as suddenly as it had started, it was gone. He breathed in and staggered a little. Nizhoni did too, staggering against him, grabbing his arm. He held her back, and looked in her eyes.

"Are you ok?" he said.

"Jump disorientation," said Trichallik from behind him. "You'll get used to it."

And then without another word, she walked off.

"Are you ok?" Fintan repeated.

Nizhoni nodded and said nothing.

"What happened, back there, before the-"

"Nothing," she snapped. She then sighed. "Sorry. Not now. Later, ok?"

Fintan nodded, concerned and curious at the same time.

She leaned against him and he wrapped his arms around her. He must have grown a little because she was short enough to bend forward slightly and rest her head on his shoulder.

Something large and red appeared in the window on their right. As the ship turned, the planet Mars came into view. It was breathtakingly beautiful. Nizhoni turned, but stayed in his arms to see it. She gasped.

"Beautiful," she said. "So…"

There was no word for it. Fintan agreed. She turned to look back at him.

His chest was pounding, it felt like something was lifting him up when she looked at him like that. It made him feel ten feet tall and powerful enough to lift the planet in his arms.

She looked at his lips. He looked at hers.

Should I? he thought. *We're too young for this*!

But they were too young to be astronauts flying to Mars, and that didn't seem to stop it from happening. She lifted her chin upwards slightly, eyes searching his. He bent forward slightly, lips ready to meet hers.

"Oh *there* you are!" said Zack. "Have you seen Mars? Doesn't it look cool?"

They broke their embrace quickly. Nizhoni looked away, embarrassed.

"What?" said Zack, and then "Ouch" as Ayako kicked him on the shin.

Chapter 33: Mars

Pretty soon the surface of Mars dominated the viewport. It was a million shades of red, dotted with mountains, canyons and seas of deep rust colors. In the distance two white points of light were her satellites, Phobos and Deimos.

Ayako pointed as a huge dimple appeared on the horizon, and as it rotated towards them they could see a snow tipped mountain that was enormous.

"Olympus Mons, or Mount Olympus," said Ayako. "It's the largest mountain in the solar system, over three iumes the height of Mount Everest and nearly ninety thousand feet above the rest of the planet."

"Wow," said Zack. "I'd heard of it, of course, but to see it in person!"

The planet continued to rotate below them, and Mount Olympus dominated both the view and the conversation. "It's also a volcano – you can see the caldera in the center," said Ayako. "That baby is nearly 40 miles wide and twice as deep as the Grand Canyon."

They watched in awe as they orbited over the volcanic crater. There was simply nothing they could say, they were so dumbstruck by its beauty.

A klaxon blared.

"Attention," said a voice from a speaker over their heads. "We'll be hitting atmosphere in ten minutes, the observation lounge is now closing. All hands please report to landing stations."

A lighted passageway led them towards a room, which appeared, to Fintan at least, to be right at the core of the ship. It made sense – should something go wrong with atmospheric entry, the crew should be as far from the edge of the ship as possible, where the friction of the atmosphere would be reaching extremely high temperatures.

They took seats with over-the-shoulder harnesses that held them snugly in place.

There was an excited buzz in the air as they sat. Large monitors at either end of the landing stations showed the view from the ships nose as they nudged against the atmosphere.

A thrill of fear ran through Fintan's body as the ship rocked gently and then bucked a little. On the monitor they could see the deep red sands of Mars right in front of them.

The ship rocked again, and Fintan felt his stomach lurching. He was glad he hadn't eaten.

"For an atmospheric entry, this is pretty smooth," said Simon. The ship lurched again, pretty violently this time and Fintan was sure that Simon turned slightly green.

Fintan turned to talk to Nizhoni. He still felt awkward since their earlier moment, but she was sleeping. On the far side of Nizhoni sat Ayako, who met Fintan's look with a smile.

"That girl can sleep anywhere," said Ayako. "Better sleeping than enjoying all this!" She strained to stretch her hands out against the harness.

The jolting continued for several more moments and they felt the ship leveling out. Blue sky showed through the monitors, with a sun that looked too small lifting above the horizon.

From the cameras they could see that they were veering northwards, away from the equator.

"We'll be landing in Cydonia in about fifteen minutes," said the voice from their speakers.

"Cydonia?" said Zack. "No way, this is too cool!"

"What is Cydonia," asked Ayako.

"It's where the face on Mars is," said Zack.

"The what?"

"The face on Mars," he repeated. "Early NASA missions to Mars took photos of the surface. In Cydonia they found a mountain that from orbit looked like a face. Lots of people think it's a sign of ancient alien intelligence on Mars, and they carved a face so that it could be seen from orbit."

He shrugged. "Of course it was all debunked using later photos, so nobody believes it anymore. But it's odd that we're going to Cydonia now, of all places."

Nizhoni had woken up. "I remember reading about it once. It's at the edge of a heavily cratered area to the south, but super lightly cratered to the North. Many folks believe that the relatively smooth landscape to the North was a water ocean which evaporated long after the atmosphere was gone, explaining why there are less craters there. If that's the case Cydonia would be on the coast. A great place for a city, right?"

They were flying low now, gliding over the surface of the planet. They crossed a long plateau, with several craters at its bottom. In the distance they could see mountains, and as the ship turned eastwards, they could see mountains either side as they cruised to land in a deep rift between them. Finally they saw signs of life and civilization in the form of a cluster of domes.

Iara was at the far end of the room, and she spoke up. "We put the domes here for several reasons. First of all, there are many devastating dust storms on Mars, and here the mountains protect us. Secondly, and perhaps more importantly, the valley is almost completely obscured from earth-bound telescopes. That way we can do our work in secret – and we don't have the luxury that the moon base has of always being invisible to Earth."

The ship touched down gently. "Be warned," she shed, "that Mars gravity is about 40% of Earth Gravity, so tred carefully, and girls, you're going to love it!" She winked.

"I think I'm going to love it too," said Zack under his breath, watching Iara in admiration as she unstrapped herself.

*

As he exited the ship, Fintan felt like a great weight was lifted from him. He walked out of the artificial gravity field and initially felt like he was beginning to float away, but his feet were firmly rooted on the ground. It was oddly disconcerting, like being in an elevator going downwards really fast. His stomach felt like it was in his throat.

Again he was thankful he hadn't eaten, and when he looked up he nearly laughed at several of the girls who were frantically holding their skirts down, thinking that the skirts were going to float upwards, but of course they didn't as gravity still pulled them down.

Zack was smirking at their discomfort too, but stopped after a glance from Ayako. "Kick me in this gravity and I think I'll fly away," he said.

Ayako replied "I think you are giving me more reasons to kick you and not less."

"You've been hanging too much with Nizhoni," he laughed. "You're getting violent."

Fintan stood back as both girls faced him down, hands on hips.

Zack tried to have a straight and sorry face, but couldn't help himself. He laughed out loud.

"Sorry," he said between giggles. "But you guys look so cute when you're mad."

The girls walked ahead of him towards the entrance of one of the domes.

"Smooth," said Fintan. "Real smooth."

*

They assembled in the largest of the domes, and Fintan noticed that they were actually inflatable, as opposed to being hard-edged like the ones back on Earth. Fintan pointed at the bottom of the dome – it wasn't sealed and under its edge they could see the rusty Martian landscape outside.

"Air pressure inflates the dome," said an adult, who from his bulk, and his uniform, was some sort of soldier.

"The Earth-air being pumped in pushes the Martian-air out underneath the dome. It's basically a big tent," he added.

"What about heat?" asked Nizhoni

"There's a heating element in the floor," he said "which serves the purpose of heating us and expanding the air to increase the pressure."

It was simple, and elegant. Fintan was impressed.

Mister Sinclair, as squadron leader, was also leader of the expedition. He gave the expected long boring lecture on safety, following instructions, staying within the marked boundaries ad nauseum before finally going offstage.

Iara also had some announcements, which perked Zack up as she took to the stage. Ayako and Nizhoni shrugged. She demonstrated how their pressure suits work, including how to make emergency repairs.

Finally she ran through the schedule for the trip. They'd be spending three days and two nights on Mars. The rest of this day would be free time, and they'd head out to the 'dig site' early the next day tomorrow. They'd spend a couple of nights on the dig site before heading back to Earth.

"But how long is a day on Mars?" asked one kid.

"Good question," said Iara, "and unfortunately it's not much longer than a day on Earth, being about 24 hours and 40 minutes long. We keep Earth time on Mars, and as a result, the clock stops at midnight and starts again 39 minutes, 35 and a quarter seconds later. We call this time 'the witching hour'. Enjoy it!"

Many of the students laughed.

As they dispersed towards their sleeping quarters to drop their stuff and get their pressure suits, Zack called to Ayako and Nizhoni. "Meet back here in half an hour to go for a hike?"

The two girls looked at each other, and then back to Zack. They nodded 'yes'.

*

Their pressure suits were light-fitting and easy to wear. They were one-piece, blue grey jumpsuits that they zipped themselves into. They wore hard boots on their feet, and the helmet was built into the suit itself. Several small oxygen tanks were efficiently spread down the sides and across the back.

"You look like you have a bubble on your head," said Zack, laughing.

"It's a lot lighter and easier to move in than a traditional astronaut suit," said Fintan. "And this fiber is like nothing I've ever seen before. It must also protect us from the atmospheric and radiation conditions on Mars in the same way as a traditional space suit. Must be some form of alien technology."

"Cool."

They left the boys dorms and found the girls near the airlock.

"I definitely preferred them in skirts," said Zack. Nizhoni sighed.

The airlock was pretty simple, a tech unzipped the door, and they walked into a small space between the main tent and an outside one. The tech then re zipped the door, which was now inside of their position, and Zack unzipped the door in front of him. Outside it Fintan could see a red, rocky valley.

"We're on Mars!" he said.

"Well duh," said Zack.

"Now I really feel like I'm here," said Fintan.

Ayako nodded in her suit. "Well, what are we waiting for? Let's go!"

They walked out through the airlock, and Zack zipped the door closed behind them. They were in a wide valley with a slope leading up at about a twenty-degree angle to their right. On their left was a steep cliff that climbed maybe a hundred feet.

The ground was made of a red substance that was coarser than sand, but finer than gravel. It was littered with different rocks of different sizes, but of a pretty uniform dark grey color. The cliffs to their left were the same red as the ground, but in places darker rocks were peeking through.

"Wind erosion is pretty bad," said Ayako. "We'd better not be here if there's a dust storm."

"I don't think they get them here very often," said Zack. "Otherwise we wouldn't be living in a tent."

They walked along the valley towards its end. The cliff was getting lower now, and after about a quarter of a mile, it was gone. They looked back along the valley they had walked out of, and could see the main dome that they had left stretching across it from end to end. Beyond it they could see the other domes as well as the ship they had arrived on towering over everything.

Zack reached down and dug some dirt away. A few inches down he found something and prodded it with is finger.

"Frost," he said. "Water ice. I guess that answers one of the big questions about this place."

"Yeah," said Fintan. "I wonder if there's life on Mars, or if they've answered *that* question."

"Well we know the answer now, don't we?" said Zack

"We do?" said Fintan.

"Err. Duh" said Zack and pointed at himself, then Nizhoni, then Ayako and then Fintan.

"*We're* the life on Mars now!"

*

They backtracked and walked along the cliff top overlooking the base.

"I'm tired," said Nizhoni. "I think I'm going to sit for a bit. Go on ahead."

"No," said Fintan, and he sat, legs dangling over the cliff, he held up a hand to help her sit beside him.

"Ok," said Zack. "Rest stop."

"No," said Ayako. "We can keep walking."

"But Nizhoni and Fintan have stopped, and there's a beautiful view. Why don't we stop and enjoy it with them."

"No," said Ayako, evenly. "We can keep walking."

"Huh?" said Zack. "Oh. Yeah. Ok. Let's keep walking."

Ayako rolled her eyes and winked at Nizhoni. She took Zack's arm and practically dragged him along with her.

From where they sat, they could look down over the valley, across to the plains on the far side. Dusty mountains lined the horizon. Nizhoni pointed and said "Can you see the crater?"

Fintan squinted to see, but couldn't. She pulled him a little closer to look along her arm towards what she was pointing at, and then he saw it. It was a perfect bowl shaped crater, with the rim on one side lit brightly by the sun, while a deep shadow crept across the other.

"You know," said Fintan. "Have you ever had the feeling that you were waiting for something? Like my whole life I knew that where I lived and what I did wasn't my real life? And that something better was waiting out there?"

She smiled a little and nodded.

"Well, one of the first thoughts that came to my head when I got to the school was that my life is now *starting*. It's starting for real. But even then it didn't feel right."

She turned to look at him. The bright spot of the sun, and the red of the landscape reflected beautifully in her faceplate.

"I was wrong," said Fintan.

She raised an eyebrow.

"It's only here, now, sitting with you that I feel that. I feel that my life is finally starting, that I'm finally making my own way in the world. And that it's because you are here sitting with me. How do I say this Nizhoni? But I feel like I can't imagine living without you. I feel that I-"

She put her hand up to his faceplate. She smiled again. "I feel that way too. I knew it for sure when I saw how you interacted with my family. You're a pretty slow learner."

Fintan laughed and took her hand from his face. She held onto his hand and didn't let go.

"Oh," said Zack, who had approached from behind. "Don't try to kiss, ok? It's not going to work with the helmets on!"

"Ewwww," said Nizhoni and threw some sand at him.

"Now what did I say?" said Zack.

Chapter 34: The Dig

The following morning they got onto a transport to head towards the dig site. They would be escorted by Simon and Red Two in their saucers.

"All aboard the big yellow school bus," said Simon as they began to board. "Next stop, the face on Mars!"

They boarded and sat in rows of forward facing seats. "It really does look like a school bus," said Zack.

It lifted off and headed out of the valley towards the mountains that Nizhoni and Fintan had been looking at the night before. After twenty minutes they landed near a number of smaller dome shaped tents.

Iara was their driver and tour guide. "So," she said. "The dig that we're going to visit is something that we started a few years back. It appears that some form of alien must have visited Mars a few thousand years ago. They left some evidence here, and we can't help but wonder if it they did it deliberately near the mountains that, from orbit, would look like a face. If you squint real hard that is. But don't worry – they didn't *really* carve a face."

"Who were they?" asked Zack.

"We have no idea," she replied. "And neither do Trichallik's people. This is why we're digging here – to find some signs of their occupation and see what we can learn."

"Trichallik really doesn't know?" asked Fintan, looking Iara in the eye.

"Well, that's what she tells us," the teacher answered. "Or, if she does know, she isn't telling. Maybe she wants us to figure it out for ourselves."

They exited the bus and walked through an inflatable airlock into one of the tents. There, they activated their pressure suits and made ready to enter the underground tunnels.

*

As Fintan entered the tunnels, he was still in awe that he was on Mars, but underground it was like anywhere on Earth. The tunnel was dark, though not quite damp.

"Zack found permafrost under the surface near the camp," he said. "How come there is none here, yet we're going deeper underground?"

Iara answered. "Good question. It appears our camp was near an ancient ocean and there are still signs of water underneath. This was further inland, so any water that was here is long gone."

The tunnel led downwards at a shallow slope, a line snaked along the ceiling and had perfectly normal lamps attached to it at regular intervals.

"It's a long way down," said Iara "and as you get closer to the end, the tunnel will get narrower and lower, so watch your heads."

It took them a long time of carefully picking their way, but they finally made it into a wide red cavern.

In the center of the cavern, they could see the top of an elevator shaft. The elevator was waiting for them, and was big enough to hold them all, but with a bit of a squeeze. Once they were all in, Iara reached over a grinning Zack to push the 'down' button.

The elevator lurched into life, and they were moving downwards. It was an unusual feeling in the Martian gravity. After a few minutes the door opened and they were in a larger cavern.

"The walls are smooth," said Simon "like they've been built and not dug."

Iara found a wall panel and flicked on the lights. They revealed a room that looked vaguely familiar to Fintan. The walls were made of huge red stone bricks and they led up about forty feet to an angled ceiling. At the far side of the room was a large doorway.

"No," said Nizhoni. "I don't believe it!"

"What?" said Fintan.

"We're in a geofront aren't we?" said Nizhoni. "Like the one in Nevada!"

The others looked around, shocked. Iara raised an eyebrow at Nizhoni. "Lucky guess?"

She strode forward to the wide doors. Now that Nizhoni had said it, the room they were in was almost identical to the one in which he had met Bob, back in the Nevada city.

Iara led them through the doors and lit some spotlights that shone into the darkness.

Through the gloom they could see some buildings and a similar platform to the one in Nevada that they had stood on to watch the welcoming ceremony only a few months before.

"It's a geofront all right," said Iara. "But as far as we can tell, it's been deserted for a long time."

*

They had each been given different assignments. Iara had paired Fintan with Nizhoni. She smiled and said "for obvious reasons". They weren't actually going to be in the geofront itself, but would instead be helping with the excavation of some tunnels nearby. "We found some artifacts there," said Iara. "See if you can find some more."

*

Nizhoni and Fintan followed the path Iara had given them, to find another dark cavern. A ramp sloped downwards, turning back onto itself, and on the far side was a cave. Nizhoni grabbed a couple of lanterns from a bucket near the entrance to the cave and they walked in. The cave was still partially dug out, and there was a huge pile of debris on the far side. Nizhoni shone her lantern at the wall.

"Look at this, Fintan," she said. There were shapes scratched on the walls.

Many of the drawings were of figures. There also random shapes such as circles and spirals. Dominating were three large semi-circles, inside of which were more stick figures.

"They look like geofronts," said Fintan. "And there are three of them."

"More than that," said Nizhoni. "These are just like Anasazi carvings, commonly called petroglyphs. There are many of them back on Earth, drawn by my people and other related tribes. I'll show them to you someday. But what are they doing here?"

Chapter 35: Discovery

Working with Nizhoni on the dig was hard, but pleasant. They had never spent so many hours together and they worked well, almost as one. Little by little they dug their way through the new tunnel exploring each rock or large chunk carefully, in case it was artificial. As they cleared their way along one rock wall, they could see more petroglyphs taking shape, so Nizhoni chose to dig in that direction.

"I think," she said "it's telling some kind of a story. It's almost like..."

"Like what?"

"I'm not sure. Give me a few minutes."

Fintan nodded and continued digging beside her.

They heard some banging and rattling behind them and turned to see Simon entering the cavern.

"Yo nuggets!" he said. "Check this out!"

He held up a device about the size of a large power drill.

"This," he said, "is a nuclear powered stone cutter. This sucker has a tiny little nuclear reactor in it and it packs a hefty punch!"

He smiled and walked through a side cavern. "I'll be down here with Red Two. We think we found the remains of a ship, but it's buried deep and likely thousands of years old!"

*

The hours blew past, and after a brief lunch break on the surface, Nizhoni and Fintan returned to work. She was carefully and slowly uncovering the carvings.

"Did my father tell you of the Diné origin stories?" asked Nizhoni. "Of the worlds of the insect people and how they came to what we now call the Navajo nation?"

There was a deep rumble above and behind them.

"Simon's having fun," said Fintan. Nizhoni smiled.

"It's a story of a people that we call the insect people and how they left their world, to come to ours. But there were a number of stops along the way," she said.

The rumbling grew deeper. Fintan thought he heard someone shouting too.

Nizhoni stopped, cocked her head to listen. "What is that?" she said.

Fintan shrugged. "Probably someone goofing around."

"And Zack is no doubt involved," she laughed.

Fintan laughed along with her.

"Anyway," she said. "if you look really closely, you can see that there are colors on these pictures. They're ancient so they've mostly faded, but much of what we see here had a blue or turquoise tint at some point, right?"

Fintan squinted. In a few places he could see some faded blue or ochre. "Yes," he said. "I see that."

She led him to a line that ran from floor to ceiling. "See how the color changes here" she said. "The blue is gone, and there are traces of yellow."

"The line isn't solid," said Fintan. "There's a gap here," he pointed. "And what looks like a tube linking the two sides. Reminds me of the wormhole we travelled through to get here."

She nodded, gravely.

"What is it?" asked Fintan. "What does it mean?"

The rumbling returned but now it was much louder and their cavern shook. Rocks started to fall from the ceiling and a cloud of dust rose up. Fintan was glad he was wearing his pressure suit or he wouldn't have been able to breathe.

He punched his bracelet. "Zack, come in."

"Yo," said Zack. "You guys having fun yet?"

"Something's going on down here," said Fintan. "Did you feel the ground shaking just now?"

"Negative," said Zack. "But the city is likely to be well insulated."

The ground shook again, and more rocks fell. Nizhoni grabbed his arm and pulled him away from one particularly large one that landed with a bone jarring thud close to where Fintan had been standing.

"Fintan," said Zack "What was that?"

"We'd better get out of here!" shouted Nizhoni.

There was another shake and the entrance to their cavern collapsed. The only way out was to go down the side cavern that Simon had taken earlier.

The lights flickered again. Nizhoni clicked on the light at the forehead of her pressure suit. It was a good idea, Fintan followed suit.

They frantically searched around, but there seemed to be no way out.

A voice came from behind them. "Fintan!" it said. "Run! Get out of here!"

Simon came clambering over some rocks to their left. He was carrying the torch in one hand and a bracelet in the other. He pointed up a slope to their right.

"Go that way!" he said. "They got Red Two! They got him!"

"Who did?" asked Fintan.

Simon threw his bracelet into Fintan's hands. "Take this and just run!" said Simon. "Run!"

Nizhoni grabbed Fintan's arm and they started clambering up the slope that Simon had indicated. There was a dark hole near the top that Fintan hoped would lead them back to the elevator cavern.

There was a sound, and Fintan looked back to something *huge* moving in the darkness. It glistened with wet brownish skin.

"Hurry!" said Simon shouting back to him, before activating the stone cutter and charging the creature.

Nizhoni and Fintan reached the top, and there was an exit. Fintan looked back to see the creature throwing Simon across the cavern. He hit the floor, and his faceplate cracked.

"Run you fools!" he said and held the stone cutter high as the creature covered him with darkness.

There was a flash, and a glow from the underside of the creature. It screamed and raised itself high, before slamming downwards, crushing Simon and the stone cutter.

"No!" shouted Fintan. "Simon!"

"He died giving us a chance," said Nizhoni. "Let's not waste it."

They crawled up through the hole to find the ramps that led down to the cavern that they had been working in earlier. "Just up here," she said, "and we can reach the elevator shaft."

Fintan activated his bracelet. "Can anybody hear me?"

"Yeah," said Zack. "I hear you loud and clear. What happened earlier, you got cut off?"

"Red Two is dead, Simon is dead. There's *something* down here. Get everyone to the school bus and get them out of here straight away!"

Again there was a loud rumbling, and the ground beneath them shook. "Quickly!" yelled Fintan.

Nizhoni had reached the top of the ramp, Fintan a few steps behind. She stopped and looked through the carved doorway to the next chamber.

Tricnollak walked through the door, calmly. His small body walked with deliberate calm and demeanor. He didn't need a pressure suit in the Martian atmosphere.

Nizhoni didn't look at him, didn't talk to him.

Fintan ran up the ramp to face the alien, panting. "Something is down there," he said. "It killed Red Two and Simon!"

The alien nodded and walked calmly towards the hole that led down to the cavern where Simon had died. "Leave this place," he said. "I will buy you some time."

Nizhoni didn't argue and immediately ran out the door. Fintan scrambled to keep up.

"You really have to tell me what it is between you and him," said Fintan as they reached the elevator. This cavern was below the main entry building that Iara had led them to earlier, and a much smaller elevator led upwards. Nizhoni punched the button to call it.

"For another time," she said. She punched the button again. "Come on!" she said. "Hurry up!"

Their bracelets chimed and they heard Iara's voice.

"We're almost finished loading the school bus," she said. "We'll be out of here in a couple of minutes. What's your ETA?"

"Just go!" said Nizhoni. "We have Simon's bracelet, so we can fly his and Red Two's saucers. Get out of here as soon as you can."

They heard something far above them. Then they heard Iara screaming over the intercom.

Zack pinged them. "We've had a cave in up here. Iara is hurt. Hurry up!"

Nizhoni repeated. "Go without us, we can get to the saucers."

"I'm not leaving without you and Fintan!"

The ground shook again, and Zack was cut off.

"I hope he chose this moment in time to get a brain," said Nizhoni. "And do the right thing."

Finally they could hear creaking from above them. The elevator was coming.

But then something scurried in the darkness around them.

"What's that?" said Fintan, moving around to illuminate the shadows with his helmet light. Several times something small moved out of the light and hid against the rocks. "Is someone there?" he called out.

"We *were* the only ones down here," said Nizhoni, fear creeping into her voice.

The elevator reached bottom and the doors opened. As they ran in and closed the door, Fintan thought he saw the silhouette of something moving in the darkness. It was small, with a large head and a slender body. It reminded him somewhat of a smaller version of Trichallik, but he couldn't be sure.

Chapter 36: The Chase

The elevator banged upwards and led them to another cavern. It was a quick and easy walk to the entrance to the geofront from here, and the elevator to the surface was already waiting for them.

"Good old Zack," said Fintan. "He sent it down to us so we wouldn't have to wait."

Nizhoni nodded. "I think I'm too hard on him sometimes."

She got inside and pushed the up button.

"Just as long as this place doesn't fall apart while we're going up," said Fintan.

"Actually, the elevator shaft is probably the safest place, as there's no ceiling to fall down on us."

Fintan nodded.

"I saw something back there," said Nizhoni. "Near the elevator. There were creatures in the darkness. They looked like-"

The elevator jarred to a stop. "Later," she said. "Let's get out of here now."

They ran through the domes to the landing area. As they reached it they saw the yellow school bus just lifting off in a cloud of red dust.

"Good," said Nizhoni. "They're safe."

Fintan and Nizhoni ran to the two saucers. Fintan used Simon's bracelet to get into the first one, and used its command overrides to open the second one for Nizhoni. They strapped in and launched as quickly as they could.

"Zack," said Fintan, once they were flying. "Come in?"

Zack's face popped up on Fintan's display. "Good to see you buddy, now can you let me know what's going on?"

"Later," he said. "Wait a minute, are you flying the schoolbus?"

"Yep," he said. "Iara hurt her leg, so I'm going to be her hero and fly these mutants out of here."

"Fly low," said Fintan. "And fast. We have to get back to base camp."

"Ok, but would you please explain what is going on?"

"We were attacked, and we don't know if it is over yet."

Something pinged on his scanners. "Nizhoni?" said Zack.

"I see them too!" she said. "Three of them approaching from the north east," she paused a moment. "They're not ours. Fintan. Stay with the school bus, I will hold them off and buy you some time."

"No Nizhoni, stay together!" said Fintan.

"Negative," she responded. "They'll be on top of us in a couple of minutes, and the school bus is defenseless. You can get the bus back to base camp in about ten minutes. I can hold them off long enough for you to get them out of harm's way and then come back here and help me finish them off." Her saucer dropped back.

"No," said Fintan. "I can't leave you."

"You can," she said calmly. "And you will. I will not let you leave the people on the school bus defenseless. What if there are more of these creatures?"

"Leave me now," she continued. "I need to concentrate. And Fintan, don't worry. They cannot hurt me. They cannot harm me. They cannot touch one who has dreamed a dream like mine."

She smiled and then her face vanished from his display.

*

"Zack," said Fintan. "There are more of whatever attacked us approaching. Nizhoni has dropped back to hold them off. Give it everything you've got to get back to base camp."

"I've been trying to raise them on the intercom," said Zack. "But someone is *jamming* us."

"Do you have any flares or anything to signal them?"

"No," said Zack. "When we get into visual range we can do a tight beam to wake them up, but that's still a few minutes off."

"Then stay low," repeated Fintan. "And fly fast."

He moved his display to track Nizhoni. Instead of waiting for the creatures to attack her, she had moved to intercept them. *The best defense is a good offense* she would say. It made more sense that way, and would buy Zack even more time.

He adjusted his magnification and finally saw their assailants. They were three of them, each maybe forty feet long, brown and segmented. At one end was a huge sharply toothed maw. They looked just like giant bugs, but were flying without any discernable wings. Unmistakably these were the creatures they had seen in the caverns below the geofront, the ones that killed Simon.

Over the intercom he heard a blood-curdling battle cry from Nizhoni as her saucer flew like a blur right into them. She aimed headlong at the lead bug, spinning her ship like a buzz saw blade. At the last moment she broke off her headlong charge, ducked to the left and started firing her lasers as she spun into the creature's side cutting through it in a shower of blood.

It reared up and screamed, turning around to swipe at her ship as she dodged away. She dodged upwards, but another creature was trying to cut off her path.

She was quick enough to see it, dodging downwards, flipping her saucer around to face it and open her main guns. They shot like a machine gun into the creatures sides. Its skin was armored, and Fintan could see many of her shots being deflected, but some hit, causing the creature to lurch and bleed.

She then twisted around again and dove for the ground, heading away from the school bus. Two of the creatures followed her, but one stayed on course to follow the bus.

"Eight minutes," said Zack. "I don't think we're going to make it. You are better off going back and helping her out. The odds will be much better with three against two."

"But there might be more of them," said Fintan. "I can't leave you. Besides, would you like to make the girl that did *that* mad?"

Fintan spotted a canyon that led roughly in the direction of basecamp. It was a longer way, and would add to their time, but it provided cover.

"Zack," he said. "Check out the canyon at ten o'clock. Can you get down into it and fly through it. It will provide visual cover."

"Better to go straight. If we go that way, it will take more time."

"Four minutes," said Fintan, looking at the output from his tactical display. "But you'll be under cover."

"Uh oh," said Zack. "Two more bogies at three o'clock. Inbound on our position. ETA three minutes. I guess we have no choice!"

Zack turned and made for the canyon. It would take him away from the new incoming ships, and buy some more time. Fintan followed, flying as close to the school bus as he could to keep a low radar profile.

He checked back on Nizhoni. She had turned to pursue the one craft that had broken off to follow Fintan, and was attacking it from the rear. Her saucer was belching smoke now, but she still seemed to be in control of it. The other two were rapidly gaining on her. The lead bug broke off the chase to avoid her shots, but she got a couple in, drawing more of its blood.

"She's good," said Fintan. "She's *really* good!"

"Good news," said Zack. "I think those new bogies were spotted by home base. They're scrambling ships to intercept."

Fintan moved his display to look towards home base. He magnified to see several battle saucers launching.

"Here comes the cavalry," he said. "Thank God!"

*

He made a calculation.

"Zack," he said. "I'm staying with you for two more minutes; at that point the battle saucers will be closer to you than the bugs. You'll be able to get cover from them."

"But that's four more minutes that Nizhoni will be on her own against them," said Zack. "Leave now!"

"No. And we're not going to discuss this, ok?"

The canyon was leveling out, so Zack lifted the school bus up and turned back towards home base. Fintan was trying to see what was going on with Nizhoni, but she was out of range now.

"Home base this is school bus one, mayday, mayday!" Zack yelled into the comm.

"Nothing yet, no response."

"Fintan," said Zack. "Check out your heads up display."

He could see that the two new incoming bugs had broken off their intercept course of the school bus and were moving to engage the battle saucers instead. Also several battle saucers had broken off and were heading towards the school bus.

"They see us," said Zack. "You can go!"

"They're still a couple of minutes out," said Fintan.

"It's ok," said Zack. "Look, I know you want to protect us, but it's ok. We're going to be fine now, and those extra couple of minutes might make all the difference for Nizhoni."

Fintan was frantically trying to adjust his display to see what was happening with Nizhoni, but there was nothing.

"Ok," he said. "I'm sorry Zack, but I can't leave her any longer."

"Go!" said Zack. "Go. And if she gets mad at you over this, I'll stand by you. I don't think she can beat us both up."

"Don't bet on that," said Fintan, and turned his saucer away to head back towards the dig and Nizhoni.

Stay safe Nizhoni. I'm coming.

Chapter 37: Fallout

He dove down to hug the landscape and pushed the saucer as fast as it would go. There was still nothing on the display. He came within range of the dig camp and put his scanners on maximum magnification.

There was nothing there. No bugs, no Nizhoni. *Nothing.*

Where are you Nizhoni. His hands moved in a blur as he reprogrammed the scanners, trying to squeeze as much power out of them as he could.

Suddenly, the scanners blanked out. He screamed inside, thinking he had damaged them, but outside there quickly a flash of intense white. His visual scanners dimmed to protect his eyes but they didn't hide the huge fireball that erupted over the dig site. He watched in awe as the superheated air climbed into the sky, sucking dust up into a mushroom cloud.

Nuclear weapon. Someone is nuking the dig site. He fought back panic, but the interior sensors showed no radiation – either the saucer was shielded, or he was at a safe distance. Choking back the fear, he knew that he had to focus on finding Nizhoni.

There was another flash, and another. Two more mushroom clouds climbed into the sky. One of them was *close and* the shockwave hit Fintan's saucer slamming him backwards.

He ignored the pain in his back as he fought to regain control. His best option was to gain as much altitude as possible and to be above the blasts and shockwaves.

As he climbed he watched the hellish scene below. The first cloud had bloated and swelled, and through it he could see a firestorm as the rocks of the surface melted. The other clouds were growing slowly, reminding Fintan of a TV show he had once seen where scientists demonstrated how plants grew using time lapse photography.

His sensors came back online and pinged. They showed two objects, climbing into orbit, and moving fast. One of them was giving off Nizhoni's transponder signal. But if the other was one of the bugs, why was she chasing it? There was only one way to find out, so he pushed the saucer as fast as he could in a pursuit course. He *had* to get there whether it killed him or not.

They were moving more slowly as they reached the upper levels of the Martian atmosphere. Fintan's ship was shaking like crazy – he was clearly pushing it harder than he should, but he didn't care. He was gaining on them.

Finally they came within visual range. He magnified and gasped when he saw that the two ships were *both* bugs. The lead bug was slowing and looked to be trying to open a wormhole outside the atmosphere. The trailing bug was giving off Nizhoni's transponder signal.

He zoomed in on it and saw that it had her saucer in gripped with its legs. It looked like a giant grub or worm, and as it flew it was trying to tear her saucer apart to get at what was inside.

No thought Fintan. And then "NO!" he screamed at the darkness.

Calm down Fintan. You can't help her if you panic. Calm down. There's a solution to this.

The transponder was still active, which meant that the pilot's core was still active. She was still alive in there.

The lead ship had succeeded in opening the wormhole; Fintan could see the bright point in the sky ahead of it, which then stretched into a hole. In only a few seconds, both ships would enter the wormhole, travelling to an unknown destination. She would be *lost*.

He was flying in Red Leader's ship, which meant that he still had the override codes for hers. That gave him an option – he could use the emergency eject command for her saucer which would send the pilot's pod away from the ship. But, the bug was trying to get at her, with only the shell of the saucer protecting her. If he ejected her pod, she would be defenseless and it would tear her apart. If he did nothing, she'd be taken away, and probably killed anyway.

He knew what he must do. She would have ejected from her ship if she could, and there was still a chance that the systems were still active. She might be unconscious and unable to eject.

But there were only a few seconds before the lead bug would reach the open wormhole. He had to work quickly.

Chapter 38: Falling Down.

There was only one thing that was going to work. He would have to eject her pod, and then somehow destroy *both* bugs. A plan crystallized in his mind – but he had no time to think it through – he had to act.

With a push of a button he beamed the codes over to Nizhoni's saucer. A green light showed acknowledgement, but he did not have time to check if she was clear before he unleashed a full volley of fire on the bug holding her saucer.

As the saucer was shooting, he was frantically programming an intercept course for the lead saucer. He would have to ram it – it was his only hope. With satisfaction, he saw Nizhoni's pod eject from her saucer and spiral down towards the red surface of Mars.

He felt like a spectator, watching the scene unfold on his monitors. His ship, on an intercept course for the lead bug, was tracking and shooting at the trailing bug, preventing it from intercepting Nizhoni's escape pod.

An instant before his ship impacted with the lead bug, there was a sickening thump in his stomach as his escape pod accelerated away, but he was glad for the speed because when his ship collided with the lead bug, it exploded instantly, blowing the bug to pieces, and the debris was sucked into the wormhole.

The wormhole expanded and then began to collapse. He could see the arcs of lightning reaching out to touch his pod and the other bug.

It felt like his pod had been grabbed by a giant hand, stretching and writhing as it was sucked towards the hole. Suddenly a huge white flash and explosion blinded Fintan and rocked his escape pod. There was a feeling of weightlessness as it was thrown free of the wormhole by the blast. However the shockwave hit, and Fintan was thrown from his control pedestal.

He had an odd sense of slow motion as he fell, and he put his hands up to break his fall. There was a sickening cracking sound as his head hit something. He wasn't sure what it was. Something wet was trickling down his neck. Blood.

He felt oddly relaxed. Everything was distant now. The sound of the shipboard alarms were now muffled and soothing.

"Boom" Tricnollak had said. *"Really big boom"*

More shuddering and rocking and somewhere deep in his mind he realized that he had entered the atmosphere.

I'm blacking out

He smiled to himself, surprised at how analytical this was, under the circumstances. *Probably concussion. Must stay awake.*

He hit atmosphere hard. He was beginning to feel hot, and worried that the pod didn't have atmospheric heat shields. He could burn up and die here.

His mind was blurring, the dizziness making him queasy.

I'm falling he thought. *I'm falling. Is there someone out there that can help me? Help me Help me Help me.*

And then everything went black.

*

His eyes opened to see a white, tiled, ceiling.

Where am I?

He tried to move, but couldn't. He drifted back down into darkness again.

Nizhoni? Nizhoni are you there?

He opened his eyes and turned his head. People were all around him, but they were blurred. He couldn't see. They were talking to him. This was oddly familiar.

There was a girl sitting near him. The blurriness resolved and she came into focus.

"Nizhoni," he croaked.

He felt a hand on his. It was cool and dry to the touch.

"Nizhoni," he repeated and looked at the girl. He blinked several times, trying to clear his vision.

But it wasn't Nizhoni. It was Ayako, and she was crying.

*

"Fintan," she said. "Can you hear me?"

"Nizhoni," he repeated. "Nizhoni?"

"Fintan, I'm sorry. I'm so very sorry."

"Nizhoni," was all he could say. "Where?"

She put her head down, crying more. His head was clearing now. He blinked again and squeezed her hand.

"Ayako," he said. "What's happening?"

"We're back on Earth," she said. "Nizhoni's *gone* Fintan. She died saving us."

"No, I saw her eject."

"They found the wreckage of her ship in orbit. You destroyed whatever it was that attacked us and killed her. Together you saved us."

"No," said Fintan weakly. He felt strength gathering in his voice. He shook his head to clear the tears. "No!"

"I'm so sorry."

Someone else was coming into the room. Fintan turned to see Trichallik and Mister Smith. Zack was standing in the doorway.

"Please leave us Miss Katsuragi," said Trichallik. "We need to speak with Fintan in private."

Ayako nodded, and squeezed Fintan's hand. She got up and ran into Zack's arms, burying her head in his chest. He led her out and quietly closed the door.

"Fintan," said Trichallik. "I am sorry for your loss. I know that you and she were very close. But you must understand that her sacrifice was not in vain. She saved much more than just the children from the squadron. She might have even saved all of mankind."

"Did you find her escape pod?"

"You destroyed a wormhole. It's a miracle *you* survived," said Smith. "No pod other than yours made it to the surface. Hers was broken up and burned in the atmosphere."

"I can't believe she's gone," said Fintan. "She can't be!"

"Fintan," continued Trichallik. "I know this is hard, but what we have to say is important. You must tell *nobody* what happened up there. Most of the squadron doesn't know. Zack only knows a little – he doesn't know what attacked, and you must keep the secret. Otherwise her sacrifice could be in vain."

"Why?"

"We call them hunters. They are semi intelligent creatures that scour the galaxy looking for civilizations. When they find signs of a civilization, they return to their masters who come here and destroy them. You see there are many civilizations in the galaxy, and many of them believe that the best way to avoid future conflict with other races is to destroy them before they reach the stars. Before they become a threat. The hunters come from one of them. They destroyed my world in the same way."

"But why keep it a secret?"

"Some of my people will want to leave this place, and leave you to the hunters if they think Earth has been discovered. We want to help you, but we're not going to fight a war for you. That you must do yourselves, and you are not yet ready."

"And you?"

"I am here for you and your people, as was my mate. He died to buy Nizhoni and you time to escape. I know your loss of her is great, but you are young, and you only knew her for a few short months.

Tricnollak and I were life mates for hundreds of years. His absence is an emptiness in my soul."

A wave of grief shook over Fintan's body again. He began to sob. *She's gone.*

*

He must have fallen asleep then, because when he opened his eyes, Trichallik and Smith were gone. Ayako and Zack were sitting at the base of his bed again.

"Good morning sleepyhead," said Zack, trying to inject some cheer into his voice, but not succeeding.

Ayako reached out and held onto Fintan's hand.

He rubbed his eyes and looked at them. Ayako's eyes were puffy and red, and Zack looked tired and empty.

"It wasn't a dream was it?" asked Fintan. "She's really gone, isn't she?"

Ayako nodded and lowered her head.

"Fintan," said Zack. "I'm sorry if this is insensitive, but what really happened out there?"

He remembered what Trichallik had said. "I'm sorry," said Fintan. "I don't really remember that much."

"But what attacked us Fintan?"

"I don't know."

"Fintan?"

"Zack, I can't talk about it, ok?"

"Can't or won't?"

"Does it matter?"

"Of course it matters it-"

Ayako had put her hand over his mouth. "Now isn't the right time Zack. Give him some space, ok?"

Zack nodded and also placed his hand on Fintan's. "Sorry."

*

After a few days, Fintan checked himself out of hospital and returned to the Red Squadron dome. He felt empty as he entered. The crowds at dinner just made him feel lonelier.

He returned to his sleeping dome, and Zack was there.

"How are you doing?" he asked.

"Not good," said Fintan. "Seeing everyone reminds me not of her sacrifice to save us, but of the fact that she's gone."

Zack nodded. "Sorry."

"What is worst is that I feel selfish in thinking that I would prefer her to be here instead of everyone else."

"I understand. It's hard to let go."

"You don't understand!" yelled Fintan. "Nobody understands! She just can't be gone. She can't! I can feel her," he pointed at his chest. "Here. Stronger than ever."

His body shuddered again as grief overcame him once more. His foot brushed against something. He picked it up and looked at it. It was the Christmas singing alien that Nizhoni had kicked across the room a lifetime ago.

"Everything just reminds me that she isn't here anymore," he said, putting it down. He lay down on his bed and put his head under the covers. "Just leave me Zack. I want to be alone."

*

Time passed in a blur. He couldn't eat or sleep. He forgot all about classes and about Zack's comings and goings.

I can't stay here anymore he thought. *I have to leave this place.*

And he knew how. He made his way out of the dome, and into the city. He followed the streets to the terminus for the train that went to the edge wall. He rode it, alone, in silence, lost in his thoughts.

Every so often he would look outside and see something nice and turn to talk to Nizhoni, but she wasn't there. And she would never be there again, but no matter how many times he reminded himself of this fact, he'd make the same mistake again and again.

The train reached the end of the line and he walked towards the building. When he reached the door, he realized that Nizhoni had never told him the combination. But it didn't matter. The door was open.

He entered and made his way to the hangar.

Bob was waiting for him there. "I was wondering when you'd show up," he said.

Fintan embraced the big man, who didn't return the hug.

"What happened to Benally's daughter?" said Bob.

"I can't tell you."

"I'm the one who had to go back and tell him," said Bob, his voice beginning to crack. "I'm the one who had to watch him break down and cry for hours at the loss of his beloved daughter. I'm the one who had to hold his wife and Nanabah and tell them that she's never coming home again."

"I'm sorry."

"They wanted to know where you were, and why you didn't protect her."

"I tried. But I couldn't."

"What happened out there?"

"I can't tell you," repeated Fintan. "I'm sorry, Bob. Please forgive me."

Bob drew himself up to his full height. "My name is *Standing Bear*." He walked out of the room without a backwards look.

There were several saucers still there, so Fintan got into one of them and took off. He climbed as high as he could, before realizing he didn't know where to go. He clearly wasn't welcome back in the Navajo nation anymore, and he didn't want to go back to school.

He hated it, but there was only one place left for him. He laid in a course for Ireland.

For home.

*

Do you think he can keep the secret?

Yes.

So how much time do you think we have?

Four years. Maybe more maybe less.

And you think they'll come?

Yes. They will, and we will need to be ready.

But the lives that were lost. Was it worth it?

Yes. Simon and Red Two did what they had to do and Tricnollak knew what he was doing. It was a good sacrifice.

But what about Nizhoni?

TO BE CONTINUED IN
"THE MILLION YEAR JOURNEY"

Visit us at http://www.destinypress.net

Printed in Great Britain
by Amazon